ADVAN(

ALL I E

"Jane Lo's debut novel *All I Ever Wanted* is a heartfelt Hong Kong love story. She writes with lyrical precision and finely observed emotions of the private lives of ordinary people with candor, wit and vision."

—Xu Xi, author of *Habit of a Foreign Sky*

"Charming, authentic and moving."

—L.A. Larkin, author of *The Safe Place*

"Jane Lo has written a book many big names can't touch in terms of feeling, warmth, and outright fun. I could not put it down. I don't have children but her description of motherhood made my heart ache, it is so poignant. She is funny and her loving portrayal of Hong Kong, especially its markets, defied my Westerner's view of the city as an overcrowded metropolis. The book revolves around love and every paragraph is tender."

—Christopher G. Bremicker, author of *Eagle Claw and Other Stories*

"*All I Ever Wanted* explores the rich territory of parenthood—the illness of children, social isolation, and the struggle with mothers-in-law—set against the backdrop of Hong Kong. It's quietly beautiful and deserves your attention."

—John Matthew Fox, author of *The Linchpin Writer*

"Lo's novel expertly examines the collision between tradition and modernity, familial duty and romance, in a thoroughly enjoyable novel. It recalls such novels as Christos Tsiolkas' The Slap in its ability to reveal the deep motivations of people via the quotidian events that define our lives."

—Dr. Patrick Holland, Assistant Professor of Humanities and Creative Writing at Hong Kong Baptist University and author of *The Mary Smokes Boys*

"*All I Ever Wanted* is an engaging novel about the challenges of new marriage and parenting across cultural divides. Its many local references will enlighten newcomers to Hong Kong and delight natives with its mentions of familiar places and the fissures between generations, social classes, languages, and backgrounds. Ultimately, readers will learn that familial love is never simple and that a Chinese mother-in-law can be a formidable opponent when an only son and grandson are at stake."

—Heather Diamond, author of *Rabbit in the Moon*

"Jane Lo's *All I Ever Wanted* is a poignant, incisive exploration of motherhood, family, and the challenges of navigating a marriage that spans class and cultural differences. She does a masterful job of giving us insight into two characters who want desperately for their relationship to work, even as they face obstacles that seem insurmountable. This thoughtful, moving novel poses a universal question with a complicated answer: what happens when you get all you ever wanted, yet realize that to keep it, you'll have to find the courage to make choices you never dreamed of?"

—Emily Colin, New York Times bestselling author of *The Memory Thief*

"Jane Lo has written the book many of us wish we'd had years ago, no matter our culture or background. Even better, her book comes with an endearing Hong Kong backdrop that shows the beauty and struggles of people who believe that love truly conquers all."

—Susan Blumberg-Kason, author of *Good Chinese Wife*

"In *All I Ever Wanted,* Lo folds faces of doubt into small red envelopes and turns them into luck. If love can be a mother or a partner, can it also be the self? How much of our language is our own, and which parts have we learned in order to not become swallowed up by the world's terrifying silence? Whether in Hong Kong waiting rooms, cabs or classrooms or childhood homes, Lo is there to soothe our flaking, reddened skin with her truth—that we belong somewhere much more beautiful than the hells we once imagined."

—Daisuke Shen, author of *Funeral*

"*All I Ever Wanted* is a rare and genuine depiction of early parenthood. There is joy and tenderness here, as well as anxiety-inducing in-laws, health issues, and the pressure of earning one's keep in a major city. After reading it I found myself missing the characters that inhabit this novel, I re-read passages of it, just to spend more time with them."

—Caitlin Thomson, author of *Incident Reports*

ALL I EVER WANTED

JANE LO

EARNSHAW BOOKS

All I Ever Wanted

By Jane Lo

ISBN-13: 978-988-8769-91-9

FICTION

EB180

Published in Hong Kong by Earnshaw Books Ltd.

Chapter 1

JOEY SHOOK his head roughly against his mother's front, leaving a large snow-like patch on her black cardigan. His hands were covered in thick scratch mitts, and further constrained by the tight straps of the baby carrier, so he got relief in the only way he could. He smiled a gummy smile up at her, and Norah wanted to smile back, but she was so troubled by her six-month-old's angry, inflamed skin. She kissed the top of his head instead. Before leaving for the pediatrician's clinic, she had coated Joey's skin in a thick layer of the colloidal oatmeal cream her mother sent from Vancouver, but it was already flaking off again. Joey continued rubbing his cheeks desperately against her chest.

"Let me hold him, Norah." When her mother-in-law, her *Nai Nai,* dug her hands into the carrier and tugged Joey out, green manicured fingers clutching at him like talons, Norah allowed her to do so without protest. A line from a long-forgotten Tennyson poem sprung to mind, something about an eagle clasping at a rock, a *crag,* she suddenly remembered, with crooked hands.

Joey was no rock, of course; he was a pudgy little dumpling, koala cub-like in his clinginess and affection. Nai Nai, on the other hand, did bring to mind a falcon, an eagle, some such bird of prey. Norah had seen pictures of her mother-in-law in her youth, when her eyes were kinder, her expressions as she gazed at the photographer coy. Her sharply angled nose was the same, though; Norah supposed in some circles it might be considered an attractive feature, but Norah had always felt that it resembled a beak.

A Chinese idiom Norah had often heard growing up was this: *to love the house is to love the crow*. She loved Ben, her first and only boyfriend, lover, now husband, her house and home, with an intensity, a ferocity, that sometimes frightened her, but when they were dating, Ben's mother had been openly critical of her and repeatedly tried to set him up with the daughters of her friends. She had often attempted to convince Ben of the desirability of these young women even with Norah sitting at the table. Norah had reminded herself that houses *always* come with crows, that ancient Chinese wisdom was infallible, didn't you know, and that she wasn't going to give up her house, her Ben, just because a very difficult crow was attached to its roof.

"You really shouldn't dress him in these zip-up jackets," Nai Nai was saying, unzipping the front of Joey's hoodie and revealing his *Mama's Little Dude* onesie underneath. "See how it's irritating his chin?"

Before Norah could answer, she began reading loudly, obnoxiously, from one of the many Peppa storybooks on the coffee table. There were several other children and their mothers in the waiting room with them, but no one noticed. It was such an upscale clinic that there was enough to keep everyone occupied: in this corner there was a sizable wooden train set, in that one, a full-service play kitchen. In the back there was even a Nintendo Switch; a woman was playing some kind of fitness game on it as her son watched, embarrassed.

It was their first visit to this fancy clinic, and Norah was thankful that they were able to get an appointment as quickly as they did. Joey's skin had grown increasingly irritated in the last two weeks. Their friends and relatives were quick to recommend various remedies, from soaking him in parsley to coating him in cold-pressed extra virgin coconut oil; apple cider vinegar in his bath, oatmeal in his bath. Norah and Ben had gamely tried each remedy, keeping careful tabs on the effects in a notebook, but for all their efforts, Joey's skin only grew worse. He no longer slept through the night; he had before, as a newborn. Now, he scratched and scratched, sometimes quietly, sometimes not. Occasionally he left long, angry gashes on his little cheeks.

When Ben's boss at the studio recommended Dr. Chan, swore that he could fix any baby with any problem of any kind, Norah called immediately. And when the nurse told her they were fully booked for the next three months, she'd cried and cried, until finally the nurse relented and told her she could perhaps squeeze Joey in the following day after all.

"Joey Tam Chun Yin, please come in," a young woman's voice announced on the intercom, and a door—one of those integrated doors that looked like they were part of the wall—slid open with a soft *swish*. Nai Nai walked in with Joey, and Norah hastily grabbed their bags and hurried in behind them just before it closed again.

"Please, sit down," the doctor said, scribbling a few final notes on the previous patient's file before turning to face their little trio. Norah had always been a little mistrustful of very young people in positions of authority or influence, and was relieved to see that the doctor was in his late sixties, possibly early seventies. He could be her grandfather.

He peered at Joey through his wire-rimmed glasses and said, "Hello, Baby Chun Yin. Is that what your mama calls you?" He gently removed Joey's scratch mitts and handed him two small rattles. Joey squealed in delight and immediately shook them like maracas.

Norah cleared her throat. "Nice to meet you, Dr. Chan. We use his English name at home, Joey. I'm his mom, and this is my Nai Nai, Joey's Maa Maa. We're here because of Joey's skin."

The doctor leaned forward and studied Joey's face without speaking. "How long has he been like this?"

"About two weeks. We've tried lots of different creams and home remedies, but nothing has really helped."

When he took Joey from his grandmother's arms, Joey did not cry. He continued shaking his rattles cheerily as the doctor examined his neck, his arms, his back, his tummy, his legs. Norah's eyes followed the doctor's, and observed, not without pain, that the eczema had been very thorough; it had left no part of her baby untouched. "Well, little Joey, I've seen lots of itchy babies, but you might be the itchiest one yet. Is he breast-fed? Have you started him on solids yet?"

"So far he's only tried plain congee, and he seems to like it. He doesn't nurse too well at the breast, so we supplement with formula about half the time." The words came out in a tumble. "I—I wish we didn't have to, but..."

"Is it the formula that's the problem, doctor, or her breast milk?" Nai Nai interrupted, her tone accusatory. "I keep telling her that she should avoid the common allergens—shellfish, you know, that sort of thing, because she'll pass them on through her milk. I mean, just look at him!"

Norah hadn't had any seafood since the time she ate one *har gao* early in her pregnancy, before she even knew she was expecting. Her mother-in-law occasionally attributed Joey's eczema to that shrimp dumpling. The rational side of Norah knew this was crazy talk, but in moments of weakness, like now, when Joey, her sweet Joey, was trying once more to scratch at his scabby cheek with one of the doctor's yellowing rattles, she wondered if that cursed *har gao* had not somehow destined her son to a lifetime of misery.

"Doctor," Nai Nai continued, "would you recommend that Joey switch to formula completely? I've heard there are hypoallergenic formulas available now? Would that make sense, given Joey's skin condition? It's not just a matter of contaminated milk, or her not making enough milk. I don't know if I'm overstepping the line here, but I think you should know what the real problem is. It's her breasts. Her nipples, I mean. They're completely flat. Have you ever heard of a baby drinking from a flat nipple?" She let out a snort, as though she had cracked a good joke, and was expecting the doctor to laugh with her, but the room was silent but for Joey, who was beginning to whine.

Norah watched, comforted, as Dr. Chan smiled at her mother-in-law with his lips but not his eyes, as he said, "If you're asking for my opinion, Maa Maa, and I think you are, here it is: breast is just about always best. In my experience, many mothers find the breastfeeding journey challenging."

Norah glanced at her mother-in-law, saw her shifting uncomfortably in her seat, a frown on her face.

"Hypoallergenic formulas are indeed available," Dr. Chan continued, "and I will give you some samples so you can see how Joey responds when you're supplementing. But, no—don't stop breastfeeding. It's too early to say for sure, of course, but I'm pretty sure I've got what he needs to make a full recovery. I'm glad you brought him in so soon after it flared up."

He prescribed three different kinds of cream, to be applied in a specific order twice a day, and a large green bottle of pine tar solution for baths. "Come back in a week, and we'll see if we need to make any adjustments."

Norah didn't speak as she slid Joey into the carrier and buckled the straps on her mother-in-law's back. She planted a quick kiss on Joey's nose as she did this, then opened the taxi door for them. "Thank you, Nai Nai," she muttered as she closed the door behind them. She waved at Joey, who looked out the window, blew him kisses, and started walking downhill towards Central MTR station to take the train to work.

The urge to slam the door behind her mother-in-law had been overwhelming, her anger at the woman building by the second, but it wasn't worth scaring Joey. And she wouldn't give Nai Nai a reason to complain to Ben.

He loved Norah, of course he did, but when his mother spoke, he listened.

About a year into their relationship she had asked Ben, playfully, why he did everything for his mom when she was not even that old, certainly no older than her own parents. Norah had observed how he always immediately picked up his mother's calls when he and Norah were out together, as though anxious about a potential emergency, how he refilled her teacup with her beloved *pu erh* tea continuously throughout every meal.

Norah remembered the way he took her hands in both of his, the way he had looked directly at her.

"She's not very easy to love, I know," he said. "But she raised me by herself, she worked her whole life for me and I owe everything to her. You understand, right?"

Sometimes, Norah thought Ben had already repaid his mother in full, and then some; she had never seen a man so devoted to his mother's well-being and happiness. Norah herself had been adding to that debt by requiring her mother-in-law's help with Joey when she was at her part-time job, but there was no alternative; they couldn't afford a domestic helper, and even if they could, her Nai Nai would never allow a stranger to live in her home; she had enough trouble as it was with Norah. There was no other support system since Norah's parents lived in Vancouver.

Dr. Chan's clinic was in Central, only a few train stations away from Jordan. Fifteen minutes later, Exit C1 of Jordan Station spilled her out onto the sidewalk, where a number of middle-aged ladies wearing visors immediately thrust flyers at her. Norah had learned the only way to dodge these professionals was to avoid eye contact as she muttered, "No thank you," repeatedly under her breath, her hands firmly at her sides. Soon, she was taking the very long escalator from the lobby up to her castle in the sky, Future English.

Future English was not the biggest adult learning centre in Hong Kong, not by a long shot, but as far as Norah was concerned, it was the best. She saw the familiar glass walls of the centre coming into view, the purple carpet with the orange hexagonal pattern, Susan fielding calls at reception. Best of all, she saw the "regulars", the convivial middle-aged crowd that always hung out in the social area drinking instant coffee and milk tea out of paper cups and discussing the latest gossip in effortful English.

Her manager, Ivan, took her on when she was a fresh graduate with no credentials to her name other than a B.A. in English Literature and Creative Writing from the University of Hong Kong. And although she had worked hard for that degree, had won scholarships and gone to Melbourne on exchange and done local service learning projects and volunteered for two summers at a school for orphans in Yunnan, her C.V. had not attracted the attention of any school principals or centre managers, anyone really, although she had sent out over twenty applications. Anyone, that was, apart from Ivan, who had called and invited her to her only interview.

She had attempted to dress up in an effort to look older than twenty-two. Her mother had FaceTimed her the night before, and together they had chosen a floral blouse, a beige A-line skirt, and brown loafers. As she waited, she could see in the glass reflection that the clothes made her look frumpy, not mature. But Ivan had not commented on her age or her clothes. He had asked her about the students she'd taught in Yunnan and at the tutorial centre for ethnic minority children, her time in Melbourne, the books she enjoyed reading.

"You have no accent, none whatsoever," he had said, finally, in his own heavy Australian accent. "Why is that?"

"I attended a very good secondary school, one of the best in Hong Kong," she responded, and she realized she was not boasting, simply relaying a fact. "All my teachers were from somewhere else, Canada or the States, mainly, and they taught me to love English, learning, and...life, I guess. My parents felt strongly that the local system wasn't right for me and paid a lot of money to send me to an international school."

"Well, it was worth it, clearly. When can you start?"

Norah could remember staring at him, speechless, her eyes bright with happy tears.

Ivan had responded for her, clearly touched. "I suppose you could say, 'In the Future.' Here, that's the answer for pretty much everything."

That was three years ago. Her parents were always nagging her to get her education diploma so she could teach at a "proper" school, one with a principal, report cards, yearly salary increases. However, being in Vancouver, they were only able to do so long-distance, once a week via FaceTime, and so far their nagging had come to nothing. She loved it here.

Ivan was approaching the table of regulars now, his signature juggling balls hidden behind his back. He had lots of great stories for the students about the year he spent in Shenzhen working at a circus and was forever performing another trick for them. Anything to get the students to speak in English in the Future; that was their rallying cry in the staff pantry. Initiatives for encouraging English conversations had included everything from the wildly popular egg tart bake-offs last year to the bubble tea taste testing sessions held just last month.

Norah scanned her staff card and locked up her backpack at reception, where Susan was speaking with a student on the phone, a perplexed expression on her face. She smiled when she saw Norah, then continued murmuring, "Yes, I understand."

"How many balls do you think I can keep in the air? How many?" Ivan cried as he juggled three at a steady clip. Norah and the students watched, enraptured, as he added a fourth, a fifth, then a sixth, with the easy grace of a seasoned performer. The act complete, he allowed the balls to fall into his cupped hands and took exaggerated bows to the students' hearty applause.

"Hi everyone," Norah called. "How's everyone doing in the Future? And wasn't that fantastic?"

Ivan continued muttering, "Thank you, thank you," before relinquishing the group to Norah and returning to his desk.

"How's the baby doing, Norah?"

"Can you check my homework, Norah?"

"I made some red bean pudding for you to try, Norah."

"Want to see a picture of the girl my son's dating, Norah? I don't think she's anything special, but—"

Norah gazed with great affection at the eager faces. "I've missed you, too. Thanks for asking, Ming: a little better, I guess, we just took him to a specialist this morning. Tim, everything looks good except for numbers two and four. Looks like you might have mixed up the answers for those. This is *so* good, Kitty, thank you...Oh, she's pretty, Siu-Fong! She's a doctor, then?"

She gladly allowed these retirees, these lifelong housewives, to soak in her attention and praise. She was only in the centre two afternoons and one morning a week now; the part-time arrangement was at her request, so she could stay home and be with Joey as much as possible. But when he was asleep, and she was alone in the flat with her mother-in-law, the tension and discomfort were almost more than she could bear.

When her assigned hour in the social area was up, she went to the resource room to pick up her clipboards and materials for the afternoon: one Orange class in Room B with two students, both brand-new, and one Purple class, the highest level offered at Future English, with four students, all long-timers who had clearly booked the class together.

She switched on the light and air-conditioning in Room B. As was her usual practice, she wrote her name on the right side of the whiteboard in cursive, and after underlining it, wrote the names of the two expected students beneath hers.

As she waited for Echo and Icy, she marveled at how she no longer giggled at these odd names. Weird English names were an epidemic in Hong Kong, and as a greenhorn she sometimes had to turn to the board to stifle giggles when calling on students with names like Hulk, Dolphin, or Fantasy.

Hadn't Ben's first class at Future English been in Room B, too? She was pretty sure it was. He had arrived after his classmate, that pretty yoga teacher with the strange name, Baby. A new teacher at the time, the name had initially struck Norah as hysterical. "It's such a pleasure to meet you, Baby," and "Can you tell me a little about yourself, Baby?" sounded knee-slappingly funny in her head and even worse when she tried to say them out loud.

It had been hopeless; she remembered how she excused herself, feigning a headache, and rushed to the staff pantry. She laughed hysterically, tears streaming down her cheeks, until she was sure she had gotten all the giggles out. When she returned to Room B, the second student had arrived. He was slim, dressed in a checked flannel shirt and black jeans, and wore rectangular glasses with no rims.

Back in control of herself, Norah flashed her best professional smile at him, and said, "You must be Ben. I'm sorry to have kept you and Baby waiting."

She remembered the way Ben had furrowed his brow before responding carefully with, "No need to apologize, Miss Norah."

"Thank you. Please, call me Norah. Now, shall we get to know each other a little first, before we start with Lesson 1? What do you do, Ben? Baby told me earlier that she's a yoga instructor. Isn't that fantastic?"

He nodded politely at Baby before quietly telling them that he liked running, and that he took pictures, mainly family portraits and touched up photos for people's CVs, at a small studio in Kwun Tong. He had blushed when Norah called him a photographer, as though it were a title he did not deserve.

Much later, he explained to her that Snapshot was an ultra-budget studio, a place where families pay $399 for a one-hour shoot, all digital files included. Holding her hand, he shyly shared his secret dream of taking wildlife photography someday, perhaps in Borneo, India, even Kenya.

Norah noticed that Ben mispronounced her name, made it sound like *Laura*, but she didn't mind. She rather liked the way he looked at her intently each time he said it, the way he always courteously allowed Baby to speak first when Norah invited them to answer a question, the way he held his mechanical pencil between his thumb and forefinger, the tip hovering a centimeter above the page, always at the ready, the way his writing was small and neat, like a sans serif font.

It was twenty minutes past three, and there was no sign of

either Echo or Icy. Norah quickly scribbled 'no show' next to each student's name, resenting the wasted hour. She headed back out to the social area, where Tony, a part-timer like herself, was teaching students how to write limericks. Norah joined them for a few minutes, helping a little, giggling with the students at the silly rhymes they had come up with.

Tony, a retired schoolteacher who couldn't stay away from teaching, had joined Future English around the same time she did, and was on an aggressive campaign to introduce literature to the students—short stories, poetry, bits and pieces of Shakespeare, all kinds. It was no easy feat, given that so many of the students at the centre had never read a line of English literature in their lives, but Ivan was overwhelmingly supportive of his efforts, and Norah and the others helped with his little workshops when they could.

About a month after that first lesson with Ben and Baby, Norah found in her pigeon hole a photograph of a stunning sunset, and written very neatly on the back, these seventeen syllables:

You are beautiful
Breathtaking, like a sunset
Pink and red and gold

Norah knew it was Ben, had recognized his handwriting immediately.

Chapter 2

On her way to the bus stop Norah passed by Reclamation Street, one of her favourite places in the world. The open-air wet market was always bustling with housewives clutching cloth shopping bags or pulling collapsible shopping trolleys noisily against the asphalt. Norah was one of the few exceptions; she just had her leather tote bag with her, the one Mom and Dad had sent over from Vancouver in congratulations when she got the job at Future English. She wasn't really here to buy anything. Living with Nai Nai, Norah didn't do any cooking at all; she was considered next to useless in the kitchen. Nai Nai didn't think she knew much about anything—babies, breastfeeding, anything at all.

But here at Reclamation Street, Norah felt light and unfettered by the weight of Nai Nai's criticisms, the sounds of the market like music to her ears. She enjoyed the sellers' familiar cries as they advertised their wares—*Five for one! Ten for three! Quick hands'll get some; slow hands won't*—and the inevitable spirited banter as the customers attempted to bargain.

Norah loved the glistening mounds of cherries and kumquats, the neatly arranged piles of mangos, dragon fruit, and persimmons and, further on, the vegetable stalls spilling over with every kind of leaf—bok choy, amaranth, watercress, kale, choy sum—and root, from daikon and jicama to a rainbow of sweet potatoes, yams, and carrots.

Norah liked to pretend that she was a housewife here to do her shopping for her family. She'd make silky smooth steamed eggs, a little dash of soy sauce and a sprinkle of chopped green onion on top, or maybe dumplings with napa cabbage and sweet corn. She'd serve the dumplings with rice noodles, and mix up a deceptively simple dipping sauce with the perfect balance of soy sauce and Chekiang vinegar. Or maybe she'd surprise her husband with a fancy seafood paella and a lobster bisque—with puff pastry on top!—and whip up a pie for dessert—perhaps apple? Or blueberry?

And once Joey could eat solids—Norah tried not to entertain the frightening thought that for some children, eczema was a lifelong condition—she'd make him those clever pasta sauces that secretly contained seven kinds of vegetables, and muffins sweetened with nothing but bananas and applesauce, and all those amazing things in her *My Nourished Child* cookbook.

One day, Ben promised that they would move out and have a home of their own—and when that day came, she would cook for Ben and Joey every night. She would come back to Reclamation Street Market with her own collapsible shopping trolley, fill it up with good and nutritious things, and she would cook.

Norah could hear the faint tinkling music from Joey's rainforest Jumperoo the moment she stepped out of the elevator.

Joey loved that Jumperoo, could spend hours on the mesh seat, sometimes bouncing with gusto, his feet thudding against the thickly padded playmat, and sometimes just sitting and admiring the flashing lights intently. Norah rather liked its cheerful music, often found herself humming along to it, and had no doubt that her memories of Joey from this period would always have that little ditty playing in the background. She once spent a feverish thirty minutes looking up what that song actually was, and learned that it was an old folk song called 'Froggy Went A-Courtin' that once featured on an episode of Tom and Jerry. Her parents sent it over for Joey's 100th day celebration.

"Is that you, Ben?" Nai Nai called from the patio. "Get me a few more hangers from the bathroom, will you?"

"It's just me, Nai Nai, hi." Norah spoke Cantonese cautiously, the way her students spoke English, but at home, there was no other choice; Nai Nai didn't understand a word of English.

She kicked off her flats as quickly as she could and slid them out of sight under the shoe cabinet with a stockinged foot. Joey was in the Jumperoo, not jumping, just swaying to the music, and idly batting at the swinging toucan with one of his mitted hands. His face lit up when he saw his mama. Norah planted a kiss on the top of his head before hurrying to the kitchen sink to wash her hands. "I'll go grab the hangers now."

"No need," her mother-in-law said shortly. She stepped back into the living room, the old rattan laundry basket in her arms. "I'll get them myself."

These first few moments when she came home from work always made Norah felt intensely uncomfortable, like she was walking on egg shells. Nai Nai avoided making eye contact with her as she strode into the bathroom.

"Thanks so much, Nai Nai. Did you two have a good day?" Norah smiled bravely for Joey's sake as she scooped him out of the Jumperoo. When Joey rubbed his face against the front of her dress, Norah knew it was partly out of love for her, but mostly because his skin was still so itchy. "Hi, baby," she murmured. "Missed you."

Nai Nai paused mid-step and turned around to face her. Her expression was pinched, as though she was sucking on a salted plum. "Yes, we did."

"Well, alright then," Norah whispered to Joey after Nai Nai was out of earshot. "Good to hear it."

"Thank you again for your help with Joey today, Nai Nai," Norah said politely, placing the choicest piece of char siu in her mother-in-law's bowl. "Say 'thank you, Maa Maa', Joey."

The baby, seated in his plastic high chair at the head of the table, immediately touched his chin with one palm and smiled proudly as everyone applauded.

Nai Nai pursed her lips. "Taking care of my own grandson is not helping you, but you're welcome, Joey. Also, I can serve myself."

"You must be tired, Ma," Ben said. "This char siu is delicious. How did things go at the clinic today?"

Norah focused her attention on Joey, who smacked his lips loudly after each bite of congee.

"The doctor seems very radical," his mother finally said. "But the pine tar bath seems to be helping a little. I hope you don't mind that I bathed him already, Norah."

Norah *did* mind. She had told her mother-in-law a million times in a million roundabout ways that she should wait for her, that bathing Joey herself was important to her. But she said thank you, told her she was grateful and meant it, because if Joey was scratching less that was all that mattered.

After dinner, everyone assumed their usual positions: the matriarch sat on her leather throne before the television, the volume turned up high as she watched yet another trope-filled TVB soap. Joey snored softly, asleep in his crib. Ben and Norah retreated to the kitchen to do the dishes together.

It was a small, cramped space, and ordinarily she giggled when they bumped elbows, relishing the closeness, but tonight she was silent.

"How did things go at the clinic today?" he asked. Finally alone, he switched back to English.

Norah could hear herself breathing more loudly than usual above the sound of the running water. "Why is Joey's eczema so bad, you think? Is it really my breast milk?"

"Why would you think that?"

"Your mom seems to think so. She told the doctor my milk is making Joey sick. She thinks Joey should just drink formula from now on."

"And what did the doctor say?"

"He's pro-BF."

"That's fine, then. You don't have to stop breastfeeding."

"It's not fine. None of this is fine!" She was almost shouting, but Ben regarded her calmly.

He turned off the tap. "Why are you so upset?"

"Why am I so upset? Did you just say 'why am I so upset'?"

"Joey's better, isn't he? You and Mom both said so at dinner."

"Your mom—"

"Honey—"

"Your mom also told the doctor I have flat nipples. She went on and on about how flat they are, and insisted that the reason Joey can't nurse properly is because my nipples are so flat."

At this, Ben dried his hands briskly on a towel and reached out to embrace his wife. "*I* don't think your nipples were flat. I like them exactly the way they are."

Norah struggled momentarily in his arms, but she was so tired, and it was good to be held. When he leaned down to kiss her, she let him.

Chapter 3

Ben sat up immediately when he heard the wailing from Joey's crib. Ben had always been the lighter sleeper, the one to wake in the middle in the night to change Joey's diaper or prepare a bottle.

When he switched on the bedside lamp, he found his son scratching mercilessly at his face, his fingernails claw-like and bloody, his cheeks a maze of dried blood and fresh tears. When Ben leaned down to pick him up, Joey smiled weakly at the familiar face, and Ben felt a sharp pinching pain blooming in his gut, the sort he had only known since becoming a father, the kind he only experienced when Joey was hurt.

There was that night, not so long ago and not so unlike this one, when Joey had woken up hungry, and Ben had placed him beside Norah's sleeping form. He had woken her, gently, had asked her to keep an eye on Joey for a minute—just one minute!—and she had nodded, sleepily, draping an arm around the whimpering infant.

He had rushed to the kitchen, switched on the electric kettle, and taken down the can of Aptima from the shelf, when he heard a dull thud coming from their bedroom which was immediately followed by a piercing wail. Then, "Ben! Ben!"

His insides had twisted then, and hurt the way they do now,

as he ran back to their bedroom in his slippered feet. Joey was in his mother's arms, crying. Norah was patting him, her face pale with shock and guilt.

"I didn't realize I fell asleep again—one moment he was on the bed next to me and the next he was—he was—"

Ben had felt a flash of anger so hot that he had to turn away. When he spoke again, he did so in low, measured tones. "I was gone for less than a minute, Norah—"

And perhaps Norah would have responded with an apology, or perhaps some further attempt at explanation, but she didn't have the opportunity to do so, because the door of his mother's bedroom suddenly swung open, and she stood there in her doorway in her silk pajamas.

"What happened?"

And in that instant he and Norah had looked at each other, and Ben had said, softly, "Everything's fine, Ma. Please go back to sleep."

"I thought I heard crying—"

"Yes, Joey needs a bottle. I was just on my way to the kitchen."

"The kitchen light is already on."

"I must have forgotten to switch it off earlier. Please, Ma, it's very late."

She had glared at Norah reproachfully then, as though she knew the truth of the matter, and returned to her bedroom without speaking.

And now, as Ben shook Norah, waking her, he felt the same sharp anger. "Norah, wake up." When she didn't, when she rolled over and her soft snores continued, he switched on the room light. "Norah! Get up!"

"What's going on? What time is it?" Her eyes adjusted to the light and she saw Joey curled up, sniffling, against Ben's shoulder. She gasped when he held the baby out to her. "Oh, Joey!"

"He's not wearing scratch mitts."

If Norah sensed his reproach, she chose to ignore it. "He was before. He must have taken them off in his sleep." She held Joey close, nuzzling his forehead until he laughed. "Let's go and get this little man cleaned up, shall we?"

Ben watched as Norah held Joey in the crook of one arm and gently washed Joey's cheeks with cotton balls dipped in warm water. She sang 'I'll Love You Forever' to him as she did, and by the time she was applying the third layer of cream, Joey was asleep. With skilled hands she swiftly changed his diaper, zipped him up in his sleeping bag again, and laid him down in his crib.

"I'm sorry, baby," Ben said softly, watching as his wife dug out the discarded pair of scratch mitts from beneath Joey's comfort blanket and put them back on the little hands.

She didn't answer; she turned off the light and lay down, facing the wall.

"I was so worried about Joey, and I was so mad that maybe we'd forgotten to check if he was wearing the mitts—"

He heard and recognized the soft snuffling sounds that Norah always made when she was trying not to cry, and Ben feared he himself was on the verge of tears. "I'm sorry, Norah, I'm really sorry—" He tried, clumsily, to embrace her, but she struggled out of his reach and covered her head with the blanket.

"I didn't forget," she said, her voice thick with tears. "I didn't forget."

Ben woke to the familiar drone of Norah's favourite breast pump, the one she called Eeyore. She had several, including an expensive one she ordered on Amazon and had shipped over from America at staggering cost but decided she didn't like, a cheap one she found on a local online store which was compatible with the parts from the expensive American brand, a second-hand pump from one of her students' daughters, and a manual pump that she brought to work with her in a little ice-pack lined bag so she could pump during her break and bring the milk home. Eeyore was the cheap one with the expensive parts.

Ben supposed he liked the sound of this one best, too; its steady *heeee-haw, heeee-haw* was soothing, almost therapeutic. It was very early, perhaps not even 6am. The room was bathed in a soft, grey glow; the day was just waking up, the parted curtains letting in a few weak rays of light.

Joey was awake, kicking his little feet and keeping his mother company in his crib as she pumped. Every time Norah said, "I love you, my little pumpkin pie," or some such endearment, Joey cooed in response, content, as though he was saying, *Yes, Mama, I know.* His heart swelled with affection for the two of them, his world, as this little scene repeated itself over and over.

About fifteen minutes later, she switched off the pump, and silence descended on the room. "What do you think, little guy? Eight ounces isn't too shabby, huh?" she said, clearly pleased, as she detached the two bottles of expressed milk from the flanges and screwed the yellow caps on. She never forgot to do that anymore, not since that one time she spilled an almost full bottle.

When Joey didn't answer, Norah peered into the crib, and she and Ben both saw that he had curled up at the foot of his crib and fallen asleep again. He really was a dream baby, eczema or not.

Norah suddenly spun around, as though she had only just sensed Ben's presence. "I thought it might be you," she said softly, and Ben knew he was forgiven. "Look, honey, eight ounces."

"I love you," he murmured, taking the two bottles from her hands and setting them gently on their bedside table. She lay down again, re-hooked her nursing bra, and gazed at him, her eyes wide and unblinking.

He kissed her tenderly on the neck, the way she liked; his fingers pitter-pattered up and down her back. He sensed his body responding to her quickened breaths. She had learned to be so quiet. He remembered how he used to always have to cover her mouth with one hand when she cried out. He had even considered adding soundproof paneling to their bedroom but was too afraid of his mother's inevitable questions. In this apartment they were never alone. Perhaps one day, he thought, perhaps one day they will have their own home, their own space. But what about his Ma? Perhaps...

He shook his head roughly, clearing these unwanted thoughts and focused his attention back on Norah, who had turned on her side to face him, her features aglow in the growing morning sunlight. "Again," she was saying. "Kiss me again."

Their Saturday morning routine was well-established. As usual, Ben sat on the aging leather sofa, bouncing Joey on his lap as Norah fussed in the kitchen, heating up breast milk and cooking congee.

He and his mother had lived in this flat on Dumbarton Road all his life. Five hundred and thirty-two square feet for two people was quite spacious by Hong Kong standards, and he had loved the view of the little playground downstairs since he was a boy. They lived on the second floor, so close to the ground that when the osmanthus shrubs at the park were in bloom, their sweet fragrance could be enjoyed from their flat. The sounds of children playing could be clearly heard in their living room in the mornings, and in the late afternoons: the *thwhack! thwhack!* of shuttlecocks colliding with rackets; the squeaking of the rusty swing set, the old blue and orange see-saw; the screams and shouts of a game of tag or hide and seek. As a child he often played there himself, his mother waving at him from the window, calling him up for meals.

Sometimes Norah brought Joey there to play. In Ben's mind the old sounds of his childhood mingled with the new ones of his wife and his son laughing together as she pushed him slowly on the swing, or inched down the narrow metal slide with him wrapped in her arms. He watched them from the window, his heart so full he thought it might burst.

The flat itself was cluttered but clean. Everything was showing its age, from the peeling wallpaper and the yellowing watercolor paintings that hung upon it to the cushions on the grey sofa, whose covers had survived a thousand washes or more. There was old junk in various corners, evidence of Ma's tendency to hoard; here, a clunky second-hand Osim foot massager that no longer worked but which she insisted could be repaired or sold again; there, an entire bookshelf filled with old copies of Chinese editions of *Reader's Digest,* dating back to the mid-1980s. She had told him many times that she couldn't bear to throw them out because one of his schoolteachers once told her *Reader's Digest* was essential reading for cultured, educated people, and she so wanted her son to be a cultured and educated person.

His mother was in her bedroom, getting dressed for their weekly 'private time' at the nearby dimsum restaurant. Ben hated the term 'private time', but had given up trying to get her to stop using it. It was unnecessarily exclusive, combative even, but Norah didn't seem to mind. She was usually busy, anyway, FaceTiming her parents or one of her friends from uni. She didn't normally get much privacy, so Ben supposed it was her 'private time', too.

"Do you want me to bring anything back for you, honey?" Ben walked to the kitchen, Joey in his arms.

"Maybe chicken noodles from that Shanghai place? And a

plain steamed bun for Joey? It's just flour and yeast. Do you think he'll have a reaction to it?" Norah squealed when Ben wrapped Joey's arms around her shoulders.

"It should be okay. I'll get you that black fungus drink you like, too. Tell your parents I said hi."

"Thanks," she said, pecking him daintily on the cheek. "Say 'have a good time, Baba', Joey." When Joey gurgled something unintelligible at his daddy, they all laughed.

Suddenly, Norah gasped. "Ben, look!"

"What? What is it?"

She gently tugged at Joey's bottom lip, revealing two white lines, barely visible, on his bottom gums. "What do you think, Baba?"

Ben's eyes grew wide. "Joey! You big boy! Wait, let me get my camera," he cried, rushing to their bedroom. On his way back to the kitchen, he bumped into his mother, who had dressed for the occasion in a bright purple cardigan and matching pants. There was a silk scarf around her neck, and her hair was freshly curled. "Ma! Joey has teeth! Two!"

Her face broke into a broad smile and they hurried together to the kitchen. "Maa Maa, look," Norah was saying, tickling Joey's chin so he would open his mouth and show off his new teeth again.

Ma ignored Norah and reached directly for Joey. Holding him close, she kissed him soundly on the forehead. "Two teeth already, my big boy!"

Ben snapped a few close-up photos of his son's gums with their new treasure, then took photos of Joey's beaming face, of Joey in his grandmother's arms, and finally, of Joey in Norah's arms.

Norah hovered by the doorway with Joey as Ben and his mother put on their shoes. Ben kissed his wife and son goodbye, and Ma said, "See you, Joey," as they left.

Ma slipped her arm in his as they took the elevator down to the lobby, where the elderly security guard, the one Ben had always called Uncle Chung, was fanning himself with a folded newspaper. The electric fan hanging from the ceiling was on, but its blades, caked in dust, were rotating with no great urgency.

"Your son taking you to dimsum again, Mrs. Tam?" he said. "Such a good son. And how many months is the little one now?"

"Six months," she responded, proudly. "And he has two teeth already."

Uncle Chung shook his head in mock disbelief. "Already, already!"

They exited the dark lobby. It was a beautiful day, balmy and breezy, and Ben could feel his mother basking in his attention like a flower in the sun. He held out an umbrella for her to shield her skin from the sun's rays, the way he had done since he was tall enough, about fourteen.

The orange firecracker vines which lined their street were in full bloom. Ben had always loved the vibrant clusters of funnel-shaped flowers, the way they unapologetically spilled over onto the brick walls, the sidewalk. When he was little, he would sometimes pick up a few flowers from the sidewalk to bring home to Ma on his way home from school.

Today, as he and Ma walked together, she chattered about Joey, about the new supermarket that was opening in their neighborhood, about the peach resin and papaya sweet soup she planned on cooking for him that evening for dessert. "I've been soaking the peach resin since last night," she was saying as Ben pushed the glass door of the Chinese restaurant and they were enveloped by the icy air-conditioning.

The manager himself rushed out to greet them, then seated them at their regular table beside the abalone and lobster tank.

He was dressed in an old suit, a frayed purple tie around his neck. "Pu-erh tea as usual, Mrs. Tam?"

Ma nodded happily. "Yes, please."

"And shall I reserve an order of the baked char siu buns for you as well?"

Being the only dimsum place in their area, Golden Phoenix Seafood Restaurant got crowded on the weekends, and their specialty items sold out quickly. It was not ten o' clock yet, but there were only a handful of empty tables left. His mother nodded again, pleased. "That would be wonderful, thank you."

"I've chosen the perfect papaya for this sweet soup," she continued once they were alone again. "Sweet, but still firm, so it will not break apart so easily when I am boiling the soup. I still need to soak the snow fungus when we get home, but that part is quick, just twenty minutes. I'll add the snow fungus, along with the apricot kernels, and the rock sugar, but not too much of course, Ma knows you don't like things too sweet..."

Ben looked up from the order form. His mother only referred to herself in the third person when it was just the two of them. "That sounds delicious, Ma. *Har gao* and beef *cheung fun,* right? I'll get some chicken congee, too. Do you want anything else? Oh, they're doing a special on the braised pig trotters."

"Yes, yes, order anything you want. Ma has money. Ma is treating today." This, also, was something she only said when Norah was not with them. It was a throwback to when Ben was a little boy, and dining out was a rare luxury, but his mother would allow him to order freely from the menu, as though money was no issue at all. In her eyes he saw that her love for him was the same as it was then.

Ben attempted to attract the attention of a waiter by waving the pink order form in the air. His was one of many pink slips fluttering like tiny flags in the air; everyone was trying to put in their order at the same time. A moment later, the manager set the promised plate of char siu buns on their table and picked up Ben's form. "They're very hot, fresh from the oven. Please eat slowly!"

Ben picked up the largest of the three buns with his chopsticks and placed it in his mother's bowl before getting one for himself. The bun's syrupy top was his favourite part, and he licked it the way he would an ice cream cone. When he took a bite, the hot filling oozed out, nearly burning his tongue, but it was delicious, savoury and sweet at the same time. When he looked up, he saw his mother's bun was still in her bowl. She was watching him, a smile on her face.

"Eat it while it's hot, Ma," he said, pouring fresh tea into her cup.

She replied, "I will, I will," but she continued watching him, smiling.

The other dimsum arrived, and they ate in companionable silence. The food finished, Ben listened as his mother told him stories of his childhood that he could recite from memory. "It was just you and me, son," she was saying, the way she ended these stories every time, "but somehow we made it through."

When the manager came by with their bill and Ben laid down his credit card on the black tray, his mother protested, saying this meal was her treat, but they both recognized this as an old charade. Adult Chinese children, the filial ones, did not allow their parents to pay for meals.

By the time they left the restaurant it was nearly noon. Leaving Ma to choose oranges at the fruit stand, Ben walked into the brightly lit Shanghai restaurant and placed Norah's order, adding six potstickers, a red bean pancake, and the thick black fungus drink that Norah liked to slurp up with her stainless-steel straw.

He found his Ma waiting by a fruit stall holding a bulging plastic bag. "Ma, did you get any crystal pears for Norah?" he asked.

Her expression hardened immediately. She gestured at his bags of takeout. "Haven't you bought enough for her?"

"I'll just go see if they're fresh," he said, even though they always were. "If you're in a hurry, go ahead, Ma. I'll catch up. And let me carry those for you." She allowed him to take the bag of oranges from her, but she didn't say anything.

The Korean pears were expensive, but he chose the three largest ones, checked that they were free of spots and bruises and, satisfied, handed over a hundred-dollar bill and received a single ten-dollar coin in change. He loved peeling these pears for Norah, slicing them into uniform wedges and arranging them into a flower for her to find in the fridge.

They walked on in silence. When Ben tried to tell her about a new family he was photographing at work, about how their baby was just a few months older than Joey, her responses were curt, so he stopped.

Soon they were home, but the living room was empty and their bedroom door was closed. Ben could hear the sounds of his wife still on the video call with her parents, speaking English so quick that he couldn't really understand much of it. Norah's parents were Chinese, but as graduates from elite secondary schools, they spoke English with a cultured British accent. Ben sometimes felt like he was talking to royalty when he spoke to them in his own imperfect English, but he tried his best.

He wondered if she was talking about him, and whether she was saying good things about her life here in this little apartment with him and his mother, or if she was saying she wished she lived in Vancouver with them.

Chapter 4

"Have you put on some weight, Norah?" her mother asked, squinting her eyes at the camera. "I don't remember you having a double chin before. Is that a recent development?"

Norah rolled her eyes. "Mom, it's just the angle. Here," she said, jutting out her chin, "that better for you?"

Norah's dad held up their beige poodle, Oatmeal, and Joey clapped his hands in delight, laughing when his grandpa made Oatmeal kiss the camera over and over. Norah would have loved to get a little puppy for Joey to grow up with, but she knew Nai Nai would never agree to keeping a pet in their flat, never in a million years.

"Stop getting the laptop all slobbery, Patrick," Mom said, feigning annoyance, but Norah saw a smile playing at her mother's lips before the white blur of a paper towel filled their screen.

"So how are things at home? Ben treating you right?" Dad asked, only half-jokingly, as he sat down beside Mom at the dining table. Norah missed that roomy mahogany table, its quaint lazy Susan in the middle. That table could fit six comfortably, eight in a pinch. It was quite unlike the cold, glass-topped square in Nai Nai's flat that always felt cramped even though it was just the four of them. Her dad often played the piano after dinner, serenading her mom with her favourite Teresa Teng songs.

Her parents had always been rather embarrassingly open about their affection for each other. As a teenager, she was self-conscious about the way they held hands in public, or the way Mom sometimes kissed Dad's cheek if he said something she found charming or amusing. She realized now that it was a good and rare thing to have a marriage like that.

"Of course, Daddy," Norah laughed, but her eyes were welling up.

She felt homesick for her parents' home in Burnaby. It was a home they had owned for less than a decade, and one that she only ever stayed at during her Christmas and summer holidays. Each time Canada had felt familiar, like home, but better, because it also felt like an adventure.

Norah was seventeen when her father was offered a position to teach Chinese Literature at Simon Fraser University, after fifteen years at Chinese University in Hong Kong. Mom and Dad both found the offer irresistible. Her mother's older brother, the one Norah called Big Uncle and who had lived in Vancouver all his adult life, was ecstatic to hear that his baby sister might be immigrating, finally.

Her parents had urged her, then in her senior year, to apply to universities in Vancouver, and when she was accepted to both Simon Fraser and UBC, they thought the family move was meant to be. But then the offer from HKU came, a full scholarship in tow. It was decided, then: her parents would move to Vancouver first, Big Uncle would help them find a home in Burnaby, by the university, and Norah would follow after her four years at university were complete. In the meantime, she would visit during her holidays. All went according to plan until she started working at Future English, until Ben. She missed her parents so much.

"Have you thought any more about moving over here?" Mom asked, as though she could read her mind. "You could stay in your old bedroom, like before, or if you want more privacy, there's always the basement suite. There's plenty of room."

"And of course, once you get settled, you could find your own home," Dad added. "Not too far away from us, hopefully!" He laughed, but his eyes were sad. "Well, anything would be closer than having you in Hong Kong."

It was tempting, but she knew Ben could never just pack up and go. He was tethered to life in Hong Kong, but to Nai Nai most of all. *This is my home now,* she reminded herself firmly. *My whole world is sitting on my lap, right here in my arms.* She nuzzled Joey's back, hiding behind him as her eyes welled up. She drew comfort from his little giggles. Her parents laughed, too.

"Maybe one day," Norah said, looking up with a renewed smile. "Anyway, everything's great. Our second anniversary is coming up! We're thinking of traveling somewhere with Joey, maybe Phuket? Hainan Island? We're still thinking about it. It'll be his first flight." The idea of a trip had only just occurred to her, but it helped take her mind off her longing for her parents and their home in Burnaby.

"Phuket is so dreamy," Mom said. "That sounds…"

Dad cut in, undeterred. "And your mother-in-law, is she still making trouble for you?"

"Daddy," Norah said in her best little girl voice, the one that had gotten her out of trouble with her father countless times. "Everything's *fine.* Don't worry about me. You keep asking when I'm moving to Vancouver, but when are you visiting us again? This little guy misses his Gong Gong and Paw Paw, you know. You haven't seen him since he was a newborn. He's getting so big."

"We were hoping that you might bring Joey in the summer

and spend a few weeks with us here," Mom said eagerly. "July would be perfect; Vancouver's so beautiful in the summer. We could go to PNE! Joey will be nine months, right? Do you think that's too young for a long-distance flight?"

"Of course not! That sounds amazing. Let me talk to Ben, but I'm sure he'll say yes."

"Let us know the dates that work best for you guys when you can. Have a good week then, daughter," Dad said. "We miss you."

"And keep thinking about what we said about moving here," Mom added. "We love you."

"We miss and love you, too," Norah replied, holding Joey up so his cheek was touching hers and the two of them looked like Siamese twins on the computer screen. "Say goodbye to your Gong Gong and Paw Paw, Joey." And Joey obliged, as always, and blew them both kisses before Norah ended the call and her parents' faces disappeared.

Norah was holding Joey in the football position, the way the breastfeeding app taught her, coaxing him to latch, when Ben opened the door a crack and popped his head in. His face lit up when he saw the two of them.

"Hi, honey," she said. "Come in. How was dimsum?"

He sat down on the bed beside her and his familiar smell filled the room—Dettol body wash, and the Cussons bar soap he used as shaving cream. He stroked Joey's cheek with his thumb. "Pretty good. Your parents doing well? Want to come have lunch now?"

She grinned. "Yes and yes. Did you get the noodles?"

"Of course. And the buns for Joey, too. Come eat while the food's still hot."

"Give me another minute; I'm trying to see if Joey will nurse a little, but he doesn't seem very interested." She squeezed her breast, squirting a little milk at the corner of the baby's mouth, but he turned away after licking at it tentatively. She switched arms, repeated the trick with her other breast, but Joey yawned. "Maybe my nipples are too flat, huh?"

Ben didn't laugh. "You're doing great."

"I don't know about that," she said, handing Joey to his daddy. "Maybe he's not hungry enough yet? I'll try again after lunch. Oh, and Ben?"

"Yes?"

"Our anniversary's next week. Can we do something special?"

"We could go somewhere nice for dinner," he said. "Ma could watch Joey for the night. Didn't you say you wanted to try that steak house in Quarry Bay? What was it called? Harry's?"

She kissed him on the cheek. "I can't believe you still remember that place." It had been nearly a year since they walked past that little bistro, the glowing candles and shiny silverware beckoning. Since Joey arrived, they rarely ate out. "I do want to go to Harry's, but not for our anniversary, and not without Joey. I was thinking of a weekend trip. What do you think? Phuket? Hainan?"

After a moment's silence, Ben nodded slowly. "Hainan might be better; it's closer. A shorter flight will be easier on Joey, don't you think? I think my mom has a cousin who lives in Sanya."

Norah swallowed. "She... she wouldn't want to come with us, would she?"

"Silly," he said, tucking a lock of hair behind her ear. "I thought you said this trip was for our anniversary."

She rested her head on his shoulder for a moment, content. "Oh, honey, you're the best." Then she sat up quickly again, her phone in hand. "We won't even need our passports for Hainan, just our mainland travel permits."

"Good thing we got Joey's travel documents sorted out, otherwise he wouldn't be able to come with us," Ben said.

"Silly," she laughed. "I wouldn't dream of going anywhere without him." She shows him the calendar app on her phone. "We'd better book something quick. It's next week. Do these dates work for you? Friday to Monday?"

When he nodded, Norah continued, emboldened. In a focused frenzy, she chose a flight and resort package, added the free Wi-Fi and breakfast buffet options, requested a crib and baby bottle sterilizer, and pressed her thumb against the home key to confirm the purchase. The whole process took less than five minutes, and when she looked up again at Ben, her eyes were bright. "We're going, we're really going!"

The food was good, greasy and flavorful, and Norah was happy that Ben bought her potstickers, too. They were a little soggy from sitting in the Styrofoam box for so long, but still delicious. Her mother-in-law was sitting in her armchair, still in the special outfit she chose for her date with Ben, the one Norah privately thought of as her Barney suit. Joey, who did not care for the steamed bun, was bouncing in the Jumperoo. Nai Nai watched him, a frown on her face.

Ben was sitting across from her at the table, peeling a crystal pear. A thin, winding strip of brown ribbon flowed, like magic, from his hands.

"How was dimsum, Nai Nai?" she ventured tentatively. She was not sure if she was responsible for her mother-in-law's sour mood, but she could not think of anything she had done this morning that could be construed as offensive; they had barely seen each other. She set down her chopsticks, took a little sip of her black fungus drink, which was so thick and sweet it was more dessert than beverage.

"Fine."

"Did the manager save you an order of the char siu buns as usual? I know how you both enjoy them," she tried again, glancing at Ben. He shrugged. He had begun slicing the pear into wedges.

"Of course he did. I've known him for years, haven't I?"

"Yes, Nai Nai," Norah muttered, giving up. She finished her meal in silence. She wondered again how it was that her students at Future English competed for her attention, yet her own mother-in-law found conversations with her so irritating and unnecessary.

Norah was wiping off the table with an old washcloth when Ben suddenly broke the silence. "Ma, Norah and I will be traveling next weekend," he said, more loudly than necessary, and Norah felt a great surge of pride for him when she realized that he had been working up the courage to say this, to present it to his mother as an established arrangement rather than a request. He cleared his throat. "Yes, next weekend."

Nai Nai gazed steadily at Ben, then Norah, her frown deepening. "What did you say?"

"It's our anniversary next Saturday, Ma," he responded, his voice quivering ever so slightly. "We wish to go to Hainan Island to celebrate."

Norah, afraid to look at either of them, hurried over to scoop Joey out of the Jumperoo. "Come and pump with me, Joey," she said brightly. "Nai Nai, we'll just be inside." Her mother-in-law frowned at her, but didn't speak.

Back in the safety of their bedroom, she laid Joey down in his crib. She unhooked her nursing bra, screwed the flanges onto the empty bottles. When she held the flanges to her breasts, she took a few deep breaths, the way her breastfeeding app had recommended, but her milk refused to let down. "What do you think, Joey?" she whispered to her baby, who was watching his monkey mobile. "Do you think she'll try and stop us?"

Joey yawned.

"Why, you little dumpling," she scolded him playfully. "This concerns you, too!"

Finally, she heard the initial *plink plink plink* of her milk flowing. The dropped began to fill the bottom of the bottles with growing speed and she relaxed into the pillow behind her.

A few minutes later, Ben knocked quietly before opening the door. "Is Joey asleep?" he asked softly. "Ma's gone to her room for a nap."

"He just fell asleep a minute ago. Is everything okay?"

His forehead was shiny with sweat and his cheeks were flushed, but he smiled bravely. "Of course. She was just surprised, is all. And she wants us to bring a little something for her cousin." He paused. "So, does anyone need a new swimsuit?"

Chapter 5

"I HEAR Hainan Island is very beautiful, Norah," Kitty said as she sniffed at her steaming thermos. When she finally took a sip, the Future English long-timer coughed theatrically, as though the beverage was toxic. "My daughter-in-law bought me these new tea bags, said they're good for my fatty liver, but they taste terrible."

She held out the thermos to Norah and Siu-Fong, another one of Norah's favourite students. The three of them were sitting together in the social area, chatting and passing the time before Norah finished her time in the centre for the day. "What do you think? Rotten?"

Norah and Siu-Fong leaned towards the thermos at the same time. The tea certainly smelled unusual for Chinese tastes, Norah thought, a bit like chai, perhaps. She did not care much for Chinese tea, though, and found her mother-in-law's preference for pu-erh, which was muddy in both taste and appearance, baffling. Whatever kind of tea was in Kitty's thermos certainly smelled better than Nai Nai's pu-erh.

"It does not smell delicious, but I do not think it is rotten," Siu-Fong said with her usual forthrightness. Norah nodded in agreement. "Where in Hainan are you going, Norah?"

"Sanya," Norah responded, grinning from ear to ear. She liked the way the word sounded, a little like it could catch on as a baby girl's name. She wondered if anyone had ever named their daughter Sanya? It did not seem so unthinkable, given baby names like Brooklyn, Paris, and Vienna. "Oh, ladies, I'm so excited!"

Kitty nodded eagerly. "And the baby? Is he coming too?"

"I could never go anywhere without Joey, Kitty," Norah said, realizing this sounded like an exaggeration, but it was not. Like Lyra and Pan from *The Golden Compass*, it was as if she and Joey were connected by some thick invisible thread. It hurt to be apart. Even now, she wondered whether her baby was awake or asleep; whether her mother-in-law had reheated her breast milk for Joey, as Norah had requested, or gone straight for the can of formula. She thought of his eyes, how they disappeared into slits when he laughed, the way his little palms felt against her cheeks.

"Of course not," Siu-Fong agreed. "This will be Joey's first trip?"

Norah nodded, laughing. "We were going to just bring two carry-ons, you know, since it's such a short trip, just two nights. But his diapers alone took up half of one of the suitcases, and then when we started packing his bottles, and my breast pump, not to mention his clothes, we realized that was not going to work!"

As Kitty and Siu-Fong laughed, Tim, another regular, sauntered up to their table and pulled up one of the plastic chairs, a paper cup of coffee in hand.

"Hi, Tim," Norah said warmly. "I was just telling Kitty and Siu-Fong about my family trip this weekend."

"She's going to Sanya," Kitty added. "With the baby, too!"

"Just the three of you, right?" Tim asked. He took off his backpack, set it down on the floor beside his chair. "Your mother-in-law isn't coming, is she?"

"Not this time, she isn't big on beach holidays," she responded cheerfully. "Ben said maybe we can take her on a trip to Tokyo, somewhere with lots of shopping, another time."

She was careful not to say anything that could be interpreted as negative about her mother-in-law; some of these students knew Ben from when he was a student here, and even now he occasionally came to pick her up from work. He was never a 'regular'; Kitty, Siu-Fong, Tim, and some of the other older students treated Future English as their second home, their social club, but Ben had only come to the centre for his lessons with her, occasionally participating in one of Tony's literature workshops.

"When my wife and I visited Hainan twenty years ago, all anyone could sell us was coconut candy," Tim said. "Every souvenir shop was overflowing with coconut candy, always packaged in the same blue and white wrappers. Good stuff."

"Do you mean gummies? Or hard candy?" Kitty asked. She had begun taking tentative sips of her tea. "Perhaps this is not so bad, after all. I've got to think of my liver, you know."

"Hard candy," he replied, "smooth and creamy. I've never seen it sold in Hong Kong, and believe me, I've looked."

"Thank you for the recommendation, Tim," Norah said. "I'll be sure to bring some with me on Tuesday when I'm back at the centre." Norah glanced surreptitiously at the clock hanging behind the reception area; it was nearly time to go meet Nai Nai and Joey at the clinic for his follow-up appointment with Dr. Chan.

"You're leaving at four today, aren't you, Norah?" Siu-Fong said, smiling.

"Go on, then," Kitty added. "Don't keep Joey waiting."

"That would never do," Tim agreed, eyes twinkling.

At one time, Norah would have been embarrassed for

being caught out by her students, but they were more than just students. When she worked full-time at Future English, her hours were such that she hardly saw anyone outside of work: she started at noon and finished at 8 or 9 at night, missing both the regular lunch and dinner time slots around which most social engagements revolved, and because her workweek was from Wednesday to Sunday, she missed the weekends, too.

Now that Norah was a mother, she felt even further removed from her old circle of friends, none of whom were married or had kids. She made an effort to stay active on Facebook, so she was still sort of in the loop, able to keep up with likes and comments when her high school friends posted updates. They tried to do the same for her, but she suspected nobody actually cared whether Joey had started sitting up unassisted, or if he'd just had his first taste of congee. Joey's developmental milestones seemed irrelevant and unglamorous compared to her friends' updates – Hannah was starting an internship at Linklaters, Cassie just got engaged after her boyfriend proposed to her during their Bora Bora trip, Kirsten had been accepted into the MFA programme at City University.

If not for her colleagues and students, or, as Ivan liked to call them, her 'Future Family', Norah would probably spend a lot of time feeling like she was missing out. As it was, her heart was full.

She smiled affectionately at her students, her friends. "Well, if you insist." She downed the last of her coffee, now cold, and stood up, smiling. "See you in a few days! I'll bring pictures! And lots of candy!"

On the radio, Karen Carpenter was singing about being on the top of the world, and in the back seats of the taxi, Norah and her mother-in-law were humming along with her. Joey was asleep in Norah's arms, his skin smoother and clearer than it had been in weeks. Best of all, Dr. Chan had told them since Joey was doing so well, he could even stop using the cortisone cream, at least for the next two weeks. And if Joey's condition continued to improve, he would make further adjustments at their next appointment. It felt as though they had won the lottery.

"Norah," Nai Nai said suddenly, clutching at Norah's arm. "Going to see Dr. Chan was a good idea."

Norah was touched. "Thank you for coming to the clinic with us, Nai Nai."

They listened to the grey-haired driver's seventies playlist in comfortable silence, Joey snoring softly against Norah's chest. By the time the driver pulled up in front of their pink and white building, Joey was awake.

Norah woke on Friday morning with a giggle on her lips. She had been dreaming of something that made her laugh so hard there were tears in her eyes—but the moment she opened them the dream slipped out of reach like a wet bar of soap.

It doesn't matter, Norah shrugged, pulling the blanket up to her chin. A silly, funny dream had to be a good omen for their trip to Sanya.

Ben and Joey were both still asleep, but she could see Joey beginning to stir. She leaned over the crib so that the moment he woke he would see her smiling down on him. She resisted the urge to stroke his cheeks, which were no longer inflamed and just a little dry. No dryer than her own cheeks, she thought, reaching up to touch her own skin with the back of her hand. When Joey finally opened his eyes and saw his mother, he immediately reached for her with outstretched arms.

"Good morning, little one," she said, scooping up her baby and inhaling his clean, familiar scent. She stroked his head tenderly; she adored his fine, wispy hair. She smiled as she remembered how little hair he'd had as a newborn. His head had resembled a peach, the layer of fuzz so thin it was barely visible. Norah nuzzled the top of Joey's head now, singing his favourite song, "Skidamarink", but she changed the lyrics to "I love you when you're peachy, I love you when you're bald..."

She told him about the trip as she changed his diaper. "We're going to ride an airplane, today, Joey, just you and me and Baba, then we're going to stay in a super special hotel for two nights! It's going to be fun, fun, fun!"

He looked at her, his eyes trusting and adoring. They were not black like her eyes or Ben's, but a smooth brown, the color of tea that had been brewing for a while.

"Ma," he said suddenly.

"Joey?" Norah felt her heart hammering in her chest. "Did you just say 'Mama', Joey?"

He smiled his trademark gummy smile at her, then, after a pregnant pause, obliged: "Ma. Ma. Ma. Ma."

"Joey!" she shrieked, delirious with happiness, lifting him above her head and kissing his tummy over and over until he laughed and laughed. "Ben, Joey called me Mama!"

Ben rolled over, rubbing his eyes. "He did what?"

"He said 'Mama'!" she paused, looking down at her baby. "Well, Ma. Ma. Like that, with a pause in the middle."

"Ma. Ma," Joey echoed agreeably.

Ben's eyes grew wide. "So he did!" He grabbed his phone from under his pillow and started filming. "Today is April 7th. Joey is six months and three days old, and he just said his first word. Can you say it again please, Joey?"

Joey furrowed his brow, looked as if he was thinking about

whether he wanted to.

"Go on, then, Joey," Norah said, kissing the top of his head. "Who's kissing you, little one?"

He didn't need to check. "Ma. Ma."

When Norah came out of the bathroom, a towel draped around her shoulders, she heard her mother-in-law's shrill voice over the din of Joey's Jumperoo: "Again, Joey, again! Ben, did you hear that? He's saying 'Maa Maa'! He's saying grandma!"

Norah stopped where she was, straining her ears to hear how Ben would respond.

Ben murmured something, but it was unintelligible; the Jumperoo was too loud.

"He did, he really did! Come on now, Joey, say it one more time for Maa Maa," she said in that wheedling tone she often used with Ben. Norah heard her switching off the Jumperoo in expectation.

Norah felt sweat pooling in her armpits.

After a very long silence, finally broken by Joey's whimpering, Nai Nai sighed in disappointment. "I'm telling you, Ben, he just said Maa Maa, as clear as anything. Didn't you, Joey?"

Norah walked into the living room, patting at her hair, as Ben was handing his mother a small stack of bills, a $500 note on top. "Ma, this is your *gayong*," he said respectfully, his head bowed.

There was a ritualistic element to their little exchange; it always took place in the morning of the first Saturday of each month, on the sofa. Ben always said "Ma, this is your *gayong*," and Nai Nai always responded with, "It's too much. It's too much," pocketing the money without counting the bills. How did she know it was too much? Norah sometimes wondered.

Was it the same amount every time?

Norah was aware of the traditional Chinese custom of giving money to one's parents, but before Ben, it had always been a fuzzy concept; her parents had never required this monetary sign of filial piety of her. As a child and teenager, she had drawn lots of pictures, written lots of cards, and knitted lots of scarves for her parents' birthdays, for Christmas. After she started working, she began buying her parents more luxurious gifts: a leather clutch for her mother, a cashmere sweater for her father, a Vitamix blender for their anniversary last year. But never straight-up money.

When they were newly married, she once asked Ben about it, asked why he should give money to his mother when she was far wealthier than he was and clearly had no need for his money, and he had responded with the sort of matter-of-factness that discouraged further questions or discussion. "*Gayong* is not about need, Norah," he had said, patiently, as though she were a child, or a foreigner unlearned in Chinese ways.

Ben's words had seemed so familiar somehow, and after a few moments, it had come to her: Ben, who had never read Shakespeare, had seemed to be quoting from King Lear—*O reason not the need!* As a teenager in English class she had felt such strong hatred for Lear's older daughters, had found them positively revolting in their ingratitude. So it was only fitting that as a young wife, she had nodded, convinced, that Ben's commitment to giving *gayong* to his mother was good and right. Now, nearly two years on, it felt too late to question the practice.

"Good morning, Nai Nai," Norah said. Her mother-in-law hastily pocketed the bills, looking up at Norah with uncharacteristic cheerfulness.

"Good morning," she responded. "Joey said his first word, Norah." She paused dramatically. "He said 'Maa'."

Norah looked at her mother-in-law, at Ben, then back at her mother-in-law. Ben was looking at her with a sort of pleading, desperate look, and the message was *Please, baby, please.*

Joey began crying then, and Norah hurried over to comfort him, but her mother-in-law clung to the baby protectively. "There, there, Joey," Nai Nai kept saying, louder and louder, but Joey kept crying harder and harder until she finally returned him to Norah with a frown.

Chapter 6

THE TAXI ride to the airport was quiet, interrupted only by the occasional buzzing of the driver's WhatsApp notifications and Joey's little snuffles. He had been unusually fussy: whimpering, squirming in the carrier, unable to fall asleep.

Ben wished he had handled the Ma/Maa situation that morning better. He had done his best, had tried not to say anything that would encourage or offend, but it hadn't been enough. Norah was sullenly staring out the window, and his two attempts at conversation, 'I think we'll have time for some ramen before the flight,' and 'I like Joey's shirt', had fallen flat.

Their taxi was crossing the Tsing Ma Bridge when Norah finally cried, "Why didn't you tell Nai Nai Joey was saying Mama, not Maa Maa?"

He thought, tomorrow will be two years. At the altar that day her eyes had looked like they did now, red-rimmed, watery, doe-like. He picked up her hand, squeezed it. She didn't let go.

"We know what he really said," he said softly. "We've even got a recording on my phone. Hard evidence, you know."

Norah's expression softens a little, and when she repeated, "But why didn't you say?" her tone was more tentative than accusatory.

"I…" Ben swallowed. "I know I should've, but I didn't want to upset her before we left on our trip. I'm sorry, baby."

Norah sighed. "Let's not talk about it anymore," she finally said. A few moments later, she rested her head on his shoulder, and Ben felt the weight in his chest lifting a little.

Sanya Phoenix International Airport looked the way Ben imagined it would look: rough hewn beams, palm trees, airport staff dressed in khakis and bright polo shirts, a giant pineapple on one of the main buildings, large banners proclaiming *Sanya: China's Hawaii*. Norah had dressed Joey in a tiny orange Hawaiian shirt and green Crocs, and he looked very much at home in these tropical surroundings.

The airport *felt* the way Ben imagined it woud, too; long rows of wooden ceiling fans were spinning lazily, adding to the rustic ambiance of the airport but doing little to ease the sticky heat. There seemed to be no air-conditioning in the airport at all. Norah fanned Joey with her passport as they waited with a small crowd of fellow tourists at the baggage reclaim area.

Joey's eyes lit up when the suitcases started sliding down the ramp onto the carousel with satisfying *thwump*! *thwump*! sounds. He clapped his hands as the bags went around and around in slow circles. When their grey suitcase finally arrived in front of them, Ben swiftly swung it off the moving belt and onto their trolley.

Ben was so thankful Eric from work had lent him the DSLR camera he now had hanging on a green strap around his neck; he couldn't stop taking photos, both posed and candid, of Norah in her bright yellow sundress, the one that flowed down to her ankles, and Joey in his little Hawaiian shirt. Joey was at a great stage for photographs; he would smile at the camera the moment his father made a silly sound, and Ben had learned a great number of these from watching Norah.

"Gambagooey, Joey! Gamba*gooey*!" he cried as they exited the airport through the revolving doors. Joey flashed Ben a bright smile over Norah's shoulder.

It was hot, humid, and surprisingly windy. Since Joey arrived, Norah almost always wore her hair in a tight ponytail, but today she had let her hair down. She looked so lovely in that dress, he thought, the wind in her hair. She had even painted her toenails; he could not remember the last time she did that, but it must have been before Joey was born.

They quickly found the taxi stand and lined up; thankfully, there were only three families in front of them.

"Take a selfie now, Baba," Norah said, passing Ben her cell phone. "We need more of the three of us."

Ben, who used to hate being in pictures, added a silly filter so the three of them were wearing matching heart-shaped sunglasses. The two of them studied the photo together on her phone, giggling like children at the effect.

"I love you, honey," Norah said, suddenly, kissing Ben's cheek. "You're so stubbly! I love it when you don't shave."

"That's why I haven't shaved since Wednesday," he responded, leaning over Joey's head and kissing her on the lips. His phone buzzed in his pocket then, and he knew, instinctively, that it was his mother, checking to see whether they had arrived safely. He considered responding later, at the hotel, but then remembered his mother's hypertension; there was no point in worrying her needlessly.

"Give me one second, Norah," Ben said, quickly taking out his phone. The message not only asked him to confirm that they had arrived safely, but to did so by calling her. He decided that a text would have to suffice: *Just landed, waiting for a taxi. Call you tonight at the hotel.*

"Is it Nai Nai?" Norah asked.

Ben looked up from his rapid typing, but she did not seem upset. "I'm just telling her we got here safely."

"I feel guilty that we didn't invite her to come with us," she said, but she did not look guilty. "Maybe next time," she added dutifully.

Probably not, Ben thought, and that was totally fine. His Ma hated swimming, hated going to the beach, hated being in the sun for long periods, so Hainan would have been a very poor choice for her anyhow.

Their taxi was bright green. The smell of cigarette smoke inside the car was overwhelming, and was made worse by the artificial coconut smell coming from the reed diffuser attached to the dashboard. Ben desperately wanted to roll down the windows, but this seemed rude, since the young, eager driver kept asking them if the air-con was cool enough. In the end, he did, for Joey's sake—cigarette smoke couldn't possibly be good for his skin. The Apple Maps app promised that the ride from the airport to the resort would only be ten minutes long, so he tried not to worry too much about it. Both Ben and Norah spent the ride taking shallow breaths and taking turns inhaling the good, familiar scent of Joey's little head.

Ben suddenly remembered a night, shortly after Joey was born, when Norah was almost certainly suffering from post-partum depression, when she was crying and crying because she was afraid Joey would lose his baby boy smell and there was no way to capture it in a photograph or a bottle, the way they could Joey's sleepy newborn smile or umbilical stump.

He looked over at his wife now, the way she and the baby were giggling as she sniffed at the back of his neck. He was thankful that six months on, Joey still smelled like Joey.

The hotel lobby felt rustic and relaxed, unintimidating. Ben took in everything with pleasure: the thatched roof, the wooden ceiling fans, the carved beams and pillars, the round turquoise cushions on the rattan sofas, the young woman in the corner serving fresh coconuts and iced towels to the hotel guests. He was not the only dad wearing a baby in a carrier; there were several young families milling about.

Ben and Joey lined up for a coconut as Norah checked them in.

"Hello, *nihao,* lei ho ma?" the coconut woman said, smiling broadly, when it was their turn. She was wearing a turquoise polo shirt which matched the cushions, and a visor, even though they were not outdoors. She looked as though working at this makeshift coconut stall was the best job in the world, and continued speaking in three languages with gusto: "Coconut, *ye zi,* yeh jee?"

"We speak all of the above," Ben laughed, responding instinctively in Putonghua; Hainan might be 'China's Hawaii' but it was still China. "Could we have a coconut please?"

The woman nodded eagerly, muttering, "Certainly, *dang ran le,* mo man tai," under her breath as she used a large cleaver to chop off the top of one of the coconuts in one smooth motion. She inserted a plastic straw, one of those silly spiral ones they had at carnivals, in the coconut before handing it to Ben with two hands. "Enjoy! *Manyong*! Man man yum!" She smiled at the next family in line. "Hello, *nihao,* lei ho ma?"

The coconut juice was sweet and icy cold. Joey looked up at him, his eyes hopeful, his tongue darting in and out like a puppy's. Ben tried to let him take a sip, but after a few unsuccessful attempted at sucking at the straw, Joey turned his head away in frustration. Ben held his thumb over the top of the straw, suctioning up a bit of the liquid, then dribbled it into his son's mouth. He laughed as his son furrowed his brow and spat it out.

"Ben!" Norah was suddenly beside them, her hands on her hips. "You can't give him coconut juice, silly! He's never had it before! What if he's allergic?"

"Sorry," Ben said, and he was. In his excitement, he had completely forgotten about Joey's eczema. "He didn't really have any, Norah, he spat it right out—"

She pecked him on the lips, silencing him. "I know he did. I'm pretty sure he'll be fine. Anyway, we're all set." She held up their room cards, feigning nonchalance. "Our villa is ten minutes away on foot, two minutes away by buggy. What do you think? Buggy, right? I think Joey would enjoy the ride."

"You booked a villa? A whole villa?" He had never stayed in a villa before. Part of him was excited; part of him wondered how much their stay here was going to cost.

She looked a little sheepish. "Um, yes." Then the rest of the details tumbled out of her, her excitement bubbling over, like champagne: "With a private pool! A Jacuzzi! A swing!" She squealed as Ben hugged her tight, Joey squirming between them.

They passed by several rows of villas, each one nestled behind a tall decorative fence, before their buggy pulled to a seemingly arbitrary stop in front of one of them. The driver hopped off, heaved their suitcase from the back of the vehicle onto the pavement and wheeled it beside the wooden door, retractable handle extended and ready. He was very young, perhaps no more than eighteen or twenty. He cleared his throat as he read the scribbled tag the lobby staff had attached to the suitcase. Then, in slow, lightly accented English, he said, "Mister and Missus

Tam, this is your villa. It is number 4-3-8." He placed a hand over his heart and bowed slightly. "I am Wen. If you dial 0 on your telephone, I will return with buggy. We can go to hotel lobby or beach, as you like it. You have access card?"

Norah nodded, thanking him warmly. "You speak such good English, Wen," she added. "You must have been a very good student at school! Or do you watch a lot of American movies?"

Ben saw the young driver blushing furiously at his wife's attention. At one point, Ben might have thought she was flirting, but he knew now this was just the teacher in her. Once, fairly early in their relationship, Ben took her on a date at Pizza Hut. He was ashamed now that he had thought Pizza Hut a suitable place to bring his pretty girlfriend for dinner, but she hadn't minded. She had never been the kind of girl to pine after luxuries, the way many Hong Kong women kept their eye on the latest designer handbag, or the newest Michelin-starred restaurant. He could see in his mind's eye the way Norah looked that evening on their way to Pizza Hut: she had walked with her arm in his, a bounce in her step, as she described in detail everything she looked forward to at dinner: the salad bar, the garlic bread, the cheesy stuffed crust.

But he also remembered how he had felt a little insecure, jealous even, when she conversed easily, unnecessarily, with the pimply Pizza Hut waiter and complimented him on his English.

"Why are you being so quiet?" she had asked, after the waiter had taken their order and it was just the two of them again.

Ben hadn't wanted to say, hadn't wanted her to think that he was jealous, but Norah had known. "You think I'm being too chatty, huh?"

"His English wasn't *that* good, was it?" And he had sounded petty even to himself.

"Oh, I'm so sorry," she had said, her cheeks reddening

immediately. "I really am sorry. Sometimes I forget I'm not at work, I guess. I'm always trying to get my students to feel confident about themselves when they talk to me. Ivan says it's my gift. Making people feel good about themselves. But now I've made you feel bad. I'm sorry, Ben." And she had looked down at her lap, making those little snuffling noises with her nose that he now knew so well, and he had felt like an idiot for being so petty and jealous.

Ben had reached across the narrow table and cupped her cheeks in his hands. "It *is* your gift," he had responded, wiping away a tear with his thumb and marveling at how the ugly jealousy had evaporated, just like that.

Ben watched his wife now, not with jealousy but with pride. She did make people feel good about themselves. He saw that young Wen was standing a little taller now.

"I watch all the Avenger movies, ma'am. Many times." He bowed again. "If you need buggy, please dial 0. I go now. Have a good day, Mister and Missus Tam, and Baby."

They tapped their access card at the reader attached to the gate, which buzzed loudly, startling Joey, who had finally dozed off. Ben patted at him gently, and Norah whispered something into his little ear, and he nodded off again.

The paneled fencing meant that the outdoor space was completely private. The pool was bean-shaped, the surface of the water glistening in the midday sun. There was a white wooden swing hanging from the roof of the porch; the seat was just wide enough to fit him and Norah both, with Joey in their arms. Through the window, he could see a large square hot tub with multiple rows of water jets.

The villa itself was bigger than his mother's entire flat, with a spacious living room area that was furnished with the same rustic rattan furniture as the lobby, and beyond that, a four-poster bed with gauzy, semi-transparent drapes. Perched on the bed were two towel swans whose entwined necks formed a heart; they were swimming in a red sea of rose petals.

Ben and Norah looked at each other then, their giddy expressions one and the same. Norah tugged Joey out of the carrier and laid him gently in the wooden crib beside their bed as Ben unbuckled the waist and shoulder straps. He plopped down on the carpet, leaning against the foot of the bed.

"Well, my love," Norah said, sitting down beside him and resting her head on his shoulder. "A very happy anniversary to you."

"Hello, Ma?" Ben was sitting on the swing on the porch, studying the mosaic designs at the bottom of the pool. Norah was taking what she called a 'power nap'; he had promised to wake her after twenty minutes. She didn't want to miss the sunset, and Joey would probably be up in a few minutes anyway.

It had been a very good afternoon. He and Norah enjoyed the hot tub immensely; it was large enough for them both, with molded seats along the sides that had strategically positioned jet streams targeting their weary shoulders, calves, lower backs.

He had gone in first, and watched as his wife studied the labels on the jars of bath salts lined up beside the hot tub. When she poured in the salt, the effect was immediate: the swirling, steaming water turned purple and the bathroom filled with the scent of lavender. She had lowered herself into the tub onto his lap, then, and it had been something new for them, being together in a Jacuzzi like that. His Ma's apartment only had a shower.

"Ma?" he said again, when she didn't answer. "Can you hear me?"

"Yes," she said shortly. "I expected you to call me hours ago."

"Sorry, Ma. Did you get my text message?"

"I was expecting you to call me," she repeated.

"It took us a while to get to the resort," Ben said, "and get, uh, settled."

There was another long pause. "Is it nice, then? What you expected?"

He gazed at their courtyard, at the bean-shaped pool. Rays of afternoon sun were dancing on the surface. "It's not too bad."

"Have you taken the tea to your Fifth Uncle yet?"

Ben checked his Timex, wondered if he could slip out for an hour before dinner if he didn't wake Norah. "I'm planning on visiting him tonight. I'll be sure to send your regards. What are you doing for dinner?"

"Don't worry; I'll cook something." The crankiness in her voice seemed to be lessening a little. "How was Joey on the plane?"

"Oh, he was amazing. Hardly cried at all."

"He's a good boy, my Joey." She paused. "Like you."

Ben cleared his throat. "Take care of yourself, then, Ma. Don't forget to lock the front door tonight."

When he went back inside the villa, he found Norah curled up on the right side of the bed, in her usual position: one leg straight and the other bent, her body forming the letter *h*. He smiled when he saw Joey awake and kicking his feet with gusto. "Hey, little guy," he said, scooping him up and nuzzling his tummy. "You were asleep a real long time."

Joey giggled, the sound sweet to Ben's ears. "Ma," he said. "Ma."

"Mama's still asleep," Ben responded. "You're hungry, aren't you? Let me get you some milk."

Ben laid a large bath towel on the carpet in front of the rattan sofa and set Joey down on it to continue his kicking while he fixed up a bottle of formula. As Joey drank noisily, his two hands clutching at the bottle, Ben checked his watch again. Perhaps he could take Joey with him to visit his Fifth Uncle, let Norah sleep another hour or so. She would be happy, wouldn't she, if he took care of the chore so they could enjoy the rest of the trip without it hanging over their heads?

He had never met this relative before. The relationship was very distant; it was his mother's great aunt's husband. According to his mother, he was a widower in his eighties who would very much appreciate Ben's visit. He scrolled up to the text message from his mother with Fifth Uncle's number and address, and picked up the receiver of the phone on the desk. As he pressed the oversized digits on the phone, he was aware that he had not touched a physical phone button in a very long time.

"Hello?" The elderly voice coughed loudly into the phone and Ben had to hold the receiver away from his ear. "Hello?"

"Fifth Uncle? I'm Ben. My mother, Sau-lin, said she told you I would be visiting you?"

"Hello? Hello?"

Ben realized Fifth Uncle must be deaf, or close to it.

"Fifth Uncle?" Ben tried again, louder, not quite shouting, but nearly. He looked nervously at the bed, but Norah's sleeping form appeared undisturbed. "I am Sau-lin's son! I would like to visit you tonight!"

"Sau-lin's son? Oh, you are Ben! Yes, please come!"

Ben sighed in relief. "I am coming now! I have your address! I will take a taxi!"

He packed his mother's three boxes of tea into his backpack, then added a diaper and the wet wipes for Joey, in case of an emergency. He scribbled a note for Norah, letting her know where he and Joey had gone, and promising to be back within an hour or so. "I love you," he added at the bottom. "We won't be long. P.S. Want to try the dinner buffet tonight?"

He left this note on the pillow beside her, then tiptoed back into the living room, where Joey clapped eagerly at the prospect of going out. Ben dialed 0, asked for Wen, and was assured of a buggy in the next two minutes.

As they waited by the gate of their villa, the sun began to set. Ben, normally a great enthusiast of sunset photography, found it difficult to look up at the mingled gold and orange hues; they reminded him too much of Norah and how he was letting her down. They had planned on that walk on the beach before dinner; he had promised. *You are breathtaking,* he thought miserably. *Breathtaking, like a sunset.*

Chapter 7

When Norah woke up, she sensed something was wrong, but her mind seemed fuzzy, like it was wrapped in a quilt. It was dark. She was in an unfamiliar bed and room. It took her several disorienting moments to remember that she was in Sanya on her anniversary trip, with Ben and Joey. According to the glowing digits of the clock on the bedside table, it was 7:37 in the evening.

She sat up quickly, afraid. Where was Joey? She switched on the bedside lamp so she could check the crib, but the moment the light came on, she saw a piece of paper on the pillow beside hers; it was a note from Ben.

As she scanned the neatly printed lines, anger swiftly replaced her fear. She could not believe that Ben snuck out with Joey while she was sleeping. Worse still, the note said they would be back by around 6, but it was already much later than that.

Norah put on her bathrobe, cinching the waist tightly. The villa was shadowy and dark, much too big a space for just her. She sat on the edge of the bed, her cell phone in her hand, wanting to call Ben, but her hands were shaking so badly she couldn't quite press the numbers on the screen.

At this moment she heard footsteps not far from where she was. She rushed into the living room, ready to open the door, when it swung open.

It was Ben, wearing Joey in the carrier. Their faces were red, their heads sweaty. Joey was sniffling, and when he saw her, began crying in earnest. He reached for her with a sort of frantic desperation, and when Norah scooped him out of the carrier, she felt the large wet patch on his khaki shorts, his swollen diaper drooping down to his ankles.

Ben stood there, his head hanging, the bulging backpack still on his shoulders and the empty carrier still buckled to his sweaty frame. "Norah, I'm so sorry."

She was silent as she carried Joey with her into the bedroom and got the bottle of pine tar solution from their suitcase. Propping Joey up in her lap, she carefully poured half a capful into the small baby tub the resort provided before adjusting the hot and cold taps, testing the temperature of the water with her elbow until it was just right. Joey dipped his fingers in too, and finally smiled a little. She laid a towel beside the tub and began to undress Joey, tugging off his soggy shorts and diaper first.

Ben continued, his voice earnest, when she didn't say anything. "I'm sorry we were gone for so long, the driver couldn't find the address on our way there, and I used up my phone battery with the screen on the whole time, but Fifth Uncle didn't have a phone charger, only a landline, and I couldn't look up the hotel number. He started cooking a whole meal for us and wouldn't let us leave until we'd tried his cooking but he cooked so slowly, and I kept wanting to leave but he kept saying just one more minute, one more minute, and we brought you lots of coconut candy, Fifth Uncle said this place was the best, he got us like ten bags to bring back to Hong Kong."

Norah knew he was afraid that she was angry. She had every right to be angry, but seeing him standing there, sweat rolling down the sides of his flushed face, she realized much of her earlier frustration had given way to relief. His eyes were so anxious and sorry that her heart ached.

"I was so scared," she said softly, looking up at her husband. She was crouching on the floor beside Joey, who she had lain on the towel beside the bathtub to undress. "I woke up and didn't know where I was. It was so dark, Ben, I had no idea where you'd gone, and I was so scared, I thought maybe—"

Ben rushed to her then, dropped to his knees and hugged her fiercely from behind. She was enveloped by the familiar musky smell of his sweat, the way he smelled coming home from a run, or after making love to her. "I'll make it up to you, Norah, we can get room service tonight, you must be starving. But tomorrow, I promise, we'll see the sunset, we'll have the buffet, we'll do everything we said we would."

Norah gently lowered Joey into the tub. He squealed, splashing the yellowy water with his hands splayed like stars. He purred with pleasure as she gently massaged his arms and legs; he was so happy to be free of that dirty diaper, clean and in her arms again. Ben crouched beside her, silent, waiting for her reaction. "Put down your bag," she finally said.

Ben untangled the mess of carrier and backpack straps, unbuckling the chest strap, the waist strap, and letting the carrier fall to the floor before sliding the straps of the backpack off his arms, too. The backpack fell with such a loud thud that Norah wondered just how many coconut candies Fifth Uncle had given them. She continued scooping the soapy water on Joey's shoulders and back to keep him warm. He was kicking now, giggling as he made little splashes with his feet. She reached out one hand to squeeze the back of Ben's neck, but it barely gave, it was so tense.

"I'm sorry," Ben said, his head bowed. "I shouldn't have slipped out without you. I should've woken you up, but I really thought it would only take an hour. I thought by the time you woke up we could just go to dinner." He looked guiltily at her. "I promised Ma I'd go tonight."

Her anger flared at the mention of her mother-in-law. "She told you to do this? Sneak off to her relative with her stupid tea while I was asleep?"

"Norah, of course not!" To Norah's ears, Ben's shock sounded affected and artificial. "Honestly, I didn't think it'd take this long; the app said the address was only twenty minutes away, but it took forever for the stupid driver to find his way. Fifth Uncle is eighty-nine, can you believe it? He insisted we call my mom long-distance, you know, but she wouldn't pick up at first. She told us afterwards when we finally got through that she was in the shower. And on our way back there was terrible traffic. Joey kept crying in the taxi, but I didn't bring any formula with us."

"If you had to go tonight, then at the very least you should've left Joey here with me!" At this, Joey's bottom lip began to tremble. "Not you, Joey, I'm not mad at you! I'm mad at your father!" But she was still yelling, and Joey began to cry.

Ben had disappeared from the bathroom and was nowhere to be seen. She lifted Joey out of the water and swiftly wrapped him in one of the thick white towels so he looked like baby Jesus in a nativity.

"Ma," Joey said, his little voice reproachful.

"I'm sorry, Joey," she whispered in response. "I'm sorry for yelling."

When they got to the four-poster bed, Norah saw that Ben had gotten Joey's pajamas, sleep sack, and a fresh diaper from the suitcase and lain them out on their bed. He sat on the edge of the bed beside the neatly arranged clothes, his head hanging low. "Norah, I'm sorry."

"I'm not mad at you anymore," she muttered as she helped

Joey put on his diaper. Her emotions were swinging wildly, in every direction, and she felt exhausted, even though she'd just woken up. *Will my mother-in-law always have this hold on me?* she wondered wearily. "I'm just frustrated at your mom, I guess. But whatever. I want to try the coconut candy now."

Ben sprung off the bed and rushed into the living room. He returned almost immediately, a clear plastic bag in his arms. "Here they are, Norah," he said eagerly, yanking out one of the packets from his backpack and tearing it open with a flourish. He unwrapped the candy, pocketed the blue and white wrapper, and held it out to her between his thumb and forefinger. "You'll like it, I know you will."

She let him feed it to her, tasted the saltiness of his fingers before the concentrated, intense flavor of the candy filled her mouth. It was creamy and smooth, just as Tim promised. That afternoon at Future English spent discussing this trip seemed like a very long time ago.

She finished zipping Joey up in his sleep sack, held him in the crook of her arm, and was surprised when he began rooting at her chest. He hadn't done this since he was a newborn. When she loosened the belt on her bathrobe and revealed one swollen breast, he sucked at it, tentatively at first, and then more hungrily. Norah felt the familiar sharp tingle that told her the milk was letting down. Norah's eyes met Ben's; she could see that he felt the wonder of the moment, as she did. Neither of them moved or spoke; neither wanted to break the spell. Joey hadn't nursed at the breast in months.

A few minutes later, Joey nodded off. Norah gently unlatched him from her breast and laid him down in his crib. She retied the belt of her bathrobe and sat down beside Ben, who was still hunched over, his elbows on his knees and his eyes staring down at the purple carpet.

"Want to make some cup noodles or something then?" she said. "I saw a few in the mini-bar. I'm hungry."

"Norah, I'm sorry," Ben repeated, penitent.

Norah cupped his stubbly cheek in her palm. "You've got to stop letting Nai Nai boss you around like this," she said. "You've got to stand up to her sometimes. For me."

He nodded miserably. "I know. I'll keep trying."

What more could Norah ask? She nodded. "Chicken or spicy seafood?"

Norah was humming 'Top of the World' as she perused the spread at the breakfast buffet. She waved at Joey, who was seated in a pink Stokke high chair, much fancier than the plastic IKEA high chair they had at home. She blew a kiss at Ben, who pretended to catch it and slip it in his shirt pocket. He was dressed in a white linen shirt and khaki shorts, and Joey's outfit matched his father's exactly. Their table was by the floor-to-ceiling windows, with a spectacular view of the resort grounds, and the long stretch of beach beyond them.

She was wearing a flowy mint green dress that swished around her ankles as she walked, and her hair smelled of the resort's coconut-scented shampoo. Ben had made love to her early that morning, when it was still mostly dark, in that four-poster bed with its gauzy drapes, and it had felt like it used to, in the beginning. After, they had fallen asleep again in each other's arms, a tangle of limbs. They had woken to Joey's plaintive cries of *Ma. Ma.* By then, their villa had been bright with the rays of the late-morning sun.

Norah, who loved buffets and had been to a great many of them, was nevertheless impressed by this one. There were the usual breads and pastries, cereals and yogurt, fresh juices in glass jugs, silver serving dishes with bacon, sausages, scrambled eggs. These were to be expected, but there was also an impressive number of stations with chefs cooking live: an omelette station with luxurious fillings like truffle slices and foie gras, a waffle and pancake station, a congee and noodle station, and what looked like a sausage McMuffin station. The fresh fruit options were fantastically exotic, with hairy rambutans, pink-fleshed dragon fruit, and mango wedges alongside the expected watermelon and cantaloupe chunks.

This is all very nice, Norah thought, pleased, but she stopped in her tracks when she saw a little girl, perhaps five or six, skip past her with three scoops of ice cream, each a different color, on a waffle cone. Ice cream for breakfast? And then she saw it—an ice-cream trolley with a striped red and white canopy, and behind it, a beaming young woman brandishing a metal ice-cream scoop like a wand. She was wearing a red apron, exactly the way Norah imagined an ice-cream scooper lady should.

"Good morning," Norah said, suddenly shy; there was no one else at this station. She wondered, wildly, what her would mother say if she saw Norah standing here at 10:30 in the morning. "You serve ice cream for breakfast?"

"Yes! For the children, and the young at heart," the young woman said, winking. "I'll be honest though. I haven't had anyone come by my station yet. Not too many parents let their kids have ice cream for breakfast."

"Good thing my parents live in Canada," Norah grinned, and the woman laughed out loud. "Can I have three scoops? Vanilla, chocolate, and strawberry, please?"

"Cone or cup?"

"Cone, please." Norah resisted the urge to clap her hands. Since she was a little girl, she had drawn ice cream that looked like this: an inverted triangle with diagonal stripes criss-crossing each other to form the waffle cone, then three circles - always white, brown, and pink, in that order. As the ice cream lady expertly balanced one generous scoop on top of another, Norah let out a little sigh of contentment.

A moment later, she was back at their table, the towering cone in one hand, a bowl of plain rice congee for Joey in the other. Joey squealed when she returned, reaching for the ice-cream. Ben was talking to someone on his cell phone. His eyes widened when he saw her cone, and he smiled at her as she caught the drips with her tongue.

"Yes, of course, Ma," he said, rolling his eyes. His free hand mimed the beak of a chatty bird, which made Norah giggle. "Of course I did. He's fine, Ma. He was very happy to see me and Joey..."

Norah gulped down the rest of her ice water before carefully balancing her waffle cone in the empty glass and positioning it right beneath her chin. She offered Joey a tiny teaspoonful of congee, but he turned his face away from it, his eyes studying the ice cream cone longingly. Norah adored the little tongue that kept darting in and out, and was so tempted to let Joey try just a bit, but she knew she would regret it terribly if he broke out in a rash again. Instead, she smacked her lips theatrically as she took a noisy bite of the congee. "Mmm, Joey, mmm, mmm good! This is so delicious! You gotta try some, Joey!"

Her baby looked up at her, his expression doubtful, but he parted his little lips and allowed her to feed him a little congee. He swallowed it tentatively, but opened his mouth wider this time, and Norah rewarded him with a kiss on his nose before serving him a bigger spoonful. Each time Joey looked away, she took big surreptitious bites of her rapidly melting ice-cream. Everywhere they'd been in Sanya so far had been hot and humid, even indoors.

"Okay, Ma, go ahead and call us, then," Ben said, sighing as he hung up. Almost immediately his phone rang, and when he tapped at it, Nai Nai's face filled the screen. He propped it up against the silver vase on their table, directly in front of Joey.

"*There* you are, Joey! Do you miss your Maa Maa?" she cried, her voice loud and shrill. Ben and Norah reached for the volume buttons on the side of the phone at the same time, embarrassed when several heads turned in their direction. Norah hastily adjusted the volume so that Nai Nai's voice was closer to a whisper.

Norah gestured to Ben to get some food. As he stood up, he mouthed the words, *Sorry, baby,* and Norah shrugged in response, a small smile on her face, as though she didn't mind.

Joey watched obediently as his grandmother proceeded to flip through the pages of *Dear Zoo*, and although Norah had turned down the volume, she could still hear her grating voice telling the story in translation, in Cantonese, with great enthusiasm, complete with exaggerated animal sounds. By the time Ben returned with two matching plates of smoked salmon, bulging omelettes, and mango wedges, Nai Nai had begun the next story, *The Very Hungry Caterpillar*. "Can you see the caterpillar, Joey? Say 'Yes, Maa Maa!' *There's* my clever boy!"

She and Ben ate in silence; neither of them wanted Nai Nai to overhear what they were saying. Ben frowned as he cut open his omelette and an odd black sauce oozed out; it took Norah a moment to realize it was the truffle mushroom sauce. *Little kids will watch anything on a screen,* Norah thought. Dirty brown rivulets trickled down the sides of her now soggy cone, forming a little muddy puddle on the table. Norah soaked it up with a napkin.

Even though Ben slid his sandaled feet to meet hers beneath the checked tablecloth, and she liked it when he wrapped his legs around hers, like a hug, Norah's mood had soured.

All but three or four of the surrounding tables were empty now, and servers were discreetly pouring the remaining food from the serving trays into large grey tubs on a trolley. Norah finally gestured at the phone and looked pointedly at Ben, who immediately picked it up.

"Ma? We have to go now," he said. "Thanks for reading to Joey."

"I'm not finished," Norah heard her protesting.

"Yes, but Joey, um," Ben coughed, "Um, we need to change Joey's diaper, er, right now."

"Well, okay," her mother-in-law said, but Norah could hear the frown in her voice. "But call me again later, when you're done."

Norah gawked at him. Surely Nai Nai was joking?

"I'll see, Ma," Ben said, clearing his throat again. "The connection in the villa isn't as good as it is here in the main building. Bye now, Ma." He flashed a forced smile at his mother before abruptly ending the call and looking nervously at Norah. "I'm sorry, baby, I didn't know she was going to go on and on like that," he paused, as though he wanted to continue, but stopped when he saw Norah looking intently at the sky.

"It's raining, Ben," she said, marveling at how quickly a magical day could go wrong. She heard Ben making some kind of apology but his voice seemed oddly distant and irrelevant. She studied the embroidered details on the waist of her mint green dress, the dress she'd bought especially for today, for pictures at the beach.

Several hours later, it was still raining, and the claps of thunder continued to grow in volume and regularity. The three of them sat quietly together on the white swing on the roofed patio, Ben pushing every few moments against the floorboards with his feet. Joey was asleep against Norah's chest, tired and content after devouring a warm bottle of formula. He hadn't wanted her breast, the way he had in the morning. Norah kissed the top of his head, stroked his wispy locks.

Norah watched as the rain hammered down on their garden, on their little pool's surface, creating tiny splashes that disappeared before immediately being replaced by more. *We will never swim in that pool, never visit the legendary beaches of Sanya,* Norah thought to herself. *We could have gone on a staycation in Hong Kong.*

"I have a surprise for you," Ben said suddenly, planting his feet on the floor so the swing stopped its gentle sway. "Do you want it now or later?" He spoke directly in her ear; the rain would have made his words incomprehensible otherwise.

She whispered back, "Let's go inside first."

The contrast in volume when they returned to the safety of the villa was dramatic; a palpable silence enveloped them when Ben pulled the sliding doors shut. Norah carefully laid Joey down in his crib before joining Ben at the foot of the bed. They had returned to their villa from breakfast to find a family of towel elephants, two big ones and a baby one, perched on their bed behind the gauzy drapes.

Ben pulled out a small silk pouch from his pocket and placed it in her hands. "Happy anniversary, my Norah," he said. He kissed her on the cheek. "Open it, see if you like it."

She untied the ribbon drawstring and carefully reached inside. Her fingers immediately found a marble-like object, quite heavy for its size, with a smooth cool surface. The ball was attached to a thin chain. She poured the pouch's treasure into her palm: it was a gold pendant and necklace. When she held the little ball between her thumb and forefinger, she noticed a ridged scratchiness to the bottom of the ball, and when she studied it more closely, saw there was a tiny engraving: *You are breathtaking, like a sunset. I love you. Ben.*

Norah, who had been trying to mask her puzzlement at why Ben had chosen such an expensive piece of jewelry that was not at all her style, suddenly grabbed Ben's face and kissed him on the lips. His eyes grew wide with surprise. She exclaimed, "Ben, it's a *sun*!"

He nodded. "It is. They said I could only choose ten words," he said anxiously. "I wanted to engrave that sunset haiku I wrote for you, do you still remember it? But they said only ten words."

Norah unclasped the necklace and held it out to Ben so he could help her put it on. "Of course I do, but Ben, it's perfect. I love it." The gold ball was cold against her skin. Ben began taking pictures of her with his phone, and, to please him, she batted her eyelashes at him, tilting her head, fingering the pendant the way she imagined a jewelry model would.

"You look amazing," Ben said, showing her the pictures, and Norah noted with relief that in the pictures there was no hint of the disappointment she was feeling about the trip. Her smiles were coy and her green dress, very low-cut.

Norah blushed. "Don't send those to Nai Nai," she said, meaning it as a joke, but it didn't come out quite right, and the warmth of the moment went. They sat in silence, trying to regain it, but not quite managing.

Finally, she muttered, "Wait here," and knelt beside her backpack where she dug past her windbreaker and Joey's spare change of clothes for the plane. She unzipped the inner compartment, where she had been hiding Ben's gift, and returned to their bed with the rectangular box in hand. "It was for the beach," she said, "but we haven't had a chance to go." This, too, came out more harshly than Norah intended.

"Thank you, Norah," Ben said, taking the box from her, his head bowed. He opened it with reverence, and immediately replaced the glasses he was wearing with the new pair in the box. "These are exactly the right prescription, and so comfortable," he marveled. "But why did you say they were for the beach?"

"They're Transitions," Norah explains, sighing. "The lenses darken in bright sunlight, so you won't have to remember to bring a separate pair of sunglasses with you when you go out. I should've given them to you yesterday, when it was actually sunny."

Ben's eyes were earnest behind the new frames. He looked different, Norah thought, more refined. "Let's not be sad anymore," he said. "*You* are my sun, remember? Never mind the weather. See how they're turning brown already?"

Norah smiled at his efforts. "Was my gold sun very expensive?"

"Was this villa very expensive?" he responded, shrugging.

"Kind of. About $4,000 a night." A second too late, Norah realized he hadn't really been asking for the cost of the villa at all.

For several moments he just stared at her, unable to hide his shock. "Four thousand dollars a night?" he finally echoes weakly.

"Including breakfast, but without, it would have been about $3,800..."

"And what about the plane tickets?"

"Oh, those," Norah said, as reassuringly as she can. "I, we, paid almost nothing for those. Like, less than $1,000 each, and Joey flew for free."

She could practically see the gears turning in Ben's head. "So, this weekend, this two-night trip, has cost us about ten thousand dollars?" He didn't sound angry at all, Norah noted with relief, just shocked. "That's like, half a month's salary."

When he put it like that, it was a lot of money. It was half a month's salary for him, but $10,000 was more than what she made each month as a part-time teacher at Future English. As she tried to comfort him, and herself, with the knowledge that the expense had been worth it, Ben's phone started buzzing urgently, and the picture of Nai Nai's vulture-like face flashed on the screen.

Norah was lying alone on the four-poster bed, struggling with a headache that was bad enough that they had canceled their original plans to go out for their anniversary dinner.

If she was honest with herself, she knew the dinner at the resort's highly acclaimed Italian restaurant would not have been quite what she had imagined, anyhow. Since learning the cost of their trip, Ben had been quiet. He was not the type of man who would intentionally give her the silent treatment to hurt her, nothing like that, but he had definitely been more preoccupied, more anxious. She caught him studying a spreadsheet on his phone several times, but each time he quickly slipped his phone back in his pocket. A small part of her wanted to apologize, to ease the tension, but most of her thought it would be silly to. Were they really that short of money?

It was just as well that Norah's head began hammering; it gave them both a reason to be apart for a while. The pain was bad enough that her eyes were watering, but she knew that actual, full-on crying would worsen the headache, so she continued staring resolutely out the window instead, even though it was dark now. All she could see was the back of the wooden swing swaying gently in the aftermath of the afternoon's storm. Just before 6 p.m., the rain had stopped as abruptly as if someone had flipped a switch.

She had tried getting on all fours and doing the cat pose,

which sometimes helped, but it hadn't done anything for her today. Ben had tried to rub her neck and shoulders, the way he did at home when her head hurt, but as usual, his hands were too gentle to bring any real relief. What she really needed was two ActiFast Panadol tablets, but although they brought all three of Joey's eczema creams, his bottle of pine tar bath solution, as well as a rainbow of just-in-case medication for him in case he coughed, got a runny nose, was allergic to something, or had diarrhea, neither she nor Ben had thought to bring any Panadol. In desperation, Ben had dialed 0, and the front desk promptly sent Wen with some pain medication, but Norah had not recognized the brand, and she studied the fine print on the back of the box doubtfully before swallowing two of the red, M&M-like pills with a gulp of warm water. Ben kept showing up at her bedside, topping up the glass with hot water each time so the water was always warm when she brought the glass to her lips.

It made her think of how Ben had kept refilling her tea cup at their first date. They were at that Shanghai place she liked so much, right by Nai Nai's apartment. She remembered how he had actually poured out the cold tea from her cup into his bowl before refilling it with hot tea. As she watched him that night, she had thought about how none of the boys in her circle of friends would ever think of keeping her teacup filled with hot tea, the way Ben was doing. They were great guys, both her high school and university classmates: funny, charismatic, self-assured. But they were not raised to think of others' needs before their own. Ben, three years older than her, was different; he was a gentleman, chivalrous, like a knight. And her heart had wriggled about with pleasure as she ate her potstickers, remembering the sunset picture he had slipped in her pigeon hole, knowing that he found her attractive, too.

She could hear the faint sounds of Joey giggling in the living room; Ben was probably tickling his tummy, or maybe the soles of his feet.

She finally fell asleep.

When Norah woke, she felt that same disorientation from the night before, but hearing the familiar snores of her husband and son on either side of her enabled her to quickly find her bearings again. *I'm in Sanya,* she thought calmly. Her head felt a little heavy, but otherwise fine. The glow-in-the-dark hands of her old Casio watch told her that it was now just past one o'clock in the morning. She reached down to pat her clothes, and confirmed what she had suspected: she was wearing her old Snoopy pajamas, not the clingy silk nightgown she had bought especially for their anniversary night. She contemplated changing into it, surprising Ben with it in the morning. First, however, she needed to use the washroom.

Norah climbed out of the large bed with some difficulty: the mattress was too soft for her liking, and combined with the ultra-smooth sheets, she felt as though she was struggling out of a ball pit.

The marble floor of the bathroom was cold, as was the toilet seat. She considered taking a quick shower, but her stomach growled in protest. She hadn't eaten since the breakfast buffet. She decided a cup noodle from the mini-bar would have to do.

The villa's carpet was thick and soft; her footsteps made no sound at all as she tiptoed out into the living room. She patted at the spot on the wall where she remembered the light switch was, and was relieved when her fingers found the little rectangular panel. She pressed it, and it took her eyes a moment to adjust to the glaring light, but when they did, she gasped.

On the glass coffee table stood two bottles of the

complimentary mineral water from the resort, about a meter apart. A piece of string had been tied to the necks of these bottles, like a clothesline, and clipped to the string were about a dozen Polaroids of Norah and Ben from their wedding day. A bouquet of pink roses was lying on its side in front of the photo display, and beside the bouquet was a small cheesecake with 'Happy Anniversary Norah and Ben' written on the top in squiggly chocolate letters. There was a little space between 'Happy' and 'Anniversary', and a pink 2-shaped candle next to the cake, still in its plastic packaging.

Norah stood in the doorway, frozen on the spot, needing to cry but afraid to because of the headache the tears would almost certainly bring. It felt like a clump of old spaghetti was caught halfway between her throat and her stomach.

She wished desperately that she hadn't gotten so upset when Ben went out with Joey without telling her, when Nai Nai called during breakfast, when it rained and rained. She wished she hadn't gotten that stupid headache. She wished she could have gone out for dinner tonight with Ben, wished she had dressed up for him and been the bubbly, cheerful Norah that had drawn him to her in the first place instead of the moody, complaining Norah she had been this whole trip.

And still he had done all this for her. She gazed at the Polaroids, remembered the passion, fiery and hot, that she had felt for Ben as they stood in their honeymoon suite, finally alone after a very exhausting wedding day. She felt tears clouding her vision and blinked rapidly to keep them at bay.

She rushed to her backpack and gently tugged out the other surprise she had prepared for Ben, the silk nightgown she had secretly purchased after work last Friday. Norah quickly closed the bathroom door behind her. She slipped into the slinky nightgown, its lace details tickling her skin. When she peered at her reflection in the full-length mirror, she was relieved to see that her figure had not changed so very much since Joey: her hips were broader, sure, but her stomach was still flat, her breasts full and round. She dabbed at one of them with a tissue and suddenly remembered that she needed to pump.

Twenty minutes later, she slipped back into bed beside Ben. The nightgown's silky fabric was cold and slippery like the resort's bed sheets, but when Norah thought how surprised, how pleased, Ben would be in the morning when he reached out to embrace her, the way he always did, just before the break of dawn, she shivered with pleasure.

Chapter 8

"You look very odd in those glasses," Ma said, frowning, as she spread a thin layer of orange marmalade on her toast.

They had returned from Sanya the night before, and Norah had already left for work. He and Ma were sharing a quiet breakfast together at home before he left for the studio, too. Joey was amusing himself in the playpen; from the squeals and coos coming from that corner of the living room, the baby was very happy to be back in his own space.

Ben coughed, taking a sip of his milk tea. He was not a big fan of the transitioning glasses Norah bought him either, but he would never admit it. In concept they were excellent; a person really would never need to bring sunglasses with him when going out, but the problem was with how sensitive the lenses were indoors as well. They reacted to the weak sunlight from a window, as well as fluorescent light bulbs, and so even now, in their living room, his glasses were a brownish tint, the color of very weak tea. He kept wanting to take them off, but he was nearly blind without them.

"They were a gift from Norah," he responded. "She gave them to me in Sanya. They protect my eyes from harmful UV rays."

His mother burst out laughing. "Sure they do. It's very bright in here."

"Ma," he protested. "Don't laugh. Maybe you need a pair yourself."

She almost choked on her toast. "Absolutely not. How was the trip, anyway?"

Ben didn't speak for a moment, as bits and pieces of the trip came to mind, like a collage: Joey's baby Crocs; the bland but ice-cold Hainanese beer Fifth Uncle had served him at his house; the squeaky white swing on their porch; Norah skipping back to their table with her three scoops of ice cream; Norah in that clingy, slippery nightgown.

"I enjoyed it," he said, finally. "The weather was awful, but we had a nice time anyway."

"I'm glad to hear you didn't take Joey to the beach or into a pool," Ma said, shuddering. "That would have been foolish, after all the progress with his skin condition. What if there had been a flare-up?"

Ben nodded; his mother was right. The rain had been a good thing, after all. He finished the rest of his coffee in one gulp and stood up. "See you tonight, then, Ma. Thanks for taking care of Joey. Norah will be home around one."

"I know, I know," she said, pursing her lips. "I know the schedule. Don't worry about a thing."

Ben glanced at the clock on his computer screen; he'd been editing pictures for nearly two hours. He noticed that time could take on a weird, elastic quality when he was editing. It was soothing to be so focused on one thing and not have the headspace to worry about anything else.

Ben reached for his phone, about to send Norah a text

message, when it rang. He grinned—it was Ricky from his old running club.

"Ben, are you coming tonight or what?"

He hadn't seen his friends from the running club in over a year, but they still called every week, just in case. He wished he could go. He missed the running, the satisfaction that came from striving for and surpassing personal fitness goals, but also the drinks and the laughs afterwards. They were misers, all of them, so they never went to a bar or anything. They just bought cold beers from 7-11 and drank them in the park.

Running used to be huge for him. As a teenager having a group of guys to hang out with had meant the world, and Ma was always been pleased with his ribbons and medals from the inter-school competitions. One time he was even interviewed on television; Ma was over the moon. She bragged about it for weeks to anyone who would listen.

He found this running club after doing the half-marathon in the Standard Chartered back in 2008. They were the fastest five or six runners in their age bracket, and someone—Ricky, probably—had suggested they start training together. How good it was to have a reason to get out of the house, to have something all his own, something that had nothing to do with either his life at home with Ma or his photography apprenticeship.

But since getting married he had only run with the club a handful of times. Norah had never discouraged him, exactly, but he knew how much she dreaded being home alone with Ma. He felt too guilty when he was running to enjoy it, especially since the group met all the way in Tai Po, a good hour away from home. Since Joey arrived, Ben hadn't run with the club even once. These days he went for a quick jog at the park downstairs when he could. The guys still called, though.

"Ben? You there?"

"Give me another couple of months," Ben promised. "I'll be back in time to train with you guys for the Standard Chartered next year, maybe earlier."

"Alright," Ricky agreed with a sigh. Then, more cheerfully, "Norah and the baby doing well?"

"Yes," Ben said, feeling that swell of pride whenever he talked about his family. "Joey's skin's gotten a lot better in the last few weeks. We just came back from a trip to Hainan Island yesterday."

"Sounds like fun. See you around then, Ben."

"Big smiles this way please, yes, excellent," Ben muttered as he snapped photograph after photograph of the family sitting on the studio's grey leather couch. It was a family of four; the children were twins, two pig-tailed eight-year-old girls in matching Disney princess dresses. One twin's name was Anastasia, and the other's was something similar. He was relieved that Norah chose 'Joey' for their baby's name; it would have been mortifying if he tripped over his son's name every time he tried to say it.

Snapshot Studio was not very big, but his boss, Eric, had done his best to furnish it nicely; the walls were creamy white, and the wooden floorboards had that trendy weathered look to them. Their furniture was all from Taobao, but not obviously so. There was just the two of them, Eric and Ben, but they did good work together. Ben was proud of the five-star reviews Snapshot got on Facebook, was always eager to share the clients' comments with Norah when they mentioned him by name.

He was about to say "Let's take a few shots of just the girls now," when his cell phone buzzed in his back pocket. He tried to ignore it, he was in the middle of a shoot, for goodness' sake, but when it didn't stop buzzing, it occurred to him that maybe it was his mother, maybe Joey was hurt.

"I'm sorry, everyone. Can we take a five-minute break?" Ben said, taking out his phone; it was Norah. "So sorry. I'll make up the five minutes to you." He slipped into the cramped storeroom behind the studio; there was no ventilation there, but at least he could take the call in private.

The moment Ben held his phone to his ear he felt that familiar pinch at the base of his gut; Norah was crying, Joey was crying. He looked down at his Timex; it was 1:30. Norah had just gotten home from work.

"What's going on, Norah? Are you hurt? Why are you crying? What happened?"

Norah didn't answer; she kept crying, and in the background, Joey continued to wail. "Norah, please—please calm down. Tell me—" He stopped suddenly, his heart hammering in his chest. "Did...did something happen to Ma?"

"Nai Nai...Nai Nai..." Norah, still crying so hard she was hiccupping, kept making false starts, couldn't get past those two words.

My ma is only sixty-two, he thought, frightened. She had only been retired for five years. He hadn't taken her to Tokyo, like he said he would. He promised years ago to take portraits of her, when he was Kenny's apprentice, but he had never gotten around to it. He had about a thousand photographs of Norah, and even more of Joey, but he had never taken those portraits. He had never known a world without his Ma, had never even really considered it as a possibility. Thinking of it now promptly turned his legs into Jell-O, and he slumped on the floor, staring at the dust on the wooden floorboards. No one ever swept in here.

Sweat rolled down the sides of his forehead as Norah continued crying softly on the other end of the line. In the four years that he had known Norah, he had never once shouted at her, but at this moment Ben struggled to keep his frustration in check. "Is she hurt? Is she…" He swallowed hard. "Conscious? Have you called an ambulance?"

"She's…she's n-n-not hurt. She's f-fine." Norah finally managed to say. Then, her voice small and pleading, "Please come h-home."

He was still thinking about how he should respond when he realized she had hung up. His denim shirt was clinging to his back, and as he stood up he saw the back of his black trousers were grey with dust. He peered through the small rectangular window on the door, saw that his clients were sitting on the sofa, their four heads bowed, each one concentrating on a different mobile device. Another quick glance at his Timex told Ben he owed this family ten minutes, not five.

He took a deep breath before tapping on Eric's name on his cell phone. His boss picked up immediately. "What's up, Ben?" His voice sounded muffled, as though his mouth was full.

"Hey Eric, sorry to call during your lunch," Ben said, clearing his throat. "Um, I'm in the middle of my shoot with the Changs, you know, the family with the twin girls, but my wife just called. There's...there's an emergency at home."

"You better get going then," he responded sympathetically, and Ben felt his eyes smart at Eric's kindness. "I can be back in five minutes. Can you wait? Tell the Changs I'll finish their shoot."

"Thanks so much, Eric. I'm sorry for the trouble."

"It's no trouble."

Ben re-emerged from the storeroom, apologized profusely to the family on the sofa, and when Eric rushed in, red-faced, shortly after, Ben apologized some more, until everyone told him to stop talking and go home to his family.

When Ben opened their front door, he saw Ma sitting in her arm chair, arms folded across her chest. She was staring out the window, and when she glanced at him, he saw her eyes and nose were red. Their bedroom door was closed, but no one was crying, which Ben took as a good sign.

Ben closed the door noiselessly behind him, hung his keys on his half of the heart-shaped key holder; Norah had made the holder at a metalsmithing workshop before their wedding. For the first time he realized there was no hook anywhere for Ma, and wondered if the key holder was unnecessarily exclusive. Perhaps they should hang it in their bedroom instead. Ma's keys sat in their usual position on top of the shoe cabinet.

"Ma," he said, finally. "I was so worried about you. Are you alright?"

She turned her head slowly to face him. "Your wife wants to move out. She's packing now."

Ben stared at her. "What are you talking about?"

"Norah wants to take Joey with her and move out. She told me she doesn't want me to take care of Joey anymore." At this, his Ma unfolded her arms, revealing a soggy tissue, and dabbed at her eyes. "That's my grandson she's talking about."

He was rendered speechless by this outburst.

"Go on, then," his mother continued, pursing her lips. "I suppose I could have misunderstood her, she was practically hysterical, but I don't think so."

Ben trudged to the end of the short hallway. His hands were shaking terribly, the way they did after he'd had a coffee from 7-11; his right eye always got twitchy and his hands would shake, but the jolt of caffeine was second to none. He hadn't had any coffee today, but it was a struggle to close his fingers into a fist to knock on the door. There was no response. He quietly turned the doorknob.

Norah was leaning against the headboard, Joey cradled in her arms, and their carry-on suitcase was lying open on the floor. To Ben's relief, the suitcase was still empty.

"Hey there," Ben said, softly. "What's going on, *lo paw*?" He rarely used this Cantonese term of endearment for wife. It had never sounded natural to him, although he appreciated the sentiment: *lo paw* was literally 'old woman' and it meant that your woman, your wife, would grow old with you. When they were first married, Norah had playfully called him *lo gong* sometimes, "old man', but eventually stopped when he never responded in like manner. These terms for husband and wife had never featured in his childhood; his father had left his *lo paw*, then pregnant with Ben, for a younger woman, his secretary. His parents had only been married one year.

As he sat down on the bed beside Norah, he saw that she was still in her work clothes, a navy dress and nylons. This was out of character; normally the first thing she did upon returning home from work was change into her pajamas. "*Lo paw*," he said again, stroking her cheek, "I'm home. Tell me what happened."

Norah blinked a few times, as though just registering that he was in the room with her. She held out Joey to him, and he took the baby in his arms without breaking eye contact with her. But when Ben rubbed his hand against Joey's head, the way he usually did, he gasped. When he looked down, he saw that the baby's soft, wispy locks had been shaved away; Joey was bald.

Ben studied the little head closely, and saw that in a few spots, the razor had nicked Joey's scalp. He frowned, counting three, four, five little scratches on the little head. As Ben set the baby down gently in his crib, he was struck by how unfamiliar he looked without his hair. Would he be able to correctly identify Joey in a line-up of sleeping babies?

Norah reached beneath her pillow and pulled out an envelope. "This was all I could save from the trashcan." Ben peered inside; it was Joey's hair.

"Ma shaved Joey's head?"

Norah nodded, tears rolling down her cheeks. Her makeup was not waterproof; it looked as if someone had outlined her eyes with a thick black marker, and done a messy job of it.

"She didn't tell me she was going to do this," Ben said, feeling angry and oddly responsible. "I wonder why she didn't mention it this morning before I left for work."

He looked down at Joey's scalp, a dull ache in his chest, as he saw that although the nicks were not deep cuts, they must have hurt. Ben had been shaved as a baby, several times; his mother had taken a lot of pictures of him when he was little, and in those pictures he had sometimes had hair, sometimes not. That was fine; who was he to question his mother's parenting? But Joey was not her son.

"Ben," Norah said, suddenly, putting a hand on his forearm. The gesture startled him; her hand was so cold. "I don't want Nai Nai to take care of Joey anymore."

Ben cleared his throat, unsure of whether he wanted to agree or to convince her otherwise, but she continued without giving him a chance to cut in.

"I guess I'll have to stop working," she continued, her tone matter-of-fact.

His jaw dropped involuntarily, but he quickly recovered and closed his mouth, trying for a neutral expression. "Norah, I'll talk to Ma. She had no right to shave Joey's head. But …"

"I don't want Nai Nai to take care of Joey anymore, Ben," she said again, more loudly.

"I know you're upset. I'm upset, too. Ma was wrong, she had no right…"

She started throwing clothes and diapers into the carry-on, a wild expression on her face. "I don't want Nai Nai…"

Ben grabbed her forearms and did not let go when she struggled to wriggle free. "Norah. I heard you. Please stop."

She glared at him, hate in her eyes. "Let go of me."

He did, and she continued throwing items into the carry-on: Joey's comfort blanket, Eeyore, her own underwear and pajamas. He watched helplessly as the suitcase filled.

Finally, as she zipped up the suitcase, he said, quietly, "Where will you go?"

Norah jutted out her trembling bottom lip then, the way she always did the moment before she cried. "Ben, she hurt our baby...she took all his hair...she's a *witch,* and I…I…h-h-hate her…."

Ben took her in his arms, held her as she cried, her shoulders heaving. "I came h-h-home and Joey was c-crying, and Nai Nai acted as if she hadn't d-d-done anything…"

"Let me talk to her," he said, when her cries finally turned into whimpers. "Please, don't go."

"Maybe I should quit my job in the Future," she said, sitting up. She made the statement sound like a question, as though she was pleading with him. Norah's eye makeup was more smudged than ever.

Ben wondered how best to respond; they would not be able to live on just one salary. Surely Norah knew this.

"Things would be a little tight, of course," she continued, as though reading his mind, "but we've got our savings, and…"

"Norah," Ben interrupted, as gently as he could. "Let me talk to her first."

She looked at him, her eyes wide and unblinking.

"If she apologizes," he tried to continue, "if she promises never to do something like this again, perhaps we could…"

She stood up, backed slowly away from him. "You knew, didn't you?"

The accusation hung between them, and Ben felt anger, hot and dangerously close to the surface.

On their wedding day one of Norah's cousins had read a passage from the Bible, and he, who had never gone to church, had liked the words, that lofty description of love, how it was kind and patient, how it never got mad, never held a grudge. How it always persevered, always protected, and never failed. As he and Norah stood at the altar, listening, she had squeezed his sweaty hand as her cousin read, had leaned over to whisper in his ear, "That's a perfect description of *you*!" Her veil had brushed against his cheek, tickling him, and he had smiled at his pretty bride, flattered but slightly afraid: it was too high a standard. *Oh God, help it be true,* he had thought.

Norah often told him how much she loved his mild temperament, how he never lost his temper or got upset. It was true that he did not shout; his mother had taught him from a young age that 'making a fuss' only led to 'consequences', sometimes even 'serious consequences', but he did get upset inside, sometimes very much so, and some nights he lay awake wondering if he might one day explode from all the unspoken, pent-up frustration he harbored inside. He was upset now.

"Of course I didn't," he said, finally. "I would've told you. I would've stopped her. You know that."

"You seem so calm, like this is nothing to you, like you don't care at all."

She must know it was not true. His world was collapsing around him like a clumsily built sandcastle. *No,* he thought desperately. *We were supposed to grow old together.* He looked down at the packed suitcase at his feet, at little Joey, who never gave anyone any trouble, his head coarsely shaven. How dare his mother lay a razor to his son's head! How dare she!

"This is a big deal to me," he said quietly, looking Norah in the eye, holding her gaze even when he sensed her discomfort. "What happened today is not okay with me." He was angry that Norah doubted him, that she questioned his concern for Joey and for her. He was angry at himself for failing to protect his little family. He also hated thinking of his Ma as the villain, even if it was true; it felt treacherous and disloyal.

Norah was the first to look away. When she hugged her knees to chest and buried her head in her arms, her skin so pale against the navy blue of her dress, Ben ached with love for her. He reached out to embrace her, and to his relief, she didn't resist him. Her arms were so cold. For several moments they sat together like this and in the silence, something between them healed a little.

"I'm going to talk to Ma," he said softly. "I'm going to tell her this is not okay with us. Norah, please don't go."

She seemed to hear the desperation in his voice, because she nodded.

He was about to stand up when Joey stirred, rolling onto his side. "Ma. Ma," he said sleepily, as his eyes fluttered open.

"Hey, little guy," Ben said, peering down at his baby. Ben was dismayed to find that Joey's face had lost the softness that came with having a halo of hair. But when Joey smiled, seeing his father, and smacked his chubby palms together in delight, Ben wondered how he could ever had thought he would not recognize his own son. He scooped Joey up, held him close, and kissed his scratchy head.

Norah leaned in for a kiss too, but frowned as she rubbed her lips against Joey's scalp. "You feel so sandpapery," she said, sighing. "But I promised to…love you when you're peachy, and love you when you're bald, to love you when you're standing, and catch you when you fall..." This came out as a song, and Joey giggled when he heard his mother's voice. He reached out a chubby palm and patted at her cheek gently.

"I'll go talk to Ma now," Ben said, standing up.

When Ben returned to the living room, he found his mother reading an old Reader's Digest. He sat down beside her, saw it was the October 1996 edition. She was wearing her reading glasses, the gold-rimmed ones that made her look a great deal older than she was, like a grandmother from a movie.

She looked up from her reading and slowly removed her glasses. They hung on a beaded chain around her neck. "What did she say?"

"Ma, why did you shave Joey's head without telling us first?"

She pursed her lips. "I shaved your head when you were seven months old. Look how nice and thick your hair is now."

"Ma, you can't just do things like that," Ben said, frowning.

"Things like what?" She sounded genuinely surprised.

"Like shaving Joey's head. Norah is very upset."

Ma sighed. "Overreacting as usual, don't you think?"

Although he too was upset, Ben privately agreed that threatening to move out was a rather extreme response to what had happened. He kept this thought to himself. "But, Ma..."

"Anyway," she interrupted, "when you were a baby, your hair was very thin, too, just like Joey's is now. But it grew back thick and dark after I shaved it. Joey's will, too."

"It isn't about the hair, exactly. It's about not saying anything, and then doing it, and then pretending it's no big deal. Norah's been crying and crying; she's packed her suitcase. I know you didn't mean any harm, Ma, you wanted to help, but you cut him..."

"Only because he was squirming so much! You think I wanted to hurt him? That's my grandson you're talking about, Ben. Don't insult me."

Ben cowered instinctively at his mother's stern tone but recovered quickly, readjusting his posture. *I must not be afraid,* he thought. *Love always perseveres. Love always protects.* "I know you didn't want to, but you did, Ma," he said, his tone gentle. "Why didn't you stop?" *Didn't you know you were hurting him?*

Her cheeks reddened, two spots of color right under her cheekbones, but Ben was not surprised when she did not back down. In truth, it was the first time in as long as he could remember that he had confronted his mother like this. But he'd promised Norah.

"I barely nicked his scalp, no more than you might nick your chin when you shave," she said, sniffing. "It's not like you to overreact. You're behaving just like Norah. She's a terrible influence on you."

It saddened Ben to think that after so many years his mother still had not found room in her heart for Norah. He wondered if she ever would. "Ma, I love you," he said, and he was embarrassed by the emotion in his voice. "But I love her, too. She's my wife. If you drive her away from here, she will take Joey with her. As for me…"

"Where would she go?" she cuts in again, smirking. "It's just hair, for goodness sake! Just a bit of hair!"

Ben sighed. "I don't know where she would go. I hope not to her parents' place. Ma, if she flew to Vancouver, I would go with her."

She stared at him, speechless. Ben knew he had just played his trump card; it would break Ma's heart if he moved to Canada.

"Don't drive her away, Ma," he said, softly. "I don't want to have to leave you."

Chapter 9

NORAH LAY awake that night, unable to sleep. She and Ben had lain side by side in the dark, not touching, and although Ben had tried to tell her a funny story about his clients at work that morning, had laughed as he told her how long and difficult the twin daughters' names were, Norah had remained quiet, not because she was angry; she wasn't. She had overheard some of his conversation with Nai Nai, and had been proud of him for standing up to her. He almost never did. Still, she didn't feel quite ready to laugh or make love yet, and she wished Ben understood.

"Let's talk in the morning," she had finally said, gently, and he had nodded as though grateful. Moments later, his snores joined Joey's, the usual duet.

Nothing could have prepared her for what happened today; she had never expected to return home from work one day to find Joey screaming and flailing in Nai Nai's arms, Ben's Gillette razor in her hand, a crumpled tissue beside her with spots of blood from Joey's scalp. The first words out of Nai Nai's mouth had been, "It isn't my fault he won't keep still!" and it had been difficult to make out what she was saying, Joey had been crying so hard.

She missed her mom and dad, and wanted to call them, but was afraid she would slip and say something bad about her Nai Nai, or worse, Ben. She never did, even when things were hard, but she was afraid she might tonight. Her parents initially had been strongly opposed to her relationship with Ben, had felt suspicious of his ability to provide Norah with a good life. They thought he wasn't good enough for her.

"You've had a different sort of upbringing from him, haven't you, dear?" Mom had said, tentatively. "This young man, this Ben, is, I'm sure, very nice. But you told me yourself he doesn't really speak English, has never traveled anywhere outside of China, started working straight after high school, and still lives with his mother. Given his background, will he be able to understand you? Provide for you? Frankly speaking, Norah, I'm worried that—"

"That's ridiculous, Mom," Norah had snapped, quite loudly. "That's... that's... *classist*!"

They had been talking on the phone, and after her outburst, there were several long moments when neither of them spoke.

In the end her mother had said something that made her feel guilty and sad all at once: "When you have a daughter of your own, maybe you will think differently." But it hadn't been enough to stop her from falling even deeper in love with Ben. *Lai jook sum hum* was the Chinese idiom her parents used in those days when talking about her relationship with Ben. It described feet so deeply entrenched in mud that escape was no longer possible.

And so she had made it her mission to convince her parents that Ben was perfect in every way; intelligent, understanding, kind. That he made more than enough to provide for her, and anyway, she was a working woman too, wasn't she, so it wasn't really about *providing* for her. She even went as far as telling them how well Ben's mother treated her, "exactly as if I were her daughter", she had said. She knew how uncomfortable her parents were with Norah moving into Nai Nai's flat, and she had been anxious herself, but her desire for Ben had swallowed everything else.

In the end, her parents had grudgingly agreed to the marriage, and on the wedding day, her father wept as he gave her away at the altar.

Norah felt pressure to assure her parents that she was living comfortably, happily, that her marriage with Ben was all she had wanted, and more. She sent them lots of updates of where they went, what they did, how very happy she was. The fact that they lived in Vancouver made it easier.

And her marriage with Ben *was* all she wanted, of course it was. But sometimes it felt exhausting to hide the hard parts, to keep them all bottled up. One of her greatest fears was that her parents would say, smugly, "We told you so, now move back in with us", and it was her life mission to never give them cause to say that.

Still, Norah meant what she said when she told Ben she didn't want Nai Nai taking care of Joey any more. Did she have the guts to quit her job at Future English? What would they do for money if she did? Ben made just over twenty thousand dollars a month at Snapshot; Norah, half that much. They basically lived rent-free here, unless you counted the *gayong* Ben gave to his mother the first Saturday of each month, but Norah was pretty sure nobody saw that money as rent. Twenty thousand dollars was not very much; Norah knew that if she got her teaching qualification for working in a secondary school, her starting salary would be more than thirty thousand dollars. They would be able to hire a domestic helper, or rent their own place, or both.

If she could choose again, she would definitely do an

Education degree instead of choosing English Literature and Creative Writing, although at the time she had relished the luxury of reading, writing, sometimes just thinking about words and ideas. These days her mind felt all over the place. She had tried, and failed, to read books again—fiction, nonfiction, anything, really—but her attention span seemed to have shrunk tremendously.

She was not sure how serious she was about leaving this flat. Joey would have to come with her; there was no question about that. She knew that she would be lost without Ben, so he would have to come, too, but Norah suspected that he might not be willing. He denied it, but he was still so attached to his mother. She wondered whether it would be possible to rent a one-bedroom flat somewhere, or a studio maybe, something they could afford which was not terribly run-down. She was not sure a place like that existed. She wondered what her parents would say if they found out she was living in a run-down studio.

It hurt to think about her parents, about her mother leaning over the kitchen table, working at a watercolor painting, her father's long but not altogether uninteresting stories of ancient Chinese poets. She could almost see them in their townhouse with its mint green walls, their slobbery, affectionate pup running about, licking their ankles.

To talk with them, though, she would have to go to the living room so the conversation didn't wake Joey or Ben. Perhaps she could just talk about the Sanya trip. She slipped her cell phone into the big heart-shaped pocket at the front of her pajamas and slipped her feet into her slippers, but just as she was about to stand up, she heard her mother-in-law open her bedroom door. Norah reluctantly lay back down. The last thing she wanted to do tonight was bump into Nai Nai.

She sent her parents a WhatsApp message instead: *Hi Mom*

and Dad, MISS YOU!!! The trip was great, it rained a little but the villa was AMAAAAZING!! It was sooooo big and we had a gorgeous private pool too!! The buffet was to DIE for! You would have loved it, Mom!! P.S. Do you like my Hawaiian shirt, Gong Gong and Paw Paw?

After sending a picture of Joey grinning toothily at the camera along with the message, she slid her phone back under her pillow.

She closed her eyes, but her mind was racing. She fell back on her childhood trick of mentally rattling off the names of countries in alphabetic order, the more distant the better: Algeria, Belarus, Cameroon, the Dominican Republic, Ecuador, Fiji…

To her relief, by the time she reached Mauritius, she was yawning.

Norah was woken the next morning by a familiar sensation that, in her grogginess, she couldn't quite place. Upon opening her eyes she realized it was Ben, nuzzling her cheek with his chin.

"Sorry," he said, suddenly bashful. Norah was relieved to find the sharp edges of her frustration had dulled in the night. When she glanced at the crib, she saw that Joey was still asleep, and the sight of his bald head was still upsetting, but she was also relieved to wake up in her usual spot, wedged safely between her husband and her baby, instead of in a hotel.

Norah smiled shyly in return, and Ben's face lit up for a moment before growing anxious again. "I, uh, unpacked your things. I thought you might need Eeyore." He gestured to the open, empty suitcase on the floor.

"Thank you," she said, unhooking her nursing bra. She wanted to tell him how good it was to wake up beside him, how safe it made her feel, but the words got caught in her throat. What use was it to be safe in this moment, when beyond their bedroom door was her mother-in-law?

"I've been thinking about what you said about quitting your job," he said, his voice hesitant. "I understand why you would want to. But when I talked to Ma last night, it seemed like she knew how angry we were, and... and, well, do you think you can give her one more chance?" He looked at her hopefully, desperately.

Norah wanted to reassure him, wanted to make things okay between them again, but she couldn't quite seem to. The room was silent but for the steady *heee-haw, heee-haw* of the breast pump.

Finally, Norah reached for one of Ben's hands. It was sweaty and shaking. "I'll be taking care of Joey myself today," she said quietly. "Let me think about it, okay?"

Ben nodded, standing up. Norah watched as he changed into his unofficial uniform, black jeans and a checked shirt. He left the top three buttons undone, revealing the little white triangle of his undershirt, and rolled the shirt sleeves up to his elbows.

"You look nice," she said suddenly, surprising them both.

He leaned over her and kissed her forehead. "I love you," he murmured. "See you tonight."

It was Tuesday, Norah's day off from work, and Nai Nai's holiday from Joey-duty, so as usual, she had left early in the morning to do whatever it was she did on Tuesdays—have dimsum, play mahjong, get a manicure.

Norah set Joey in the jumparoo and laughed as the whole toy shook violently with his jumping. His legs had gotten so strong. She took out some congee from the fridge to reheat for him, then made a cup of coffee for herself. Decaffeinated coffee tasted different; she still hadn't gotten used to it, but for Joey's sake, she was very careful with her caffeine intake. Dark chocolate was what she missed most. Different health websites had provided different guidelines for breastfeeding moms, but with Joey's eczema, she had been going by the most conservative numbers. That meant decaffeinated coffee and herbal teas only, very small amounts of chocolate, and no soda.

After breakfast, she changed Joey into a smart polo shirt and jeans, and put on his feet striped socks that matched his shirt. She had booked a trial class for him at a playgroup in Central, not far from Dr. Chan's clinic. If Joey liked it, the lessons would be expensive, but the way Norah saw it, there was nothing more important than investing in Joey's future. In her experience, good things cost good money. Dr. Chan's costly consultations and medicine were a case in point.

Several Tuesdays ago she had taken Joey to a trial class at a children's learning centre near their home. It was free and less than ten minutes away by foot, so she had signed him up.

The centre allowed children to be accompanied by an unlimited number of adults, so some babies came to class with both parents as well as a grandparent or a domestic helper, and the classroom felt cramped and hot. There was no policy against photo-taking during the lesson, and eager mothers snapped picture after picture of their babies while the teacher tried desperately to maintain some semblance of control over the crowd of adults and the little babies at their feet. The teacher had used a very poor-quality microphone that produced ear-splitting feedback each time she gave an instruction.

Joey, normally so placid and agreeable, had refused to even clap his hands. He had stayed curled in her lap, like a real joey, and Norah had shielded his face from the photographer moms and his ears from the screeching microphone as best she could. When the receptionist tried to intimidate her into buying a package of lessons, Norah had to stop herself from laughing in the woman's face. "No thank you," Norah had said. "And please don't ever call me again."

So, although this thirty-minute trial class was going to set her back $400, Norah was hopeful it would be worth it. She strapped Joey into the carrier, swung her backpack onto one shoulder, and was about to open the front door when she remembered his baby Fedora hat. She set it on his bald head, then took out her phone to snap a selfie of the two of them.

"Smile, my little peach," she said, kissing his cheek. Joey laughed as she took the picture. Norah sent the picture to Ben with a little heart emoji. He responded immediately with three kissy face emojis, which made her smile.

Joey was asleep by the time they arrived in the lobby of the right building. It had taken Norah a few minutes longer than expected to find it, although it should have been easy; it was only about hundred meters from Dr. Chan's clinic.

Red-faced and sweating, Norah checked her phone again, confirmed that Gemma's Gym for Babies and Toddlers was on the twelfth floor, and rushed into a nearly full elevator. She stared and stared at the button panel but couldn't find a '12', until she finally realized all the numbers on the panel were odd numbers. She rushed back out, apologizing profusely. She was tactfully re-directed to the line for the correct elevator, where she watched the glowing numbers above the elevator anxiously. Glancing down at her watch, she was relieved to see there were still five minutes before the start of Joey's class.

Finally, the elevator doors opened on the twelfth floor. Gemma's Gym seemed to be the only vendor on the floor, and it had the air of an amusement park, with large rainbow-colored panels on the walls and smiling jungle animals swinging from the ceiling. Calliope music was playing faintly in the background. It even smelled good, like vanilla, or sugar cookies. Beyond the reception area, in the actual gym, Norah could see floor-to-ceiling windows overlooking Victoria Harbour. There were three children inside already, their mothers chatting in a small huddle behind them. A blond man of perhaps forty was setting up brightly colored tumble mats and a miniature balancing beam. Behind the reception counter, there was a giant photograph of a smiling woman, presumably Gemma, doing splits in mid-air. Norah sighed with pleasure. Now this was what Joey deserved.

"Good morning, and welcome to Gemma's Gym!" The young woman sitting behind the counter sort of bounced up, smiling like the picture hanging behind her. She extended a manicured hand in Norah's direction, and Norah took it, although the receptionist's green nails brought to mind her mother-in-law and the magic of the moment went. She glanced down at her clipboard and said, "I'm Erin! You must be Joey's mummy! It's his first lesson with us, isn't it? I see little Joey is asleep! What a sweetheart! Here's a gold star sticker for his polo shirt, so the teacher, Mr. Stuart, will know Joey is an extra special guest!"

Everything the receptionist said seemed to end in an exclamation mark. "Thank you, Erin," Norah smiled, attaching the gold star to the front of Joey's shirt. Enthusiasm was hard to find in Hong Kong, but here it was in abundance. "And may I ask where we should put our shoes and things?"

"Absolutely, Mrs. Tam! Shoes this way in the rainbow cabinet! Bags and other personal belongings can go inside the gym with you!"

Norah nodded gratefully at her before taking off her leather flats and Joey's Nike runners; Ben had the same pair in his own size. Joey was still huddled against her front, asleep.

The teacher, Mr. Stuart, stood up when he saw Norah and Joey approaching the glass door of the gym, and he rushed forward to open it for them. The three moms glanced up from their conversation, and nodded politely at Norah before picking up where they had left off.

"Hello, my very special guest, and mummy! I am Mr. Stuart! But please, call me Stu!" he exclaimed in that posh British accent that Hong Kong parents adore. He spread his arms, as though prepared to hug her, then brought his hands together in front of his chest as though he was about to pray.

"It's a pleasure to meet you, Stu," Norah said, smiling at him. "I'm Norah, and this is my little one, Joey. He's asleep, I'm afraid, but—"

He interrupted with a hearty laugh. "Joey! And you, the mama kangaroo! What a perfect name. And don't worry about him being asleep. He'll wake up once we get started. The babies always do. Just put your bag down over there in the corner with the others, and join us on the mat."

Norah took off her backpack and dropped it more loudly than she intended to on the floor. It was so heavy; she could never count on Joey nursing when they went out, and she had brought everything she would need to mix up a fresh bottle of formula: a baby bottle with six scoops of powder in it, a thermos with hot water, a bottle with room temperature water. And diapers and wet wipes, of course, a spare change of clothes, and Joey's creams, just in case something in the environment didn't agree with his skin. At the last moment she had packed her own battered Nalgene bottle, too, and was thankful she did. She took a big gulp of water before gently unstrapping Joey from the carrier.

Joey was still slumped against her shoulder as the opening bars of 'Do you know the Muffin Man' played on the speakers.

Including Norah and Joey, there were only four pairs of moms and babies forming a circle with Stu. They all seemed to know what to do; they all sang "Welcome to gymnastics class, gymnastics class, gymnastics class…" to the tune of 'Muffin Man', with actions, and Norah tried her best to follow along.

Finally, Joey stirred, and Norah's heart swelled with love for him as she watched him turn his head slowly from side to side, blinking his eyes rapidly but not crying. His bottom lip was trembling when he looked up at her, and he reached out his chubby arms and wrapped them tightly around her neck like a frightened koala cub.

"Hello, Maisy! Hello, Christopher! Hello, Gwyneth! And an extra special hello to Joey, who is joining us for the first time today here at Gemma's Gym!" Stu smiled and nodded at each baby in turn. When Christopher crawled onto his lap, Stu's laugh was hearty and sincere. "Why, hello, little one!"

As Stu led them through the first few activities, Norah quickly concluded that Christopher and Maisy were older than Gwyneth and Joey, they were the two who could crawl. Stu pulled out a monkey puppet after the welcome song and made the babies as well as their mothers giggle with a convincing monkey impersonation. Gradually, Joey loosened his grip around Norah's neck, and began to nod his head and clap his hands in time with the music.

Stu and the monkey got the moms to bounce the babies on their laps, to balance them on their backs, and to toss bean bags into baskets while skipping in a circle and singing 'Ring Around the Rosie'. The highlight for Norah was what Stu called 'Parachute Time'; all four babies laughed and laughed as Stu led the mothers in bringing the parachute up like a mushroom and then down again over their little heads, over and over. Joey's was the only bald one, but in the exhilaration of the moment, it didn't bother Norah.

At the end of the lesson, Norah scooped Joey up, and was packing up her things when Stu walked up beside them. "How did you like it, little Joey?" Stu asked kindly. "You did so well, especially as it was your very first time."

Joey tentatively reached out a hand to touch Stu's face.

"I think he likes me," Stu smiled, leaning forward so Joey could pat his cheek. "I like you too, big boy!"

"We had a wonderful time, Stu; thank you so much," Norah said, pleased at how quickly Joey had taken to the teacher. "Where do we sign up?"

Stu laughed. "Am I glad to hear you say that! Just this way," he said, opening the class door. "After you."

At the reception counter, Erin presented Norah with the package deals: three-month, six-month, and twelve-month options. Erin spoke very rapidly and enthusiastically, and Norah found herself nodding along eagerly. She would love to bring Joey here every Tuesday.

"Of course, the twelve-month option is the best deal. The trial class was $400, but if you buy fifty lessons at once, you'll be all set for an entire year, with two weeks off for Christmas and Chinese New Year, of course. At $16,250, you would only be paying $325 per class. That's a real steal, mummy!" Erin knew this spiel, numbers included, like the back of her hand. "This is a special offer, only for sign-ups immediately following a trial class."

Norah unzipped her wallet and was digging around for her credit card, when she paused. Their money was shared money. "Just give me one moment, please, Erin," she said. "I just want to call my husband."

She nodded understandingly. "Of course, of course! We often have daddies accompanying the children, especially on the weekends. But please remember, mummy, the special offer only applies today. If you want to sign up after today, you will be charged the regular price, $20,000 for 50 lessons."

Norah nodded, then went back out by the elevators for a little privacy. Ben picked up almost immediately. "Hello?"

"Hi, baby," he said, clearly pleased to hear her voice. "I got your picture."

"I got your kisses. Hey, we're at Gemma's Gym now. I have something to ask you."

"The playgroup place, right? Go ahead. Anything."

Joey was gnawing on the carrier strap and Norah knew she needed to sort this out quickly; Joey was going to have to eat soon. "So, Joey just had his trial class and he absolutely loved it—"

"Gemma's was the place that charges $400 a lesson, right?"

"That's the thing. It's only $325 if we buy the package." Norah paused. "But we have to buy fifty lessons at a time."

"Fifty lessons!"

Norah tried not to sound annoyed; she hadn't expected Ben to be this difficult, after all that happened yesterday, after their sort of truce in the morning. "I know it's a lot," she said, "but Joey needs to attend a playgroup. He'll need to have something on his portfolio for kindergarten applications, and Gemma's is really well-recognized. It's beautiful here, and you can come with him too, the receptionist said lots of dads—"

"But, fifty lessons, that's..."

"A little more than sixteen thousand dollars, but—"

"Norah," he said softly, "that's a lot of money. I don't think we can afford..."

"But it was perfect; Joey loved it. *I* loved it." Norah sighed. "Please, Ben."

"Can we talk about it tonight?"

"No, we can't. The deal expires the moment we leave. It'll be the full price, twenty thousand dollars, if we sign up tomorrow."

About a minute passed, when nobody spoke. Joey looked expectantly at her.

"Ben, please. Joey was hungry."

"I wish we could afford it, I really do, but we just went on that trip to Sanya, and…"

Norah hung up.

Chapter 10

Ben rested his forehead on the cold glass top of his and Eric's shared work desk, where they did their editing after a shoot. Eric was not in that day; he had a gig with a small law firm in Mong Kok that wanted professional headshots of its staff on their website but did not want to spend too much on them. Snapshot fit the bill nicely.

Ben should have been heading home; it was past seven and his mother would be wondering where he was. Norah would be too, normally, but he had a bad feeling that maybe Norah and Joey weren't home. She had ignored his messages all afternoon.

He opened up the Google sheet he had on his phone again, the one he used to track their savings and expenses. While the file was not a secret, Norah had never seen it; she had never wanted to. She told him herself that growing up she had never been taught to make or follow a budget, and had no interest in learning. It was only natural that when she started making her own money as a teacher, she just spent as she liked. There was always plenty leftover at the end of the month, so she could not see any point in laboriously noting down each item and making herself feel bad for spending too much. She had been lying in his arms as she told him this, and he had happily accepted it as part of who she was—his carefree, cheerful Norah, so very different from himself.

Sweat beads bloomed on his forehead as he typed '16000' in the lowest cell in the column with 'JOEY—MISC' at the top. In the column next to JOEY—MISC was a hidden column. He tapped on the screen and selected 'Unhide', revealing a neat column of numbers entitled 'MA'. Each cell in this column had '$10000' and there sure were a lot of them—he had been giving his Ma fifty percent of his salary since he began working at Snapshot.

The practice of giving Ma exactly one half of his salary began when Ben was fourteen. He earned a modest salary as the tutor of their neighbor's two young boys, and on the last Friday of each month, Ben would find his eight $100 bills paper-clipped together at the neighbor's dining table. During that hour, as the two boys toiled over their math workbooks, he would eye the money surreptitiously, hungrily, dreaming of the luxuries he was saving towards: a more fashionable pair of sports shoes, a graphing calculator, a smartphone that took pictures.

He stared at the screen for several long moments, thinking. He slowly typed 'Gemma's Gym Central' in the search bar of his browser. His index finger hovered over the gym's phone number, then taking a deep breath, he tapped at it.

"Hello, Gemma's Gym! Erin speaking! How may I help you?"

Ben held the phone away from his ear; the enthusiastic voice on the other end of the line was so loud. He switched to speaker phone, then turned down the volume. There was carnival music playing in the background.

"Um, hello," he said, tentatively. He hated speaking English to strangers.

"Hello, there, and thank you for calling Gemma's Gym! What can I do for you today?"

The woman was overwhelmingly cheerful; she reminded Ben

a little of what Norah was like at work.

Ben coughed. "My wife brought my son to a class today. I would like to buy lessons for him."

"Absolutely, daddy! And what is your little boy's name? I'll just pull up his file and take down your credit card information, if that's okay with you?"

"His name is Joey. Joey Tam."

"Oh, Joey! *Such* a sweetheart! Are you aware of our package deals, daddy? We have a selection of *excellent* deals for children who register on the same day as their trial class, so I'm very glad you called now! Did you know, our centre closes at 7:30! You could *not* have called at a better time!"

Ben wanted to say *I am aware of this,* but he listened patiently as she rattled off the package deals, and confirmed that Norah had not misheard the outrageous cost of a year's worth of lessons – it was indeed $16,000. He fingered the embossed digits on his credit card as she talked. By the time he read out his credit card number and expiry date, he was mostly at peace with the decision. He hoped it was enough to stop Norah from leaving.

When Ben opened the front door, the first thing he noticed was the smell: his mother had cooked curry, his favorite. Norah liked Indian curries, but he had always been partial to his mother's curry, which contained lots of carrot and potato chunks and was more mildly flavored than the masala and makhani dishes Norah ordered at Bombay Dreams. On the dining table his mother's pyramid-shaped mosquito net was guarding a covered dish, a covered rice bowl, and a pair of chopsticks.

There was no one in the living room. He slowly removed his shoes, hung up his keys and backpack. The silence was disconcerting. Where was everyone?

Ben couldn't see any light at the bottom of either bedroom door, but he knocked softly, just in case, on their bedroom door, before opening it. He was surprised to see Norah in bed, her familiar face ethereal in the glow of her cell phone. He could make out the baby's sleeping form in the crib; when he squinted, he saw that Joey was wearing the striped sleeping bag he and Norah bought together at Mothercare shortly after they found out she was pregnant. How excited they had been!

"Hi," he said, sitting down on the edge of the bed. "How was your day?"

Norah switched off her phone, plunging the room in darkness. Ben parted the curtains a little; the street lamps had just come on.

"I have something to tell you," he tried again, patting at the blanket in an attempt to locate her hand.

She rolled onto her side, away from him.

"I bought the lessons."

She sat up immediately. "What did you say?"

"I bought the lessons at Gemma's Gym," he repeated, as though it was nothing.

"You didn't!" she said, grabbing his arm. "You said…you said we couldn't afford it." Doubt crept back into her voice.

"Maybe I was wrong," he responded lightly. They would have to dip into their savings account to cover the cost, but if they were careful with their spendings in the next few months, perhaps they could slowly make up the difference. He didn't dare make adjustments to Ma's *gayong*. He wondered wildly if Ma would notice if he slipped her $5,000 instead of $10,000, if he replaced some of the five-hundred dollar bills with one-hundred dollar bills. He shook his head; she would definitely notice right away. "Nothing but the best for Joey, right?"

"Oh, Ben!" she shrieked, throwing her arms around his neck. "I knew you'd come around eventually. I just knew it."

He wanted to ask *So you'll stay then, right? You'll let Ma take care of Joey again, right?* but didn't want to ruin the moment. When he tentatively reached out a hand to stroke her back, she responded by tightening her grip around his neck. For the first time in days, the silence between them felt good again. Better than good; Ben had missed this closeness, and the air in the room felt almost electric with possibility.

"About Nai Nai," she finally said, looking up at him. "Maybe it's okay for her to take care of Joey if she doesn't try to shave his head again." She paused, chewing on her bottom lip. "I want to stay here with you."

She buried her head in his chest as she said this, and Ben wrapped his arms tightly around her, frightened by how close he had come to losing her. He saw out of the corner of his eye Norah's carry-on suitcase still standing at the ready behind the crib. That would never do. "I'll just, uh, put the suitcase away."

As Ben was about to stand up, Norah leaned towards him and kissed him on the lips. The gesture was so light, so quick, it might have been his imagination—and he was about to respond with something stronger when his stomach let out a great rumble, spoiling the moment. They both laughed.

"Nai Nai made curry before she went out again," she said. "Your favorite. We didn't talk, of course, but I could smell it cooking. I haven't eaten yet either," she added, her voice shy. "She's mad at me, so I'm pretty sure she only cooked enough for you, but I bought a few cup noodles on the way home. Can I come eat with you?"

Ben leaned against the railing outside Future English, pretending to be reading something on his cell phone as he waited to pick Norah up from work. At first he was actually reading; the news article on the latest developments in the social unrest in Hong Kong had been alarming, but he realized now that he had been reading without comprehending the same paragraph for a long time. He'd been glancing up at Norah through the glass walls of the centre instead. Normally he enjoyed seeing his wife in her element, confident and at ease. Today she was wearing a form-fitting chiffon dress that stopped just above her knees. Her legs looked impossibly long and lovely.

Norah had been talking with a student Ben did not recognize, a grungy-looking man in jeans ripped at the knee, for about ten minutes—thirteen minutes, if Ben was to be exact. It was not that she was flirting; he knew she wasn't. But that student kept leaning towards her as they talked, eyeing her legs as he did, and several times he had actually reached out and touched her arm. He acted as though he was emphasizing a point, but Ben was not fooled.

Norah seemed pretty oblivious to how attracted the student was to her; she was talking animatedly and gesturing a great deal with her hands, the way she always did when she was with a student. There was that concerned, attentive expression on her face, the one he fell in love with, the one that made people believe Norah thought the world of them.

One more minute, he thought. *If this goes on for any longer than one more minute, I'm going in there and making my presence known. That's my wife he's talking to.*

A minute later, Ben strode into Future English. He greeted Susan at reception in English, as was expected of him, then chatted briefly with Siu-Fong, one of Norah's favourite students, about Joey. Ben always found it curious how all the students spoke to each other in such effortful English here even though they could all speak Chinese. Strategically placed signs proclaimed the centre's motto: "English in the Future! English in *YOUR* Future!"

He waved hello to Ivan, who was deep in conversation with one of his sales staff.

Once Ben was in the social area, Norah saw him immediately, and the next thing he knew, she was clutching at his hands, squealing. "I didn't know you were coming to pick me up today," she said, delighted. "Have you been waiting long? I'm sorry; I was just talking to a student."

"Not long, just a few minutes," he said, shrugging. Out of the corner of his eye he could see the new student watching them, his hands stuffed in his pockets. Ben pointed at him, as subtly as he could, with his chin. "Was it him? He's looking at us."

She nodded eagerly. "Yes, want to meet him? His name was Cable, isn't that an unusual name? It's his first day in the Future. Cable was telling me all about his job refurbishing smartphones, and..."

"You must be Ben," Cable interrupted, holding out a hand; his fingernails were dirty. Ben frowned, thinking of that hand touching Norah's skin. "I'm Cable, like Cable TV."

"It's nice to meet you, Cable." Ben casually draped an arm around Norah's shoulders, then kissed her forehead. She glanced up at him, a little surprised; they were usually less physical with each other at the centre, but then she smiled shyly, pleased. Cable gave him a quizzical look which confirmed Ben's suspicions: he had been hitting on Norah. "I'll wait for you outside, okay?"

He nodded at Cable, who gave him a tight-lipped smile in return, and waved at the other students—Tim, Kitty, several others whose names he no longer remembered.

A few moments later, Norah joined him outside, her handbag slung over one shoulder, and hand-in-hand, they took the long escalator down to the lobby. Ben could feel many pairs of eyes watching them as they made their slow descent.

"Hi," she said, grinning. "This feels romantic, kind of like before we got married or something."

Ben glanced at her, wondered if he should bring up what just happened with Cable, whether Norah would think he was being petty or possessive. He finally decided it would be irresponsible not to. "So, Norah, um, that new student—"

"Oh, Cable?"

"Did he seem a little weird to you?"

Norah chewed on her bottom lip, thinking. "A little, now that you mention it. He seemed very touchy-feely, which is unusual for students here, but he was so enthusiastic, kept going on and on, and because it's his first day he didn't know anyone in the centre yet, so after the lesson I felt sort of responsible for him, you know?"

Ben squeezed her hand. "I know. Do you think maybe you should tell Ivan about him? He seemed very, uh, interested in you. He kept staring at your legs."

She shuddered. "Did he really? That's gross. I'll talk to Ivan, but I don't really want to get Cable in trouble. We might lose him as a student, and maybe...I don't know, maybe it was a one-time thing."

Ben stopped walking. "Norah, it was not a one-time thing. The guy's a creep." His tone must have been too harsh; she looked frightened, her eyes blinking rapidly. "Just talk to Ivan, okay? I want you to be safe."

She nodded.

"I booked a table for us at the Shanghai place. Potstickers and *xiaolongbao* for dinner sound okay?"

A smile broke on her face. "You mean a date? Just the two of us?" She paused, frowning. "But what about Joey?"

"Well, I called Ma before I left the studio, and she said he looked really sleepy," he said, exaggerating the last two words. He knew how torn Norah felt about leaving Joey at home while they enjoyed themselves, and all the more so after Ma shaved his head. "So, after his congee dinner he'll probably go straight to sleep, and you'll be there for his midnight feed. What do you think? We could get those fried dough balls for dessert, the ones with the red bean filling and powdered sugar?"

He could feel Norah struggling beside him—her nails were biting into his arm and she was taking deep breaths through her nose, the way she sometimes did in moments of crisis, but he didn't say anything. Finally, she leaned her head on his arm. "Okay, just this once." She looked up at him, her eyes bright. "Thank you, honey!"

"Shall we get a mango pudding for Nai Nai?" Norah asked. She had stopped walking, was peering in the window of the Chinese bakery two blocks from home.

They had ordered too much food at the Shanghai place; Ben was regretting having finished the last of the noodles, even the thick peanutty broth, but it was delicious, and more importantly, he hated wasting food. His jeans felt tight at the waist.

"Ben? Do you think Nai Nai would like a mango pudding?" Norah did this sometimes, asked the same question several ways to try and elicit a response from him, as though Ben were still her English student and needed to work on his listening skills. He had no trouble understanding Norah's questions, of course, but he was unsure why she would want to buy something for his mother so soon after their argument over Joey's haircut.

"Ben," she began again patiently, "I'd like to ask you whether you think it would..."

"Do you want to?" Ben interrupted.

"They're her favorite, aren't they?"

Ben watched as Norah walked briskly into the bakery, her

chiffon dress clinging to her hips as she squeezed through the narrow doorway. She pointed at the mango pudding cups and held up two fingers in a peace sign, then shook her head, smiling, when the store owner picked up two plastic spoons.

She came back out, the little plastic bag swinging by her side. "Okay, home time."

"You're not mad at Ma anymore?" he asked. It didn't make sense. Just a few days ago she was so angry she was threatening to move out.

Norah didn't speak for several moments. They kept walking together, her arm clinging to his, in silence. Just before they entered the elevator, Norah reached for his hand. "She shouldn't have shaved Joey's head. I really didn't like that. But she's your mom. She's Joey's grandmother. I've got to keep trying, right?"

When Ben unlocked the door, he saw his mother in her armchair, flipping through a Reader's Digest. She took off her reading glasses and watched them as he and Norah huddled about the front door, shedding their coats, bags, and shoes.

"Hi, Nai Nai," Norah said quietly. For several uncomfortable moments, Ben worried that his mother was going to ignore Norah.

"Hello, Ben," she finally responded. Ben sighed. *So this is how it's going to be.* "I gave Joey his bath. He slept at 7:30."

"Thank you for helping to take care of him," Norah said, her head bowed.

"I've told you many times that you don't need to thank me for looking after my own grandchild," Ma said, scowling. "And I thought you didn't want me to touch him anymore? Why did you come home so late then?"

Ben stole a glance at Norah, who was looking at the plastic bag with the pudding cups in her hand, as though unsure how it got there.

"Ma," Ben protested, "you knew we would be back around this time. I called you from work, remember?"

"Hmmph," Ma said, putting her reading glasses back on. "I'm happy to be with Joey, anytime. But I'm not happy about being treated as unfit for childcare. If I'm not fit, then by all means—"

"That's not what Norah meant, Ma," Ben interrupted quietly. This was not going well at all. "Look, she bought you your favourite dessert."

"I'm pre-diabetic, don't you know," Ma snapped, glaring at Norah. "Now you want to kill me too?"

Without a word, Norah dropped the bag with the puddings on the table, then walked the short length of the hallway to their bedroom. She closed the door behind her noiselessly.

"Ma," Ben frowned, sitting down on the sofa beside his mother. "Why are you so upset?"

"Unfit for childcare! Hmmph!"

"She didn't mean it. That's not what she meant at all. She just meant, don't shave Joey's head anymore. Also, since when did you become 'pre-diabetic'? What are you talking about?"

She bristled. "Well, I *am* pre-diabetic. Everybody is."

"You buy those pudding cups for yourself all the time, Ma. Just last week you were eating one."

"The real issue, of course, is how easily she threatened to leave us. Not much regard for her marriage, is there?"

Ben was rattled by his mother's words. He hadn't thought of Norah's outburst in those terms.

"That's not what she meant," he repeated weakly. "She... she was very upset." He cleared his throat, tried again. "You're changing the subject. Please stop being so mean to her, Ma."

His mother snorted. "You treat her like she's royalty, but she'd leave you in a heartbeat, over a bit of hair."

"Ma, I'm tired. Good night."

She put on her reading glasses again, picked up her Reader's Digest. Ben saw that it was the November 2001 edition. "I've upset you," she said, squinting at the words. "But if I don't tell you how it is, who will?"

Chapter 11

NORAH WAS sitting on the floor of Dr. Chan's clinic with Joey, making foam block towers for him to knock over. He could sit up without help now, the soles of his little feet touching each other in a quasi-cross-legged position. He was a sturdy, smiley baby, and especially since some of his hair had grown back, albeit coarser and spikier than before, Norah believed her Joey could be a baby model.

The clinic was quiet today; there were only two other families waiting with them. Behind Norah and Joey were Ben and his mother, chatting in low tones about a relative in China who had recently been diagnosed with a rare intestinal cancer. It was Ben's first visit to Dr. Chan's clinic. He took the day off so he could come with them to Joey's appointment, but then Nai Nai insisted on joining them as well. "Am I not welcome?" she had asked, sniffing.

She would not take no for an answer, and recently she had been so crotchety that neither Ben nor Norah said anything when Nai Nai put on her shoes and followed them out the door. Their original plan had been to take Joey paddle boating at Inspiration Lake after the doctor's appointment to celebrate his eighth month, but Norah was quite sure they would not be going after all, now that Nai Nai was with them.

Her mother-in-law had become even more difficult in the past few weeks since their disagreement over Joey's hair. Norah tried desperately to process her own emotions, to rise above the toxic environment that their home had become, but it was difficult. Nai Nai was aggressively putting forward the view that Norah had overreacted, and that in overreacting, had shown how little she cared for their marriage, or worse, how little she really loved Ben. Ben pretended not to care, but Norah knew he was heavily affected by what his mother said.

Norah continued surrounding Joey with flimsy structures that could be knocked over with a lazy swat. Joey was doing so well. He was the only good thing in her life these days: his skin was smooth and soft, and he was gaining weight at a steady clip. He was meeting all his milestones, was even a bit advanced for his age. According to mybaby.com, unassisted sitting was typically a milestone in the eighth month. Norah had felt inordinately proud when she read that.

"Tam Chun Yin, Joey," the familiar female voice announced. Norah hastily scooped the foam blocks back into the plastic tub they came from as Ben picked Joey up from the floor. They squeezed into Dr. Chan's office, and after the usual greetings, the doctor held out the yellowing rattles. Norah grinned as she saw Joey's eyes light up. Dr. Chan reached out for Joey, who willingly went to him.

"Boy, you're heavy now, little one," he said, smiling down at the baby. He checked Joey's skin with great care, even the little folds around his wrists and ankles. The room was silent apart from the faint whirr of the air-conditioner and the occasional rattle from Joey. Several moments later, Dr. Chan nodded approvingly.

"Continue with the pine tar baths," he said, smiling, "and

the moisturizers for his face and body. Be sure to keep him moisturized, the way you've obviously been doing. Apart from that, I believe my work here is done." He cleared his throat dramatically, then announced: "I declare this child itchy no more!"

Norah let out a whoop and began clapping, and Ben and Nai Nai joined in after a moment, their smiles matching hers. She and Nai Nai may not agree on much, but they both loved the baby. Joey blinked at the sudden noise in consternation, then joined in, knocking the two rattles together with a toothy grin.

"Oh, *thank* you, doctor, thank you!" Nai Nai cried.

Norah felt like dancing. It was over. The long nights of scratching, of bleeding, of crying—were over. The curse of the shrimp dumpling was over.

Norah thought of something else. "Dr. Chan, does that mean he can start eating solids? I mean, apart from plain congee?"

Dr. Chan nodded. "Indeed it does. I would start slowly, with the least allergenic foods. Rice is fine, of course; he's had congee for months. Banana, sweet potato, and chicken meat would be logical first choices. Perhaps start with those, one new food item per week, and be sure to note any changes in his skin. You can come back in a month, and we'll see how he's doing then."

Joey suddenly reached out for Ben, who scooped him up and tickled the soles of his feet with his index finger. Norah watched, content, as Joey giggled. They left the doctor's office in a happy parade, Joey first in line.

On the taxi ride home, Norah's phone suddenly buzzed, and she frantically tried to locate her phone in the mess that was her backpack. By the time she found it, buried under Joey's spare change of clothes, she had missed the call. It was her mom.

Ben glanced at her phone, then whispered, "Call her back. She'll be asleep if you wait till we get home."

Although Norah did not really want to chat with her mother within earshot of Nai Nai, she knew Ben was right. It was already 11:30 p.m. in Vancouver, later than her parents' usual bedtime. She wondered if something was wrong with Dad's health; when they spoke last week, neither of them mentioned anything, but perhaps it was an emergency?

Joey was sitting in Nai Nai's lap, and both of them were gazing calmly out the window; perhaps it would be okay to make a short call.

Norah tapped on the picture of her parents, then the CALL button. As she held the phone to her ear, she was suddenly quite certain that Mom had terrible news for her. The air-conditioning in the taxi was on full blast, too cold for comfort, but Norah began sweating. She felt a tissue dabbing at her temples, turned from the window and saw it was Ben. He smiled encouragingly at her, and she did her best to reciprocate.

"Norah, is that you?" Mom didn't sound like she was in distress, a good sign.

"Hi Mom, everything okay? It's pretty late over there, isn't it?" She tried her best to keep her voice steady. Her mother-in-law had turned to watch her as she talked. Even though Norah was speaking English, which Nai Nai didn't understand, it still felt as though everyone in the car was watching and listening to her every word. She wished the driver had the radio on, but the taxi was silent.

"Of course! I just missed you and the little guy, you know. Have you talked to Ben about flying over here in the summer? I wanted to get some dates down, because your dad, you know how impulsive he is sometimes, wants to book a cruise for us this summer. What do you think? We could do the Disney Cruise,

Norah! Wouldn't Joey love that?"

Norah glanced at Ben, hoped desperately he hadn't heard what her mom just said. Calling her mom back in the taxi was a mistake. She hadn't mentioned traveling to Vancouver to Ben at all, and after all they had just spent at Gemma's, she couldn't imagine Ben agreeing to an expensive summer trip. A cruise was completely out of the question.

"Uh, that sounds really fun, Mom. I'm, uh, with Ben and my Nai Nai right now, how about I call you back? Later would be too late, right? Would tomorrow morning be okay?"

"Well, alright, love. Tomorrow sounds fine," Mom said. "How's Joey?"

Finally, a topic Norah felt comfortable talking about. "He's doing so well! We just took him to the clinic, and the doctor said his eczema is pretty much all gone. He can start eating solids, can you believe it?"

"Oh, fantastic, I'm so glad. I miss him so much. So, FaceTime tomorrow morning? Your 9 a.m. okay?"

"Sure. See you, Mom. Give Dad a kiss for me."

"He's asleep and snoring. Can you hear him?"

Norah laughed. Yes, she could. She hung up, and was thankful that Ben did not ask what her mother had said that sounded so fun. The driver pulled up in front of their building shortly after.

Norah bought *My Nourished Child: A Cookbook* in the third trimester of her pregnancy. By then, Joey had become very real to her—much more than just a bump that Ben took pictures of each week. By this point they had named him Joey, and she spent a great deal of her time rubbing his bum through the muscular wall of her womb, telling him she loved him, imagining what he looked like.

She had begged Ben for that expensive and unnecessary 4D ultrasound, and he had refused, insisting that they should spend the $2,000 on something useful, like a crib or a stroller, or even both, if they bought second-hand. Eventually he had come around, just as he had with the lessons at Gemma's Gym.

It had been a costly but magical twenty-minute session at BabyImage. They had marveled at the moving images on the oversized monitor: there was Joey, brown and clay-like, his hands splayed, sometimes raised in an almost wave, and the corners of his little mouth upturned in a demure smile. Ben's hand had been sweaty as he clutched hers. The technician had been very quiet, offering occasional and mostly unnecessary words of commentary as he expertly guided the transducer on her belly; the gel had made it cold and slick, like the surface of a skating rink. Norah remembered how Ben had gripped her hand, stunned, when Joey languidly rolled onto his side and a little foot, with its five perfect jelly-bean toes, filled the screen. As the two of them stared at the screen, mesmerized, Joey had wriggled his foot left and right in a sort of wave. The technician murmured, "That is his foot," as though worried Ben and Norah did not know what they were seeing.

After the 4D scan, Norah had doubled down on her efforts at preparing for motherhood. This was when she bought the staggeringly expensive Medela breast pump, an assortment of organic cotton onesies, a baby carrier with the infant insert, and this baby cookbook. She had delighted in the glossy photographs, which made even the most basic of purées look appetising.

Today, Norah felt at peace with the world. Joey had had no allergic reactions, no flare-ups whatsoever in the last two weeks, and had loved the banana and sweet potato additions to his diet. This was chicken week, finally. She was so excited she could barely stand it. If Joey could eat chicken, that would mean he could eat a whole meal, a real meal: chicken congee, mashed sweet potatoes, banana slices for dessert. Joey, who for the longest time couldn't even drink breast milk without breaking out in a rash.

For Joey's first-ever chicken meal, she had purchased the best quality chicken she could find: organic, free-range, hormone-free, antibiotic-free, boneless, skinless, chicken breasts. They were expensive, but she used her credit card, and didn't mention the cost to Ben. She turned to page 34 of *My Nourished Child* and went through the steps in the 'Chicken and Sweet Potato Surprise' recipe one more time before opening the door of their fridge.

The night before she had taken out one of the chicken breasts from the freezer and placed it in the fridge to defrost, and when she poked at the meat with her pinky, she was pleased to find it was soft. Joey was watching her from the Jumperoo, a toothy grin on his face. Today he was not bouncing; instead, he kept shifting his weight from one little foot to the other, swaying from side to side, like he was dancing to the lively 'Froggy Went A Courtin' music.

She boiled the chicken breast in canned chicken broth, anxious not to overcook it, as her cookbook had warned, in capital letters ('OVERCOOKING THE MEAT WILL RESULT IN A BLAND PUREE'), but also worried about undercooking it, as she was pretty sure salmonella lurked in undercooked poultry.

As the meat cooked, she popped out two portions of sweet potato puree from the ice cube tray and placed them in the microwave. She then cut the meat into the recommended 'die-sized' pieces as best she could, burning her fingers in the process, before scooping up the chunks and dropping them into the blender. She added a bit of broth ('up to the 0.5-cup line') and was about to press the blender's '1' button when she heard a key turning in the lock. Ben and his mother had gone on their regular

Saturday brunch date about two hours ago.

"Hi honey, hi Nai Nai," Norah said, her eyes still on the blender. Her finger hovered over the '1' button as the microwave beeped. She heard the door close.

"What's that in the blender?" Nai Nai's voice was shrill. "Frozen meat?"

"It's the chicken I bought last week," Norah said quietly, wiping her hands on her apron before slowly turning around. Nai Nai, dressed in a garish sequined blouse, was standing alone, her shoes still on her feet. *Where was Ben?*

"Frozen food isn't as nutritious as fresh, Norah. You know that, don't you? If you need help, you should have asked. I can help buy fresh meat from the wet market," her mother-in-law offered, peering at the contents in the blender with suspicion. "And what are you heating up in the microwave?"

"Sweet potato puree, Nai Nai," Norah responded quietly. Out of the corner of her eye, she saw that Joey had stopped dancing, and was watching the adults solemnly. She resisted the urge to walk over and switch off the music.

"Why didn't you cook it fresh? Why keep serving frozen food to the baby? Frozen food isn't as nutritious as fresh," she repeated. Her tone was not particularly harsh, but the criticism hurt. Norah felt her eyes smarting.

Just then, the door opened behind Nai Nai. "I'm back," Ben said as he walked in, a bag of pears in his hand. Norah watched as he glanced at Norah's face, then his mother's, and his smile immediately became a frown. "Uh, is everything okay?"

Normally in these situations Norah was inclined to pick up Joey and take refuge in their bedroom, she hated confrontation, but today she was compelled to stand her ground. This was the first day of chicken week, and she was going to finish cooking this meal.

"I was just saying that she shouldn't serve Joey frozen food, is all," Nai Nai finally removed her shoes and stuffs them into the shoe cabinet. "I wasn't trying to upset anybody."

"I'm sure Norah is cooking good food for Joey, Ma," Ben said, but as usual, his voice sounded weak and uncertain around his mother.

Nai Nai sat down in her armchair. "I was only making a suggestion. Fresh chicken tastes better, is cheaper, and is more nutritious. Sweet potatoes only take a moment to cook, if you've cut them into small enough pieces. It's important that we serve Joey only the best, especially since his skin..."

"Ma," Ben interrupted quietly. "Joey's skin is fine now."

"Not for long, if Norah insists on serving him this... this..." Nai Nai waved a hand dismissively at the blender, the microwave. She let out a little snort. "We can do better than this, surely. Shall I cook for him from now on?"

Norah jammed her finger onto the '1' and the roar of the blender temporarily stopped the conversation. She did not let go until the meat and the broth had combined into a smooth beige mush. She could hear Ben and his mother talking in the background. She allowed the words to wash over her like little waves of nothing. She poured some of the chicken puree into Joey's green bowl, the one with the suction at the bottom, and the rest into another silicone ice cube tray for future meals. She took out the sweet potato from the microwave and stirred it carefully before spooning some of it onto the chicken puree to form an orange heart.

Ben and Nai Nai were still talking as she scooped up Joey from the Jumparoo and brought him into their bedroom, laying him down in his crib for a moment before going out into the living room to grab the high chair, Joey's airplane spoon, and the bowl of Chicken and Sweet Potato Surprise.

Nai Nai was saying something to Norah, but she could not make out the words, nor did she want to. She kept walking to the end of the hallway and closed the door behind her. She wanted to say "Joey, it's chicken week," but she was crying, and the words came out in a garbled mess instead of a sentence.

Chapter 12

"Ben, I need to talk to you," Norah said that night. They were lying in bed next to each other, not touching. He had kicked his half of the blanket to the foot of the bed. The air-conditioning was turned up high, and Ben had just showered, but he couldn't seem to get comfortable. Beside him, Norah was curled up against the wall, like a baby. It suddenly occurred to him that she might be sleeping like that because she was cold, and he hastily covered her shoulders with the blanket.

Ben knew his wife was hurting. Ma had been mean to her, again, this time over the frozen chicken. He could kind of see his mother's point; it did seem silly to buy expensive imported frozen meat when you could buy a fresh chicken from the wet market for a fraction of the price. But it was such a little thing, and Ma had insisted on blowing it up and insulting Norah, even calling her lazy.

After Norah disappeared with Joey in their bedroom, Ben had protested that Norah was trying her best, that Ma shouldn't be so critical, but Ma had sighed dramatically.

"I tell her one little thing, one little thing in the best interest of my grandson, and she starts crying, like she's a little girl. I just don't understand how you can stand her, she acts like an entitled child who has never received a word of criticism in her life."

He had responded, quite sternly, that she had to stop criticizing his wife. Ma snorted before settling down in her arm chair to read the newspaper.

Norah suddenly rolled over. "Ben, I want to go to Vancouver."

It felt as if she had punched him in the gut. Ben wanted to ask, *For how long?* but he didn't want her to know he was frightened. He remembered the phone call from a few weeks ago, the one in the taxi when she had said, 'That sounds like fun' to her mother. Was a summer trip what she wanted? Or was it more than that?

"I miss my parents. I want my mom."

"I'm here, baby," Ben said softly, reaching for her hand. She allowed him to hold it for a moment but let go again almost immediately. His hand fell on the mattress with a dull thud.

"I love you," she said, and Ben marveled at how these three words could sound so much like an apology. He could hear the 'but' in her voice before she said it. "But I really miss my parents," she repeated. "They were hoping Joey and I would visit this summer, but I want to leave sooner than that."

It was already mid-May. "Why?"

She sat up then, and despite the darkness of the room, the hurt on her face was unmistakable. "You're asking me 'Why'?"

"I mean, I know you're unhappy, Norah, I do. I just..."

"Sometimes I get so upset with Nai Nai it's like I can't breathe. She criticizes everything I do, especially what I do for Joey. Ben, it's like... it's like I'm dying inside. She's even... she's even..."

Ben could smell the stench of his sweat as he waited for her to finish her sentence, but she abruptly stopped talking. "What, Norah? She's even what?"

"Something's happening to our marriage, isn't it?" The words hung between them, like a black cloud of exhaust that refused to dissipate.

"What do you mean?" But even as he said this, he knew it was true. He had felt it himself. "Things have been a little tense, sure, but..."

"Do you still love me?" she interrupted.

Unexpected tears sprang to his eyes. "Of course I do," he said, unable to hide the hurt in his voice. "More than anything..."

"But you won't do anything about how Nai Nai treats me, right?"

He wanted to say, *It's not that I won't*, but he was afraid of her inevitable *Then what is it?*

His mother had indeed poisoned his marriage in some way, and he was powerless to stop it from spreading.

"Please, Ben. Let me visit my parents. Next week."

Norah had not mentioned the trip to Vancouver again in the last few days, so Ben pretended he'd forgotten about it, too—but as a result, their conversations were stifled and artificial. Sometimes they didn't say anything to each other at all, only to Joey, and to Nai Nai only when strictly necessary.

It was not surprising then, how quiet it was around the dining table. Ma had cooked curry again, and Ben had doused his rice with so much of it that the yellow mixture in his bowl resembled a thick soup. He loved meals that he could eat with just a spoon.

He glanced at Norah, who was quietly feeding Joey his congee. She just returned home from work a few minutes ago, and had changed into one of his old T-shirts, but she hadn't had time to remove her makeup. She looked lovely: her eyelashes were long and dark, framing her eyes.

Ma seemed unusually fidgety. His eyes had met hers several times, but each time Ma had quickly looked away. She had been pushing the food around in her bowl with her chopsticks for the past few minutes.

In the past, Norah would thank Ma for helping with Joey, and Ma would act offended that Norah felt thanks was necessary. Tonight, no one said anything. Ben was thankful for the silence, punctuated only by the sounds of chewing and china against china. Even Joey was being uncustomarily quiet, apart from the occasional whimper. Every now and then he rubbed at his mouth with the back of his hand as though he was using it as a tissue to dab away the congee.

Ben was ladling more curry into his bowl when Norah suddenly gasped.

"Something's wrong with Joey's skin!"

The adults huddled about Joey's high chair, and Ben saw for himself that a small pink rash was developing around Joey's mouth and chin.

This is just the beginning, he thought, then stopped himself. Why had he thought that? The rash did not look too bad, but it was upsetting. For so many weeks Joey's skin had been so good.

"I'll get a warm towel," Ma said, rushing from the table.

Norah frowned. "I don't understand it. I asked Nai Nai to serve him a banana for breakfast, and chicken puree for lunch. He's had both before with no problems."

Joey scratched at his face tentatively with one finger, then began doing so in earnest with both hands, leaving behind angry red tracks. He had not yet drawn blood, but it would not be long before he did. Ben grabbed roughly at the baby's hands, and Joey looked up at him, surprised.

"No scratching!" Ben said, louder than he intended. When Joey struggled to free himself from his father's grip, Ben repeated, even more loudly, "I said *no scratching*!" He was yelling. Joey's face wrinkled and he began to wail.

"Ben, shut up," Norah muttered. Her cheeks were terribly

flushed. "He's never had these bumps before." She gestured to the growing red ring around the baby's mouth. "See that?"

Several small clusters of bumps had sprouted around Joey's lips and on his chin, awful blistery bumps that made Ben think of the shingles Ma had had a few months before he married Norah. Ben felt a prickly sensation creep up his arms and chest, all the way up his throat, and it was all he could do not to shudder. Beside him, Norah was taking shallow breaths, and Ben knew she was on the verge of breaking down. Joey continued wailing, shaking his head frantically from side to side as he tried to rub his face against his shirt, his high chair, anything.

"What's *happening* to him?" Ma suddenly shrieked from behind them. Ben turned and saw his mother's face was ashen. "Oh, *Joey*!"

Norah's hands were shaking terribly as she unzipped her handbag and pulled out her cell phone. "I'm going to call Dr. Chan. He gave us an emergency number, for situations like—"

Norah abruptly stopped talking and looked down at Joey's bowl of congee. She blinked at it, then held it up beneath her nose. "Nai Nai," she said softly, her voice barely audible amid Joey's cries. "What did you put in this?"

"I—I—" For once, his Ma was at a loss for words. "I—well, I—"

"*What did you put in this*?" Norah was shouting now. She held out Joey's bowl to Ma, the remaining contents sloshing about, some of it spilling onto the tiled floor. Ben saw that one glistening drop had fallen onto Ma's plastic slipper.

"Fish," Ma said, her head hanging low. "I bought a grouper from the wet market this afternoon. It was so fresh, you know, it was still flopping about by the time I got home. I added a bit to Joey's congee, just a tiny bit. I never thought this would happen."

"How *could* you! Dr. Chan said bananas, sweet potatoes, and chicken! He said bananas, sweet potatoes, and…"

Ben heard the growing hysteria in his wife's voice and let go of Joey's wrists, reaching for Norah's hands instead. She was still thrusting the half-eaten bowl of congee—the *fish* congee, he reminded himself—in his mother's face, and Ma was standing there, shocked and ashamed.

"Don't touch me!" Norah growled at him, her eyes wild with anger. "*She* did this! *Your* mother!" She suddenly threw the bowl on the floor with such force that it bounced off the tiles, the cold congee splashing onto their toes and ankles.

She yanked Joey from the high chair, slung her handbag over one shoulder, and went to the front door. She jammed her feet into the work shoes she had not put away earlier, when she arrived home. Ben jumped to his feet, frightened, wanting to say something like, *Norah, don't go,* or at least, *Norah, wait,* but his wife did not look back. She opened and closed the door in what seemed like a single movement and before Ben could register what had happened, they were both gone.

Chapter 13

Norah felt like a fool as she stepped into the elevator and saw her reflection: her makeup was intact, but she was wearing Ben's old Standard Chartered T-shirt, the one with the brown stain down the front, pyjama bottoms, and her leather flats. Joey was in a short-sleeved body suit, no socks. As if on cue, he began to sneeze, and Norah hastily wiped his nose with the sleeve of her shirt. In the dim light of the elevator, Norah noticed something that made her feel faint, and she had to steady herself against the elevator wall: Joey's features seemed to be growing fuzzy, more blob-like, and his head appeared to have grown in size. His eyes were smaller than they were, not quite slits, but getting there. He looked like a different baby. He blinked up at her, fear in his eyes, and Norah swallowed hard, resisting the urge to scream. She hugged him close to her to comfort him as much as to stop his hands from reaching up to his face, and muttered, "It's going to be okay, it's going to be okay, it's going to be okay," under her breath like a spell.

The elevator doors slid open and Uncle Chung, their white-haired security guard, glanced up at them over his newspaper. "Going out so late, Mrs. Tam?" he smiled, folding his newspaper, prepared for the usual small talk, but tonight Norah, who normally always stopped and chat, merely nodded before walking briskly into the night.

She sat down on the bench outside the building and called the number Dr. Chan gave them to use in emergencies, but it went straight to voice mail. "Dr. Chan, it's uh, Norah Tam," she said, her teeth chattering violently. "Something's wrong with Joey. He's got a rash... with blisters... and he's swelling up. Pretty badly. Please call us back, Dr. Chan. It's...it's an emergency."

Joey rubbed his face against her shirt, desperately, and it occurred to her that if Dr. Chan didn't call back, right now, she would need to take him to the ER. In the glow of the streetlamp, Joey's eyes looked smaller than ever.

Norah held Joey close, willing him to stop scratching. His cheeks were so hot. She felt something breaking inside her, something crumbling and collapsing. She gasped for air, her chest heaving. It was like she was drowning.

"Joey," she sobbed. "How could she do this to you?"

The space around them abruptly grew dark; someone was blocking the street lamp. When she glanced up, she saw it was Ben, wearing both his backpack and the baby carrier. He sat down beside them on the bench, and Norah was relieved when he did not make any attempt to touch her; she would have pushed him away.

"Norah, let's go to the hospital. I've called an Uber. It should be here any minute now." He tenderly stroked Joey's swollen cheek, and Norah could see her pain reflected in Ben's expression.

Nevertheless, she was angry at him. He seemed responsible for this, too, somehow—he was the one who persuaded Norah to keep her job, who insisted that Nai Nai deserved a second chance at caring for Joey. He was the enabler, the one who caused Nai Nai to feel so self-important, so unfailingly right in her opinions. She was a stupid, stubborn witch of a woman. Ben had to be blind not to recognize this.

A white Tesla pulled to a silent stop in front of their building. "That's our ride," Ben said quietly. "Come on. Joey's in bad shape."

He was right, and she didn't need to be asked twice. They climbed into the car without speaking. When Ben reached out for Joey, Norah was touched to see the baby hold out his arms to his daddy. She helped Ben strap Joey into the baby carrier before buckling her own seat belt.

"Ma was wrong," Ben said quietly. Clearly exhausted, Joey had begun yawning. His eyes didn't seem quite so swollen closed.

Norah stared out the window. "I can't talk about it right now."

"Okay."

They continued their ride to the hospital in silence until Norah's phone suddenly buzzed loudly in her pocket. "It must be Dr. Chan," she said, relieved, but when she pulled it out, she saw it was her mother, and it was a FaceTime call.

There was a strong urge to decline the call. She didn't want to tell Mom about Joey's condition. Even though she was furious at Nai Nai, and hated her, in fact, telling her parents about the congee would feel like a betrayal. It would show she was wrong for choosing Ben. And despite everything, she was not sure she was ready to admit that.

She waited until she had missed the call and stuffed her phone back into her handbag. Ben glanced at her questioningly, but didn't say anything. She reached for his arm then, clutching at it with both hands, as though it was some kind of life line. "Ben, I'm scared," she whispered. He kissed the top of her head, like she was a little girl.

Her phone buzzed again, and Norah considered ignoring the call; she could not talk to her mother right now. But as she reluctantly pulled it out, she was relieved to see that it really was the doctor.

"Mrs. Tam? It's Dr. Chan. I got your message," the kind, familiar voice said, and it was all Norah could do not to burst into tears.

"Something's wrong with Joey," Norah said, taking a shuddering breath. When Ben held out a tissue, she took it. "His face is all swollen, and there's a rash on his face. A bad one, different from before, with little blisters that look like they have pus in them."

"Where are you now?" She was dismayed to hear that Dr. Chan sounded alarmed; he was normally so calm. She remembered the way he said *I'm pretty sure I've got what he needs to make a full recovery* and, at their last visit, *I declare this child itchy no more,* as though it were a royal pronouncement.

"Nearly at the hospital." Norah could see it just ahead, about two blocks away. "St. Teresa's."

"I'm glad to hear it. It sounds like an allergic reaction, quite a severe one. Joey's going to need a shot of epinephrine, which the hospital will promptly administer, but he will be alright after that." He paused. "What was he allergic to?"

"My mother-in-law slipped some fish into his congee without telling me," Norah said, angry and ashamed. If she had not been at work, she would have been the one to cook Joey's food. She resolved then to resign from Future English, once and for all. "It won't happen again."

"He'll be okay. Bring the little guy in to see me tomorrow, will you? I want to take a look at that rash. You could come after my last appointment at 5:30, does that work for you?"

As the Tesla stopped in front of the hospital entrance, Norah assured Dr. Chan that 5:30 worked fine before hanging up. Ben rushed out of the car with Joey, and Norah followed close behind.

The lobby of St. Teresa's Hospital was mostly empty. Strains of 'Amazing Grace' were playing faintly on the speakers as they rushed towards Emergency.

The waiting area outside the ER was busy: there were at least a dozen other patients in various states of distress. One elderly woman was clutching at her midsection, groaning softly.

A frazzled nurse with a clipboard approached them. "Name, please."

"Joey Tam," Norah blurted out at the same time that Ben said "Tam Chun Yin."

The nurse glared at them, clearly irritated. "One at a time, please," she said crossly.

"It's Joey, Tam Chun Yin," Norah tried again. She recited his birth certificate number from memory as she glanced nervously at Joey, who was beginning to stir. His eyes were still closed, but he had begun coughing.

The nurse frowned at Joey. "You'd better come with me."

To their surprise, they were ushered into the next room before the other patients, where a young doctor was bandaging a man's knee. The nurse murmured something unintelligible to the doctor before slipping out to the waiting room again. The doctor glanced at Joey and frowned.

"Be sure to keep the bandage dry," he said absently, already walking towards Joey. "You can wait outside. They'll give you some medicine to help with the pain." The patient hobbled out of the room, wincing.

"Sit down," the doctor said, brusquely. Norah held her breath as he proceeded to examine Joey's face, his eyes, with a pen light. Joey whimpered weakly in protest, but his eyes were so swollen it was hard to tell whether they were open or shut. "This is quite severe. Has this sort of reaction happened before? How many months is he? Do you know what triggered it?"

"Joey's nearly eight months. He has a history of severe eczema, b-but he's never had such a s-severe reaction to anything, n-not until..." her teeth were chattering uncontrollably. She swiped at her eyes. "My m-m-mother—"

"My mother fed him fish," Ben broke in. "It was his first time eating fish. The rash came first, then he started swelling up. It's gotten a lot worse in the last half hour."

"He'll need an injection," he said, grabbing a syringe and a small glass vial of clear fluid from the shelf behind him. "No known drug allergies, correct?"

Norah and Ben both nodded. The doctor snapped the syringe into the vial in a single smooth movement. Both the vial and syringe looked very large, but before Norah really knew what was happening the doctor was tearing open an alcohol prep pad and wiping a small section of Joey's thigh with it. "Hold him tight," he ordered. Norah had to look away as the doctor inserted the needle into Joey's leg. He let out a heart-wrenching wail. Norah's eyes welled up, and when they met Ben's, she saw that his were glassy as well.

Joey continued crying and scratching at his face for what seemed like hours until suddenly, as though someone had flipped a switch, he stopped. Joey blinked at the doctor, then frowned upon realizing he did not recognize the person he was looking at. He turned his little head this way and that until he spotted his mother. He promptly began crying again, his arms outstretched towards her, his feet kicking.

Norah scooped him up, held him close. His cheeks were so hot against hers.

"Sorry about that," the doctor said, smiling apologetically at them from behind his surgical mask. Norah marveled at how much kindness a person could convey with just his eyes.

"That should bring the swelling down. I've prescribed two antihistamines for the baby, just in case, and a non-steroidal cream in case he's still a bit itchy later tonight. Pick them up at the pharmacy beside the hospital cashier."

They muttered their thanks as they left. To everyone's surprise, Joey managed to wave goodbye through his whimpers.

Norah sat at a table in the hospital canteen, Joey snoring against her chest. It was a rather tight squeeze for the two of them, but when Norah tried to push the chair back further she saw it was bolted to the floor. She shielded Joey's eyes from the glare of the fluorescent lights with her hand. His features were not quite their normal size, but compared with two hours ago, he was looking very well. The rash around his mouth was still there, but it was pink now, not red, and the bumps had shrunk considerably.

Ben was buying something for them to eat, and she thought perhaps she could manage half a sandwich, now that she knew that Joey would be okay. Looking down at him, it was a struggle not to burst into tears again at the thought of how close she had come to losing him.

She was startled when Ben set down a brown tray with the corned beef sandwich she ordered, a steaming dish of fried rice, and two mugs of milk tea.

"You must be hungry," he said, hesitantly. He sat down across from her rather than beside her.

"A little."

He tore open two packets of sugar and poured into her mug all of the sugar from one packet and half the sugar from the other, the way she liked. At Joey's last checkup, Dr Chan had given her the green light to consume caffeinated beverages in small amounts. He stirred the brown liquid with a metal teaspoon thoroughly, forming a little vortex in the middle, before placing it in front of her. He waited until she began taking bites of her sandwich before picking up his spoon and digging into his dish of rice.

They ate without speaking until the food was gone. When they were both taking sips of their milk tea, Ben coughed. "Would you like to stay in a hotel tonight?"

Norah cocked her head. She must have misheard him. "Pardon?"

"I brought clothes for you and Joey," he paused. "And me, too."

She just stared at him. "You want to stay at a hotel?"

Ben smiled sadly. "I knew you wouldn't want to come back home with me after what happened today so I thought maybe I could go with you."

"Won't Nai Nai be mad at you?"

"Probably, but we're mad too." He tried to shrug, but Norah knew it was no small thing for him to not return home to his mother. "Please, Norah, let me come with you, don't go to Vancouver, please, I…"

"Yes," Norah interrupted. She tightened her grip around her mug of milk tea. "Yes, please. I'd like that."

Chapter 14

By the time they arrived at the hotel, Joey was awake again, and grumpy. He banged his head against Norah's chest, crying. She kissed his forehead tenderly. It was its usual size now, and the rash around his mouth was a shadow of its former angry self. She considered lifting her shirt and encouraging Joey to nurse, but she was afraid he would refuse her breast.

"We'll be upstairs in a minute, lovey," she told him instead, running her fingers through his hair, which was darker and coarser than it was, but still lovely. She bounced him on her lap until he began giggling.

INNspire was a new hotel in To Kwa Wan, one that Norah had never heard of. It was very small by Hong Kong standards, with only one elevator and a cramped check-in counter manned by just one young receptionist. It seemed clean and modern, though, with the industrial furnishings that were so hip at the moment: concrete walls, raw wooden panels on the floors, exposed metal pipes. In one corner of the lobby were two vending machines that sold cup noodles and snacks; in another were two treadmills, a stationary bike, and a couple of free weights. Norah couldn't help but smile at the name of the little exercise area: INNshape. Maybe Ben could do some running later tonight, after Joey was asleep. She hoped it would not cost too much to stay here.

The hotel room itself was tiny. The two single beds were positioned beside each other with a gap of about three inches between them. To Norah's delight, a narrow crib had been parked beneath the circular window, which was charmingly porthole-like, with a distressed bronze ring around it. The grey carpet was barely visible; there was so much furniture crowding the little room. Hanging behind the beds was a framed black and white photograph of a pile of rocks.

Ben transferred Joey into the crib as Norah went to wash her hands. In the corner, there was a tiny bathroom with fixtures that looked like they were designed with elves in mind. Everything looked clean and new, though, and Norah was very relieved to be here instead of home.

She opened the bathroom door to find Joey attempting to pull himself to a standing position in the crib. His hands were clutching at the slats, and he looked like a very small prisoner in his striped bodysuit.

On the other side of the room, Ben was pushing the beds together. He looked embarrassed to have been caught in the act. "I should've asked you first," he said, staring down at his feet, still in their socks, "but I wanted to sleep with you."

Norah found herself going to him, then, and reaching for his neck with both hands. He leaned down to reach her mouth, but paused just before touching her lips. When she opened her eyes, she saw him watching her, uncertainty in his eyes, as though unsure if she might still push him away. She tightened her grip around his neck and kissed him with a fervor that she had not felt in weeks, and he responded in kind.

Joey began crying in earnest, and they hastily disentangled themselves from each other, but Ben shot her a playful look that Norah understood to mean *This is not over*. They scrambled to fix a bottle of milk for Joey, Ben filling the hotel's electric kettle with water at the bathroom sink, and Norah measuring out eight level scoops of formula from the can of Aptamil Ben had brought from home.

Norah stood by the kettle, waiting for the water to boil, as Ben unzipped his bulging backpack and took out a diaper and a clean set of clothes for Joey. He hummed as he changed Joey out of his dirty onesie and bounced him gently on his lap until his whimpers died down.

Several moments later, Joey's chubby arms were hugging the bottle as he drank, his legs kicking idly at the foot of his crib, his expression content once more. Ben and Norah sat cross-legged on the bed beside the crib, watching him.

Norah squeezed Ben's hand. "Want to shower first? You must be tired."

He shook his head. "You first. I'll stay with Joey."

When she looked in Ben's backpack, she found her underwear and pajamas, her favourite jeans and t-shirt and a pair of flip flops. When she dug deeper, she saw that in addition to Joey's bottles and clothes, he had brought Joey's inflatable bath tub and ratty comfort blanket. "You remembered everything," she said, her eyes unexpectedly welling up.

"I love you," he responded simply. "Go shower, honey."

The bathroom door was made of frosted glass, and Norah felt a little naughty as she undressed behind it, taking more care than usual as she unhooked her bra, knowing that her silhouette was visible to Ben. Just before she turned on the faucet, she heard Ben say, "Ma?"

Any playfulness Norah had felt disappeared. She stared at herself in the mirror as she listened and frowned with displeasure at what she saw. The woman staring back at her looked fearful and insecure. Had her breasts always sagged like this? Had the areolas always been this dark, this large? They were hideous. She covered them up with the back of one arm.

"Joey's better," Ben continued quietly, as though aware that Norah was listening. "I didn't get a chance earlier," he said, then after a long pause, "I don't know yet."

Norah stopped herself from opening the door and demanding that Ben end the call. How dare Nai Nai call him! After what she did to Joey! Then it occurred to her that perhaps Ben was the one who called his mother.

"We haven't talked about that yet," she heard him say. About what? Then, after another long silence, "Don't forget to lock the door, Ma. Good night."

She hastily stepped into the shower and adjusted the taps so the blast of water was so strong and so hot it hurt. A few minutes later, flushed and clean, she roughly rubbed herself dry. She felt guilty when she saw the remains of her foundation and eyeliner smeared onto the white hotel towel. She had forgotten about her makeup; her work day seemed like a lifetime ago. She tried to remove the stains by scrubbing at them with the little disk of soap, but the black and brown patches seemed intent on clinging to the towel permanently.

When she opened the door, Ben was inflating Joey's travel bath tub, the spout between his lips and his face shiny with sweat. "Do you think it's okay to give Joey a bath so soon after his feed?" he asked, panting. "I don't remember this thing being so big."

Norah sat down beside him, peering at Joey, whose eyes were drooping shut. She switched off the overhead lights and turned on the bedside lamp instead. "We should've bathed him before we gave him his bottle I guess, but he was so hungry. Let's bathe him in the morning."

Ben nodded gratefully, setting the half-inflated bath tub to one side and digging into the side pocket of his bag. He handed Joey's tube of moisturizer to Norah, who quickly slathered a thick layer of it onto the baby's face and neck. Joey, well-accustomed to such treatment, rolled onto his side and promptly went to sleep.

The mattress was unbearably firm. The pillows, as though in counterpoint, were cloud-like in their softness. Their bed at home was the complete opposite. Ben switched off the bedside lamp ages ago, but Norah continued turning from side to side, longing for her memory foam pillow and struggling to find a comfortable position. Beside her, Ben did the same.

"I overheard you talking to Nai Nai," Norah said, finally.

"I knew she would be feeling bad about the fish," he responded, after a pause. "I wanted to let her know Joey is doing okay now."

Norah nodded in the dark.

Another long silence followed. Suddenly, Ben asked, "Can I hold you?" His fear that she would refuse him was so apparent that Norah's heart ached.

"Yes, please," she whispered.

When he placed one hand on the small of her back and gently drew her towards him, she let out a little gasp. He rested his open lips on her neck, the warmth of his breath causing desire to course through her body like electricity. He began to kiss her with an urgency that matched her own, and it was as if she was melting and falling, all at once.

When Norah woke it was still too dark to be morning. Her pillow was damp; her eyes were swollen. Through the slats of the crib, she could see Joey's sleeping form, but she was afraid to look too closely.

In her dream she was in a room not unlike this one, a dark and unfamiliar place, Joey lying in a crib that was not his own. Dr. Chan, dressed in a blue surgical gown, had appeared beside her, an apparition. *Why are you here, doctor?* Norah had asked, but in her heart, she had known what he was about to say: *I declare this child alive no more. Did I not say bananas, sweet potatoes, and chicken?*

She forced herself to take ten deep breaths, then another ten, before tapping on the flashlight icon on her phone. Joey's chest rose and fell, rose and fell, its rhythm steady. She reached between the slats and wrapped his little fist in her hand. Its warmth was reassuring, but Norah continued to lie awake. It didn't make sense but she couldn't shake her conviction that if she fell asleep again, the nightmare might somehow morph into a prophecy.

"Do you want to talk? I guess we need to decide on a few things." Ben tried to smile, but his nervousness was apparent. He was dressed for work, the sleeves of his checked shirt rolled up to his elbows.

Norah watched as he attempted to stir his coffee with a toothpick. The hotel had provided them with nearly nothing: two toothpicks, two water glasses, and two Nestle 3-in-1 coffee sachets. A large WITH OUR COMPLIMENTS card sat in front of this modest spread. On top of the safe were two cup noodles, a pack of salted peanuts, and a tiny bottle of red wine, but these had labels that read MINIBAR on them.

Norah was still lying in bed, Joey curled up beside her. Under ordinary circumstances, she would have returned him promptly to his crib after his early morning feed, but after her nightmare, she wanted him close. She glanced at his chest and was relieved to see that it was rising and falling as usual.

She propped up her pillow behind her and pushed herself into a sitting position. "So what happens next?"

He gave his coffee one more swirl before looking up again. "We have a couple of options, I think." He coughed. "We could keep staying here for now, but it will cost us $800 per night."

It was less than what Norah would have guessed, but still a lot, and more than they could afford if it was going to be a long-term arrangement. "What else?"

"I looked online yesterday for some short-term rentals, but I didn't see anything suitable. Mostly *toh fongs*, you know." Ben shifted in his chair. "Maybe not ideal."

A few years ago, *toh fong* had simply meant en suite. Before they were married, Norah had dreamt of an apartment with three bedrooms: a nursery for their future baby, a guest room for when her parents visited from Vancouver, and a *toh fong* for her and Ben, complete with a luxurious claw-footed bathtub large enough for two, or perhaps a Jacuzzi.

These days, though, when someone said *toh fong*, they meant a subdivided flat, a single room with an attached bathroom doubling as the kitchen. Norah shuddered. That was no place for Joey to grow up in. "What kind of budget are we talking about?"

"It sort of depends on you. We don't have very much money saved up, so if you stop working...but you'll have to, won't you? To take care of Joey."

Norah nodded. She would have to talk to Ivan today, tell him the situation, see if he'd let her resign. Beyond that, she was not sure. Private tutoring was an option, perhaps online. She would need to prepare some Facebook advertisements, maybe a personal website.

"The last option," he began again, once more stirring his coffee in earnest, "well, the last option for us would be to move back to Ma's." Ben did not look up. "Just for now, I mean."

"That's not the last option. I could call my parents right now. Joey and I could fly to Vancouver today." Norah didn't like the growing edge in her voice.

Ben looked up in surprise. "I didn't know you were considering that."

She frowned. "I wasn't, not until you mentioned going back to your mom's."

"Then why did you say it, Norah? I thought we were trying to work things out."

"You started it!" she cried. "Anytime something bad happens, you go running to your mother."

She had never said anything like this before. She felt wicked as she spoke, but the words kept flowing, like a dirty stream from the sewage pipes. "You want to call her right now, don't you, tell her you'll be home for dinner?" She lowered her voice in a crude imitation of Ben: "What's for dinner, Ma? Did you make curry for me, Ma? See you at seven, Ma."

Norah glared at him, daring him to respond, but he didn't say anything. His shoulders were slumped in shame, but he held her gaze, his eyes sad. She had seen him adopt this position many times in conversations with his mother, and was always angry with Nai Nai for reducing her husband to a frightened child. Norah intended to hurt him, but now that she had, she was ashamed.

"Ben," she began, reaching out to place a hand on his thigh, but he stood up, dodging her touch. "What I'm trying to say is…"

"I'll go to the front desk and book another night here." He picked up his wallet. "I bought some baby food for Joey; they're in my backpack. I checked the ingredients but maybe check them again, just to make sure."

"Ben," she pleaded. "I'm sorry, I didn't mean it. I was just upset that you thought—"

"I'm not angry at you," he said, but Norah was certain that he was. For two years she had tread carefully, had always avoided the sacred unspoken line, but today she had crossed it.

"I have to go to work. See you tonight." He leaned over Joey and kissed him on the cheek. "Baba loves you, little guy." He didn't kiss her. "See you."

He closed the door noiselessly behind him. Norah considered opening it and trying to apologize again, but decided a text message in a few hours might be more effective.

She picked up her phone and called her mom instead. Her mom didn't pick up at first, and just as Norah was about to end the call, her mother's flushed face filled the screen, a grey towel around her shoulders, her hair damp. She could almost smell her mother's bath soap and shampoo; she had always been partial to citrus scents. Norah felt a lurch of longing for her parents, for life before the complication of marriage. "Mommy," Norah said.

"Sorry, I was just getting out of the shower and..." Mom's eyes narrow. "Where are you? That doesn't look like your bedroom."

"Mommy," she repeated, her voice quavering. "I miss you."

"I miss you too, baby. Is everything okay?" Then, her tone hardening, "Is it Ben? What happened? Are you... are you hurt?"

At this, the old defenses came up. She cleared her throat, tried to laugh. "Of course not. He's great. I miss you, is all. I haven't seen you in so long." She paused. "We're in a hotel! We're on a staycation, Mom."

She walked to Ben's backpack with the phone in her hand, careful not to reveal the size of their hotel room. Unzipping it, she dug around for the baby food Ben mentioned on his way out. She found them in a plastic bag in the front compartment: three pouches from Organic Baby's expensive 'Nothing But' series. Norah held them up proudly to show her mom. "See, Ben even remembered Joey's baby food."

"That's sweet. So where is the little guy? Is he up?"

Norah switched to the rear-facing camera so her mom could see the baby, who was starting to stir, but was still asleep. Joey's skin was still a bit rougher and pinker than usual, but these blemishes would be less obvious on the phone, and Norah was quite sure her mother would not notice anything out of the ordinary. "Aww, Joey," Mom cooed. "He's gotten so big. Is his skin okay these days?"

Norah coughed. "Uh, not too bad. Pretty good, mostly." *It was doing fantastic until yesterday.*

"That's good to hear. Oh, I wanted to talk to you about something."

"What's up, Mom?"

"Your dad and I were thinking, how about we come and visit you this summer instead? I know you were looking forward to coming here, but such a long flight might be hard on the baby. What do you think?"

Norah felt her heart hammering in her chest. That was a good idea, really; she and Ben would be able to save on the plane tickets. Traveling in the summer was terribly expensive. But they didn't have a place to stay yet, and when they did, it wasn't going to be somewhere she'd want her parents to see. They would have to sort something out quickly. "That sounds great! We miss you. When are you thinking?"

"When can you get time off work? We're pretty flexible, but the first week of July we'll be going on the cruise I told you about last time." She looked sheepish. "We didn't wait for you, sweetheart, sorry. There was a special, and your dad, well, you know how impulsive he can be."

She could hardly tell her mother that she was quitting. "How about mid-June, then? Does that sound good?" That would give them a little more than three weeks to settle into a new place and make it look halfway decent.

"Or early June? We'll need a little time to get over jetlag before we go on the cruise. It'll be our first time; I'm a little nervous about getting seasick! Jetlag will make it worse, I imagine."

Norah swallowed. That wasn't much time at all. "Sure, Mom. Early June, then." She glanced down and realized that Joey's eyes were open, that he was smiling toothily at her. She stroked his cheek with the back of her hand tenderly. Her heart clenched as she remembered the wretched nightmare from the night before. How could she live if she ever lost Joey?

"Paw Paw, someone's awake." Norah held Joey up under the arms, but he didn't need much help standing anymore. His chubby legs were pretty sturdy.

"Joey!" her mother squealed. "Gong Gong and I are coming very, *very* soon! We *miss* you!"

Shortly after ten o'clock, Norah and Joey arrived at Future English. She stood just outside the centre with Joey in the baby carrier. She looked at the familiar space through the glass walls: she took in the long grey reception counter, the white IKEA tables and chairs, the metal shelves that housed the teaching binders with their dog-eared materials, the posters that insisted on students speaking English in the Future, in the future. They were early; there didn't seem to be any students here yet.

She hadn't brought Joey with her to work since she was pregnant with him. When she finally revealed the news to her students, she was already in her fifth month. The older women had delighted in placing their hands on her bump, waiting eagerly for the baby's fluttery kicks. They spent many afternoons in those plastic folding chairs discussing potential names for her baby, them with paper cups of instant coffee in hand, her with a small carton of skimmed milk.

Seeing Ivan at his desk, idly juggling several battered bean bags, she suddenly thought of the afternoon when he wheeled his high-backed swivel chair to the social area and insisted she sit in it. She must have been seven, maybe eight, months pregnant then. She had refused, but he was adamant: "There'll be no more sitting in those folding chairs for you until the baby's out, Norah. It's not safe." And there Ivan's leather chair had stayed until after she gave birth, until she returned from maternity leave as a part-time teacher. For those few months, no one ever sat in it apart from her, not even Ivan.

"Welcome to Future English," she said to Joey, before abruptly bursting into tears. She had avoided coming at a busy hour, knowing how emotional the goodbyes would be, but she did not expect the sight of the centre to elicit such a strong reaction. She should have known better; Future English was home to her.

"Mama," Joey protested, looking up in alarm. He wriggled one hand out from the carrier and reached up to pat his mother's wet cheek. "Mama."

Norah took a few deep breaths in an effort to get a hold of herself.

"Norah?" The voice was vaguely familiar, but Norah couldn't quite place it. When she turned around, she saw it was Cable, the new student who upset Ben several weeks ago. He was dressed a little more neatly today, but his hair still looked and smelled dirty. "Are you alright?"

"Hey, Cable. I'm fine, I get these allergies sometimes in the summer. I don't know if its hay fever, or what. It makes my eyes water like crazy." She felt foolish for lying, but didn't want to explain.

He pulled out a crumpled napkin from his jeans pocket and

held it out to her; it had STARBUCKS across the bottom. She took it, but was reluctant to wipe her face with it. She slipped it in her pocket instead.

Susan ducked behind her computer monitor as Norah and Cable walked into the centre together. As usual at this time of day, Susan was very busy—scarfing down her breakfast takeaway as surreptitiously as possible so Ivan would not reprimand her for eating while on duty, and applying the finishing touches to her eye makeup. She reemerged, having swallowed the mouthful of macaroni, her professional face on. "Good morning, and welcome to—Norah, what are you doing here? It's Monday, isn't it?" she glanced down at her calendar. "It *is* Monday. Hey, you brought the baby! Hi, Joey!"

As Cable settled down at one of the tables to do his homework, Norah walked hesitantly towards Ivan's desk. Although his desk was off to one side, it was only a few meters from the social area, allowing students easy access to the manager whenever they wanted to chat.

His face broke into a broad smile when he saw her and Joey. "I was hoping you'd bring the baby around one of these days. He's a handsome fellow, isn't he?"

Norah sat down in the plastic chair across from Ivan and took Joey out of the carrier, setting him on her lap. Joey leaned comfortably against her front. Spotting the bean bags on the edge of the desk, Joey reached for one, then looked up at Norah, as though seeking her permission. Norah, in turn, looked questioningly at Ivan, who smiled before placing a bean bag in each of Joey's outstretched hands. Joey squealed.

"Say thank you, Joey," Norah whispered in his ear, and he responded immediately in sign language, placing one hand in front of his little chin. Norah knew he would; her baby was impossibly agreeable.

"You're welcome, little man. What brings you to Future English this morning, Norah? It's your day off, isn't it?"

Norah swallowed. "Ivan, I have something to tell you."

"Please, go ahead."

"There's been a change in my family situation, and..." Norah felt the tears making a comeback and bit on her bottom lip to try and stop them. "I...I don't think I'm going to be able to work here anymore." Normally she appreciated the open design of the centre, but today she wished they had some privacy. "Ivan, I'm sorry."

He raised an eyebrow as he pushed the box of tissues on his desk towards her. "Is everything okay at home?"

"There's been some friction with my mother-in-law, and we need to find a new place to stay. She won't be taking care of Joey anymore," she said, but regretted the words as they left her mouth. Despite her anger at Nai Nai, she was frustrated to find that she still felt loyalty towards her; she was Ben's mother. Still, Ivan deserved some kind of explanation. "Ivan, I'm really sorry to be leaving you in the lurch like this." She dug in her bag for the handwritten letter she wrote that morning in the hotel. "I have three classes tomorrow afternoon, and another three on Thursday. Six in total this week."

He scanned the letter, wrinkling his brow as he did. "You mean you're resigning...with immediate effect?"

She nodded miserably.

"I can cover your classes for you this week, or this month even, that's alright, but after you sort of whatever it was that was going on at home, come back to us. We need you here, Norah. You know that."

"Thank you," she said, alarmed by the tremor she heard in her voice. Her insides churning with emotion, she attempted to deliver the speech she had rehearsed on their way to the centre:

"You've been so kind to me, the best manager a newbie like me could hope to have. You took me on when I was nobody, you mentored me and taught me to teach. If I could, I would teach here for the rest of my life, but my family needs me. Future English hasn't just been my workplace, it's been…" She wanted to say *It's been everything,* but the dam broke then, and she cried and cried.

She was embarrassed at this public show of emotion. She sensed people crowding around her, tissues being held out to her, Joey's hands patting her cheeks urgently, his little voice crying "Mama? Mama?"

Ivan guided her into the pantry, which Norah was relieved to see was empty. She wished they'd had their conversation in here in the first place. "Norah," he said, "I don't want to, but I accept your resignation. When you're ready to return, just call."

"Thank you. I know I need to pay a penalty for resigning without giving my three months' notice, but would it be possible for me to pay it in installments, because, well—"

Ivan held up a hand, stopping the frantic tumble of words from continuing. "Don't worry about that. This is an emergency. And anyway, if anyone from senior management asks, I'll tell them I knew in advance."

Before she could thank him again, he stood up, and she hastily followed. "We'd better go tell Susan. She'll need to rearrange your classes so they match my schedule."

When they re-emerged from the pantry, the social area was empty apart from Cable and a new student Norah did not recognize. She was thankful that she would not need to say goodbye to the regulars today; she would come back another time when she had a better handle on her emotions. She knew that just the sight of Kitty, or Tim, or Siu-Fong, would be enough to start her tears again.

Cable waved to her from his table in the social area, and Norah reluctantly waved back. He must have seen her cry. The last thing she wanted was to be grilled on why she was so upset, but the teacher in her took purposeful steps towards him. Joey seemed relieved to see his mother smiling again, and started gnawing at the teether necklace hanging from Norah's neck.

"Norah, I couldn't help but overhear. You're moving out of your mother-in-law's place?" She couldn't quite read his expression as he said this, and felt exposed that he knew something so private about her family life. She resisted the urge to respond with, *What's it to you?* She wasn't officially on duty today, but here at the centre her teacher cap was always on.

"Yes," she said, smiling. "With Joey growing so fast, we need more space. You simply can not imagine how much stuff we need for this one little baby." She nuzzled Joey's ear, and he giggled. She did not sit down. Ben was right, she thought to herself. Cable was creepy.

"Of course, of course," Cable said, but there was a smirk on his face, as though he'd overheard the part of her struggling with her relationship with Nai Nai. "I didn't mean to eavesdrop. I just wanted to tell you that I'm looking for a new tenant for my spare flat. I'd give you a discount, of course…" He unlocked his cell phone and held it out to Norah. The photograph on the screen was of a spacious, tastefully decorated apartment, all cream and chocolate tones. He swiped left every few seconds, and Norah saw the two furnished bedrooms and the washroom, where the color scheme continued. It all looked brand new. It must have been renovated very recently.

Norah liked what she saw, but she knew Ben would never approve of their renting Cable's property. Nevertheless, she took the bait. "It's gorgeous, Cable. How much would such a lovely apartment cost to rent?"

When he grinned, Norah could see that his teeth were stained and crowded, adding to his unkempt appearance. "For you, just $5,000 a month."

In this day and age, you couldn't even rent one of the dreaded *toh fongs* for $5,000, not to mention a fully furnished, newly renovated two-bedroom apartment like Cable's. He must be very wealthy.

She smiled, unsure of what to say. "Well," she finally said, "thanks for showing me the pictures."

"If you don't like this one, I have another," he said, tapping on his phone.

Another! As if on cue, Joey began to whimper, and Norah stood up. "Thank you again," she said. "See you next time, Cable."

"Wait," he called as she began walking in earnest away from him. "Here's my number." He handed her the corner of page 16 from his workbook. "Please call me if you change your mind."

Chapter 15

"What exactly are you doing?"

Ben swung around, dropping the bag in his hands. Despite his careful attempts at returning home at a time when his mother was certain to be out, she had returned unexpectedly and caught him packing their things into the large nylon canvas bags he had bought at Japan Home Centre on the way over.

Apart from the mattress, an outrageously expensive Sealy mattress Norah had insisted was essential, all the furniture in the room belonged to Ma. By modern standards, he and Norah did not own very much. He planned to call Ma after they were settled in their new home, wherever that was going to be.

A family had cancelled their shoot at the last minute that afternoon, so Ben had an extra hour to pore over rental listings on his phone. The most promising was a 200-foot studio apartment in Hung Hom. It was located directly across from a funeral parlour, which most people would not find auspicious, but Norah was so western in her thinking that he was certain she wouldn't care. At $12,000 per month it wasn't cheap, but if he adjusted Ma's *gayong*, and they scrimped, perhaps they could make it work. Maybe Norah could take on a few tutoring students in the evenings after he got home from work; she was good at what she did, and could probably make at least $400 an hour, maybe even more.

He had wanted to send the listing to Norah, but decided to wait until he was back at the hotel. He resented her nasty comments from the morning; they made him feel as though she did not recognize his efforts to fend for her and Joey, when he had been trying so hard to do so.

When he heard his mother's shrill voice, his instinct was to cower. He forced himself to stand tall and look his mother in the eye. She was standing in their doorway, her arms crossed. "I'm just p-packing our things, Ma." He could hear his voice shaking. He cleared his throat and bravely tried again: "I'm packing our things."

Ma frowned. "What are you talking about? This is nonsense. Who will take care of Joey?"

"Norah resigned today. She'll be staying home with him."

"My point exactly. You don't *have* another home. You've lived here all your life. How will you pay the rent? How will you live on one income?"

"We've saved up a little." He could hear himself breathing heavily. In truth, their modest savings were dwindling, thanks to their extravagant Hainan trip and Joey's playgroup lessons. *Thanks to Norah, you mean,* a voice in his head piped up, but Ben shut it up in a hurry. Anyway, there was always the option of taking out a loan at a credit agency. Not ideal, of course, they called them loan sharks for a reason, but it was a possibility.

He forced himself to think of Joey, his eyes swollen shut, that blistery rash around his mouth. He thought of Norah throwing the baby's suction bowl onto the floor, congee flying everywhere, her eyes blazing. They had to move.

"Don't be an idiot. You can't afford to move out, not unless you plan on living in a cage home." Ma's words were harsh, but her tone was not. "Look, I know Norah talked you into this. She's so stubborn, she's impossible. But she's quit her job, and the bank account is under your name, isn't it? What's stopping you from just bringing Joey back here?"

She sat down heavily beside him.

"This is your home, Ben. Don't be a fool. Don't pour your life savings into the ocean."

If I hold onto my life savings, I'll lose my wife and son, he wanted to say, but his mother would have some snarky response to even that. He knew Ma would never do something to intentionally hurt Joey, but she had made it clear that there were to be no compromises; she would carry on taking care of Joey the way she always had. He could see in his mind's eye more nicked bald heads, more fish congees, more confrontations. It would never end. Best to pick his battles and leave while he still could.

"You're right, Ma. I'll talk to her." He knew Ma would not suspect anything. She was smiling triumphantly; this was the response she expected.

"I'll just heat up the soup for you, I made your favorite, bitter gourd and pickled cabbage." She hummed as she walked to the kitchen, a bounce in her step.

Ben closed the door behind her and stuffed as much of the canvas bag's contents into his backpack as he could. He hastily made the bed so his mother would not think of Norah as a slob, although she could be.

"Your soup is ready," Ma called from the kitchen.

"I'm coming."

The soup was scalding hot. It was indeed his favorite: sour and bitter, mingled together with the richness of the pork and soybeans. At first, he used his soup spoon; it was too hot to drink any other way. Once it had cooled down a little, he picked up the blue and white porcelain bowl and downed the rest. He should be going soon; Norah and Joey were waiting for them. Ma smiled at him, her own bowl of soup untouched. "Seconds?"

"Thanks so much, Ma, it's so good, but I should get going. Joey's going to be waiting for his dinner."

At this, his mother's face fell. At sixty-two, she was still beautiful: her eyes were still bright and alert, and the only wrinkles on her face were the ones that appeared around her mouth and eyes when she smiled. She'd had her hair permed and her nails manicured without fail since Ben was a young child. For the first time, he wondered why she had never married again. "But, Ma," he suddenly blurted out.

She had been taking a sip of the soup, frowning, as though it didn't taste quite right. "Yes?"

"Do you mind if I take a few photos of you?" He took out his cell phone from his jeans pocket and set it on the table cloth. "I've only got my phone with me, but it's got a pretty good portrait mode."

She smiled shyly, patting her hair demurely. Ben was ashamed; how long had it been since he promised to take portraits of her? Three years? More?

"Let me put on some makeup, if you're going to do that."

Ben shook his head. "No makeup. You look great. Can you go sit in your armchair?"

He helped her untie her apron and guided her to her usual seat, by the window, where the setting sun was still casting a few rays into their living room. She sat down, smiling. She crossed her legs, then folded her hands on one knee. Ben grinned. It was clear that she had practiced this pose.

He took pictures of her sitting in the armchair, then perched on one of its arms. He was not aware that he had resorted to his usual workplace muttering: "Yes, excellent, that's it. Look this way, please—excellent. And just a few more; the light's perfect.

Excellent, you look excellent."

It all happened very quickly; within five, six minutes, the sun had set and Ma was sitting in the early evening darkness. Ben could hear children playing in the playground downstairs.

Ma squeezed his arm. "I suppose you'll want to edit those before you let me see them." She sighed. "You'd better go. I don't want my grandson starving because I was busy posing for photographs."

Ben nodded, standing up. "Remember to lock the door tonight, Ma." He kissed her on the cheek. She smelled of Pond's cold cream; she had smelled of it all his life. His heart clenched as he realized that this was really goodbye.

He abruptly stepped away from her, swung his backpack on one shoulder and headed for the door. "I'll talk to Norah," he promised, leaving before she could say anything in response.

On his way back to the hotel, Ben picked up a bucket of KFC for him and Norah, and a bowl of chicken congee for Joey, carefully specifying that he did not want peanuts, ginger or spring onion in it. The journey helped to clear his head a little; by the time he was taking the elevator up to their room, he felt considerably less guilty about leaving Ma to live on her own. Just before it reached their floor, he had a revelation: he could start transferring money into Ma's account instead of giving *gayong* to her in person. An adjustment in the amount could be made less obviously this way; he could casually mention that he had made a deposit, couldn't he, and leave it at that? Perhaps in the bottomless depths of Ma's bank account, the size of his monthly contribution would go unnoticed. And if Ma did complain about his giving her just $2000 a month instead of $10,000, well, he would cross that bridge when he got there.

The sight of Norah and Joey curled up on the makeshift double bed, singing along to a video on Norah's phone, further cheered him. Most people hated the Baby Shark song, but he didn't mind it much; whenever he heard the tune, he thought of scenes like this.

"Baba's home," Norah cried, switching off her phone and scooping Joey up so he could wave to his father. "You got fried chicken!" She swung Joey around in a little dance and Ben was inordinately pleased with himself. Every now and then he got something right.

Upon opening the lid of the KFC bucket, Norah practically swooned. She grabbed a drumstick and took a noisy bite before holding it out to Ben.

Joey watched them, drooling. "Sorry, big boy," Ben muttered. He blew on a spoonful of congee before serving it to him. Joey's eyes lit up.

Joey signed more, more, more, the tips of his fingers touching each other over and over, swallowing the spoonfuls faster than Ben could serve them. This was such an improvement to the plain congee Joey used to eat.

After dinner, the three of them flopped onto the double bed together, content. Joey let out a little fart, which made them all giggle hysterically.

"I wish we could stay here like this forever," Norah sighed. Ben liked the way Norah's hair looked spread out around her head, fan-like. He ran his fingers through the locks, idly looking for white hairs. He stopped abruptly; that was a chore his mom required of him when he was a little boy. She would hand him a wide-toothed comb and insist that he find at least five white hairs before letting him go. He didn't want to think of Ma just now.

Norah didn't seem to notice what he was doing or that he

had stopped; she was watching Joey with a dreamy expression. He had pulled himself to a sitting position, and was shuffling around the bed on his bum. Ben hastily repositioned himself so he was lying lengthwise along the edge of the bed; he wanted to be there to catch Joey if he fell. Joey shuffled from Norah to Ben, and then back to Norah again, a toothy grin on his face.

"Hey," he said, after a moment. "I have some good news. I found a place for us."

Norah propped her head up on one arm. "Really? Where? How much is it?"

He took out his phone from his pocket and showed her the listing on 28hse.com. "$12,000. It's only a studio," he said hesitantly, "and it's in Hung Hom, near the...well…"

"Funeral parlours?" Norah rolled her eyes. She took the phone from him and started swiping left. "I don't care about that, silly."

"Right." He was relieved. "I knew you wouldn't mind." Ben stole glances at her as she studied the photographs with care, zooming in on this corner, that wall.

"It looks okay," she said finally, but she was frowning. "Can we afford it though? That's more than half your salary. And I guess you still have to give Nai Nai money…"

All this was said very matter-of-factly, but to Ben, her words were accusatory, and he struggled not to defend himself. "I'm going to make some adjustments there," he began, but stopped. He had never told Norah how much he'd been giving to Ma, and he didn't want to. "Anyway, if you like it, I'll message the owner. I already downloaded the rental app."

She nodded, handing the phone back to him, but her expression continued to be troubled. "There's something else we need to talk about."

He swallowed. What now?

"My parents are coming to visit in June."

Truth be told, Ben was not particularly fond of Norah's parents, who felt their daughter had been 'settling' when she chose him, but this was a sentiment he had closely guarded and would take with him to the grave. This was a complication he really didn't want to handle at the moment, but he tried to smile. "How nice! You must be excited." He scooped Joey up on his lap. "Your Gong Gong and Paw Paw are coming, Joey! Pretty awesome, huh?"

Joey gripped Ben's thumbs and steered them like race car controls.

She watched them without speaking. "Actually, early June."

He freed one hand from Joey's grasp and glanced at his watch. It was already mid-May. "That's very soon, isn't it?"

"A little," she admitted. "It's the only time they can make it."

"Right."

She chewed on a fingernail for several moments without speaking. "Did you talk to Nai Nai about us moving out?"

"Not really." He paused. "Sort of. She doesn't think we should."

"Why doesn't that surprise me?" She frowned, looking away.

"Hey," Ben said, grabbing her hand. "Don't be like that. We're moving. I said we would." He set Joey in her lap and reached for his backpack. "See, I got our toothbrushes."

She smiled a little, squeezing Joey. He glanced up at his mama, then reached his hands up to pat her cheeks. "I love you," she said. "Both of you."

Later, after Joey had his bottle and Norah was in the shower, Ben took out his cell phone. With trembling hands he opened his Gallery app and looked at the pictures he'd taken of Ma that afternoon.

They were marvelous. His eyes welled up as he made minor edits to the portraits, adjusting the lighting slightly, cropping out the Jumperoo in a couple of them. Her cheeks were rosy, her eyes playful—or was it pride he saw? She would have made a lovely model in her youth. He wished he had taken more pictures of her when he'd had a chance, but in the last few years both his heart and his phone storage had been taken up by his wife and son.

He sent the best dozen to Ma by Whatsapp, with a message: *Ma, you look great!!!*

Then, his eyes blurry with tears, he typed a second one: *We have decided to move out. I will come back to see you. I love you and I am sorry.*

At the last moment, he deleted it.

Chapter 16

"THE SOFA bed is brand new," Mr. Wong said, waving a hand towards the checked loveseat in the corner of the studio. "The table extends, and there are two folding chairs in the cabinet."

He walked over to the kitchenette. "There's only one hob on the stove, but if you ever need a second you can use this portable butane burner. This here's the fridge." He opened the door of the little fridge, only slightly bigger than the one they had used in the hotel; it was empty apart from a plate of lemon slices.

Their landlord seemed friendly enough, Norah thought, if a little eccentric. He was one of those middle-aged men who thought they were still very young: his hair had been dyed platinum blonde, and he was wearing a ripped and faded denim jacket which might have been trendy twenty years ago.

"You need anything, just call me." He sat down at the tiny dining table, best suited for one diner, and took out a folded sheet of lined paper from his fanny pack. His handwriting was very poor; Norah couldn't really make out the words.

He scribbled something, likely his signature, at the bottom with a flourish, then handed the sheet to Ben. "I've got your first and last month's rent, so here's a receipt for that. I can come by on the first of each month to pick up a cheque, or you can deposit the rent directly into my bank account, if you prefer."

"I'll be sure to transfer the $12,000 on the first of each month," Ben said hastily, slipping the receipt into his backpack. "Don't worry, Mr. Wong."

Their landlord shrugged. "Sure. I'll be going then." He closed the door behind him with a soft click.

Norah sat down on the love seat and unbuckled Joey from the carrier. He looked around him tentatively, as though unsure of where he was. "This is home now," she said softly. "Like it?"

Joey smiled, flipped onto his tummy and slid onto the floor. Grasping the edge of the sofa with both hands, he cruised slowly from one side to the other, his expression one of pure pride.

"Isn't he clever, Mama?" Ben said, joining them on the sofa. "You big boy, you."

Joey giggled at this praise, then inched over to bury his head in Ben's lap. Ben stroked the little head gently, tenderly, and Norah's heart swelled with love for them. The studio was smaller than she imagined, but also brighter, and it was all their own.

It was true that their closest neighbor was Universal Funeral Parlour, Hong Kong's biggest and busiest, and the hubbub below—the noisy delivery of floral wreaths, the constant arrival and departure of hearses—would take some getting used to. Norah was not too concerned. Mr. Wong had installed thick curtains by the windows, which seemed to muffle the noise somewhat. In the distance stood Hung Hom Station, whose rippling roof looked rather beautiful from this vantage point, and if she crouched beside the window and looked straight up, she could see a small patch of sky.

Cleaning the studio did not take long, and by early afternoon, they were seated around the dining table, the adults slurping up cup noodles and Joey enjoying a pouch of rice and sweet potato puree. The table was only slightly bigger in its extended form, but that was alright, Norah thought. There were only the three of them, anyhow.

Norah was surprised by how nervous she felt as she waited for her first online student to join her in the Zoom meeting room. The studio was quiet; Ben took Joey down for a walk after dinner so she would not be disturbed during the lesson.

Norah was not a Luddite, exactly, but neither was she tech-savvy, and certainly not with regards to her teaching. She glanced at her notes anxiously, desperate not to make any mistakes. She was expecting Vincent, an older gentleman who was completely new to English but was eager to learn conversational skills that he could use to communicate with his grandchildren in the states. He had already paid the agreed upon $500 into her PayPal account, so Norah was feeling particularly eager to get started.

Earlier that week, Ivan had gifted her with the names of two students who desired more personal attention than could be provided at Future English. When they spoke on the phone, Ivan's voice had been kind. "What do you think, Norah? I don't mean to force this on you, nothing like that." He had paused then, and Norah knew that he knew how tight their budget was just then. He had cleared his throat, lightened his tone further: "These students could really use the help; they wanted one-on-one instruction, which I couldn't offer in the Future, but they would do well under your care, I know they would."

And when Norah protested that her current home wasn't, well, ideal for private tutoring, he had laughed. "They want to be tutored online, Norah. No one wants to leave their air-conditioned homes anymore."

Ding-dong! A man's face filled the screen. Vincent was probably about her father's age, perhaps a few years older; his hair was mostly grey. He was sitting in a very dimly lit room; perhaps the only light in the room was from his computer monitor. Norah felt like an intruder in the unfamiliar man's room, but she smiled bravely.

"Hello Vincent, I'm Norah," she said, but he frowned, shaking his head. He cups one of his ears with his hand.

Norah frantically fiddled with her webcam, her microphone, her speaker settings, but Vincent continued frowning.

"I can't hear you," he repeated in Cantonese, his tone increasingly impatient.

It occurred to her that she was having no problems hearing *him,* she could hear his impatient sighs quite clearly, but he could not hear her.

Oh! It was a light bulb moment—she located the floating control panel and clicked on the microphone icon. "I'm sorry about that, Vincent," she said, shaking her own head a little, trying to dispel the bad energy from the start of the lesson. She mopped her sweaty brow with a tissue. "I'm so sorry to have kept you waiting. It's a pleasure to meet you." She never spoke Cantonese with the students at Future English, but she spoke it now, carefully. The words sounded odd to her ears, like a poor translation of her usual teacher talk.

"That's alright," Vincent responded gruffly. "It took me a while to figure out the controls, too."

Norah smiled, grateful. "Ivan told me you've got two grandkids in California, is that right?"

At this, the old man's eyes crinkled into slits, and Norah could see him as a grandfather. "Actually, three. My daughter just had her third baby, a girl. Freya."

"That's wonderful! I love babies. And how old are Freya's siblings?"

"Jeffrey's five and Zachary's three. They're crazy about

Thomas the Tank Engine at the moment." He held up a Thomas storybook. "I got a few of these to read with the boys, but the English is too hard. Do you know much about Thomas & Friends?"

Norah laughed. "Not much, but my son's turning one in a few months so I guess I'd better start learning."

"Indeed you should! All the boys go through a Thomas phase; it's just one of those things. My daughter was dead set on avoiding it, she hates the theme song, but one of Jeff's classmates was playing with one of the engines at school, and that was that. Construction vehicles is another one. For the longest time, Jeffrey and Zachary couldn't stop pretending to be diggers and road rollers and such."

"You and your grandsons seem to be very close, even though they don't live in Hong Kong."

"We use Zoom! And before that, we used Skype. We chat almost every day." He smiled proudly.

Norah nodded, impressed, but she was also getting anxious. So much of this conversation had been in Cantonese; the only words they had been saying in English were 'Thomas' and the names of Vincent's grandchildren. She quickly typed in 'Thomas and Friends' in the search bar of her browser and found a Thomas story ('Edward') that had been scanned and uploaded in its entirety onto the Internet. It was bad for copyright but very good for her. Vincent taught her how to 'share her screen', and she and Vincent spent the rest of the lesson reading the story together, creeping along at a turtle's pace, eventually finishing about half the book by the time their hour was up.

Just as she was waving goodbye and clicking the small 'x' in the corner of the window, Ben walked in with Joey asleep in the carrier. He was snoring loudly, which made Norah smile. She quickly opened up the sofa bed and was pleased to see that it was as Mr. Wong said, brand-new.

Ben set Joey gently onto the middle of the sofa bed. Joey rolled onto his side and continued sleeping. Ben was frowning when he stood up again. He sat down on the other folding chair, then buried his head in his hands. Norah watched him without speaking. He had never been one to be dramatic, so this was frightening.

Finally, she reached out a hand to stroke the nape of his neck. It was sweaty but cold. "Ben, you okay?" She gently pried his hands from his face. "Honey?"

He looked up at her, miserable.

"You're scaring me. Is it Nai Nai?"

He shook his head. "Eric just fired me."

Norah was flabbergasted. "What do you mean? You were doing so well there."

"That's what Eric said too. But he said he can't afford the rent anymore; he's moving everything online. He'll do shoots at people's homes, I guess. He also can't afford to pay me a salary anymore. Snapshot will be a one-man band from now on."

"What a jerk. At least half of Snapshot's clients come because of you! He knows that. Haven't you tried to talk to him?" She regretted this question even as she asked it; of course he had.

"He said he's already made up his mind." He stood up, his head hanging low. "I'm sorry, Norah. I'll think of something." He slumped into the bathroom. Norah listened dully as he adjusted the taps in the shower.

Tomorrow, when he was feeling better, she would ask Ben how much they still had in their joint account. Would they be able to afford to continue renting this flat? She wondered wildly whether it would be worse to ask her parents for a loan or to take Cable up on his offer of the two-bedroom flat, but she knew either would be seen as an unforgiveable betrayal. Ben's pride was at stake.

She was thankful that she had Vincent every Monday evening now, and if all went well tomorrow, Agnes on Tuesdays. That would add $4,000 to their monthly income. Maybe it would be enough to tide them over until Ben found a new job.

Chapter 17

The airport bus was crowded and the air-conditioning did not seem to be working; the vents kept blasting out hot air.

Norah glanced down at her phone again, checking for a message from her parents. She had been doing this every thirty seconds or so for the past thirty minutes.

Beside her, Ben sensed her mounting anxiety that they were going to be too late to pick up her mom and dad at the airport but understood that there was nothing he could say that would help. He shifted a bit closer to the aisle; she was so on edge that even brushing her arm by accident had resulted in glares and exasperated sighs.

Joey was looking out the window, happy to be snuggled up against his father and oblivious to both the traffic and his mother's fragile emotional state. Joey was dressed to the nines in the vest and bowtie ensemble his Gong Gong and Paw Paw had sent over at Christmas. It had looked enormous at the time, but was almost too small now. That seemed to be the fate of a lot of his baby clothes, especially the expensive ones.

Their bus was inching along on the Tsing Ma Bridge, normally about twenty minutes away from the Hong Kong International Airport. On a day like this, with the vehicles jammed up against each other, it was impossible to say how long the rest of the journey would actually take. The bus was packed with passengers, many of them asleep. The rest were on their phones, like Norah.

He checked his watch as surreptitiously as possible; it was 6:04. According to the airport website, his in-laws' flight was due to arrive at 6:15, so including going through customs and reclaiming baggage, they should be in Arrivals no later than 6:45. Hadn't Hong Kong's airport won an award for being the most efficient in the world a few years back? Or was that Changi airport in Singapore? He hoped it was Changi.

"Oh, crap," Norah muttered, staring at her phone. Ben could see she was on the verge of tears, but she took a deep breath to steady herself.

"Are they here?" he ventured.

She nodded miserably, causing a solitary tear to escape. "They're going to be so disappointed that we're not there waiting in Arrivals." More tears fell as she texted a reply.

Ben patted her thigh awkwardly. "I'm sure they'll understand. We left two hours ago. You couldn't have known there'd be traffic like this. Even if we took a..." He stopped, feeling a sudden warmth in the carrier. He glanced down at Joey, who was no longer looking out the window, but smiling up at his father. "Did you just poo?"

The baby smiled up at him. "Baba," he gurgled proudly. In Joey-talk, that meant yes.

"Great," Norah said, halfway between laughing and crying. "That's just great."

The bus pulled to a stop outside the airport at 7:26, the engines sighing heavily, as though relieved the long ordeal was over.

They rushed through the towering automatic doors and speed-walked to the Starbucks by check-in Aisle A, where Norah's parents had said they'd wait. They had sent Norah a selfie of the two of them in front of the Arrivals Hall B sign, and Norah had wept some more when she saw it.

Joey needed to be changed, desperately, he was smelling foul indeed, but first they had to meet the grandparents.

Norah broke into a dash. "*Mommy! Daddy!*" They embraced, all three of them. From the fifty-meter or so distance, Ben could see that she was crying again, happy tears, of course, but also tears of apology. She hated to let her parents down, hated to look bad in front of them. Ben tried not to think about how he made her look bad.

He hoped his in-laws would not ask too many questions, although they almost certainly would. They were always deeply interested in how he was doing financially, always finding roundabout ways of seeing whether the pauper their daughter married had improved his lot since the last time they met. They always seemed disappointed with his responses, but never before had he had to tell them he was unemployed.

He was thankful that in the last few weeks there had been some freelance work. Norah, always the bolder and braver of the two of them, had encouraged him to create a simple website advertising his rates and services ('Passport and School Photos', 'Family Sessions', 'Engagement Sessions', 'Work Functions', 'Children's Parties'). On the website he had posted photographs of Joey in his sailor suit, of Norah, with Joey propped on her knee, on the loveseat. The lighting in the studio was not ideal for photo-taking, but he had managed to get some pretty sweet shots of the two of them.

Norah had blasted the link on her social media accounts and in all her Whatsapp groups. She had called Gemma's and asked if they would be so kind as to post a link to Ben's website so that interested parents needing affordable and high-quality photographs could reach him and they had grudgingly agreed after she called three times. Ivan had of course agreed immediately to tack the poster to their bulletin board.

Norah's marketing worked. At first it seemed odd to not be able to give an address either on his website or when he spoke with potential clients on the phone, but they did not seem to expect one.

"I'll come to you," he learned to say, with growing confidence. "I can shoot quality photographs in any location." In the ultra-budget spirit of Snapshot Studio, he charged a more-than-fair price for his pictures, and word of his services spread, so that he began to feel surer of himself. More importantly, he was able to feel less ashamed that Norah was the sole breadwinner and that he had gone from depending on one woman to another. So far it seemed like his photography business would draw an income that would allow them to live in this studio comfortably. Of course, they would need to find someplace better once they could afford to.

He desperately hoped Norah's parents would not insist on visiting them at their studio. The first week or so of living there had been odd for Ben. He did not consider himself superstitious at all, and yet he found himself fearful at night when he heard the increasingly familiar sound of the hearses pulling to a stop in front of the funeral parlour. He always tried to block out the sound with the blanket around his ears, but sometimes he had nightmares about the corpses. Sometimes the corpses looked like Ma. He never mentioned these fears to Norah, who seemed to love the little space and the privacy it afforded them, and had no qualms whatsoever about either ghosts or dead bodies. The nightmares had finally, thankfully, receded after the first week, but still, each night Ben tried his best to fall asleep before Norah did.

He missed Ma. Two days after settling into the new flat, he had finally worked up the courage to send her another text message, one that said they would not be moving back to her flat. Ma had responded with a frowny face emoji, and had stopped communicating with him from that point on. Ben could see the double blue checks, so he knew she was reading his messages, but she never wrote back, not even when Ben sent her photographs and videos of Joey. He had stopped by 25 Dumbarton Road three times in the last few weeks, but each time he lost his nerve before he had made it into the elevator lobby.

As he and Joey approached the trio, Ben smiled, tried to look suitably happy about his in-laws' arrival. He had never really known what to call them. He knew 'Mom' and 'Dad' was the accepted norm for the wife's parents, but when he tried, the words always got caught in his throat. Knowing they did not approve of him made the terms feel saccharine and disingenuous. His in-laws seemed as uncomfortable as he was whenever he used the terms. But there was no alternative; to use their first names would be unthinkable in Chinese culture, to use Mr. and Mrs. Kwan, impossibly formal. He would have to go with Mom and Dad.

"Mom and Dad, so sorry to have kept you waiting! How was your flight?"

"*Joey*!" his mother-in-law cried, ignoring Ben. She scooped him out of the carrier eagerly, but Joey, with his heavily soiled diaper and after the two-hour bus journey, began bawling.

"There, there, sweetheart," Norah murmured, stroking his head tenderly. "This is Paw Paw, remember? And here's your Gong Gong." She was flustered when Joey continued crying. Ben sensed her disappointment that Joey had not performed better at this much anticipated reunion.

"No worries, Ben, we didn't wait long. Anyway, what's thirty minutes after a fourteen-hour flight?" His father-in-law laughed heartily, clapping Ben's shoulder with unnecessary force. "Joey's grown so much!"

Ben tried not to wince. He nodded, smiling with all his strength. "He just turned nine months last week." Unsure of how to segue to the pressing issue of Joey's soiled diaper, he coughed. "Excuse me. I need to use the restroom. I'll just change Joey's diaper while I'm there."

Norah looked gratefully at him as he took the baby gently from her arms. Ever the agreeable child, Joey was now only whimpering, but he desperately needed to be changed.

Ben sighed as the two of them walked to the baby room, Ben holding Joey straight out in front of him, under the arms, so his bum wouldn't be squashed up in poo any more. Two weeks until his in-laws flew home. "That's thirteen days left, my little man. Are we going to make it?" he whispered.

Joey, smiling once more, responded with his trademark "Baba, Baba."

"I sure hope you're right. But don't tell your Mama I said that."

Chapter 18

THE DIMSUM restaurant Norah's parents chose for their first proper meal together was in the basement of their hotel. Norah appreciated the muted, understated refinery of the place; there were no gaudy chandeliers or fake floral centerpieces. The marble walls were inlaid with jade in the shape of bamboo stalks, and as Norah and Ben meandered through the tables, looking for Mom and Dad, it felt as though they were walking through some ancient bamboo forest. Norah squeezed Ben's hand, and he smiled back at her and Joey, but she could see that he was nervous about the meal—the cost, the conversation, everything. She tugged at his arm until he stopped walking, then kissed him quickly on the lips.

He blushed, surprised, but then he smiled. They continued making their way to the back of the restaurant, and finally spotted Mom and Dad. Mom jumped to her feet and rushed out to meet them, her arms outstretched for Joey.

"Good morning, my darlings," she cried, embracing both Norah and Joey. Ben murmured his good mornings, and Joey greeted his Paw Paw with a regal wave.

When Norah lifted Joey out of the carrier and handed him to Mom, his smile was tentative, but he didn't cry. Mom held

Joey close and started talking quietly to him, pointing at the large seafood tanks with their fish and lobsters. After a moment, Joey nodded, and Mom took him over for a closer look.

"Morning, Daddy," Norah said. When she hugged Dad, he hugged her back, tightly.

"Good morning, Dad," Ben echoed quietly as he sat down. "Did you and Mom sleep well?"

He nodded, folding his newspaper in halves, then quarters. "I got about six hours, Mom a little less, I think. Not bad for our first night."

"How's Oatmeal?" Norah asked. Dad immediately pulled out his phone and tapped on his Gallery app, showing off the poodle's latest haircut. She nodded appreciatively; her parents loved the dog to bits. "Who's dog-sitting him these two weeks?"

"Our neighbor; she's got three dogs of her own, so Oatmeal will have plenty of company. Did I tell you I've planted a fig tree in our backyard?"

Mom and Joey returned from their visit to the water tanks, their faces bright with excitement. Norah was pleased to see that Joey had taken to his Paw Paw and was looking up at her adoringly. After Norah had attached Joey's Totseat to the chair between Mom's and her own and strapped him in, Mom started folding him a paper boat out of a receipt from her purse.

Out of the corner of her eye, Norah watched as Ben studied the menu, feigning interest in the dimsum selection but probably balking at the prices. A waitress dressed in an embroidered cheongsam stood attentively by, refilling the teacups immediately after anyone had taken a sip.

Mom and Dad would be expecting their son-in-law to treat them to their first proper meal in Hong Kong; it was the filial thing to do. Norah gently tugged the menu from Ben's hands. "Silly, you don't know what my parents like to eat. I'll order. Let me see, spring rolls for Dad, *siumai* for Mom, custard buns, of course, Dad likes those, and Ben, too… we won't need congee for Joey, we brought our own today… Mom, he can have minced pork now! Tomatoes, too, did I tell you?"

Norah kept ordering, offering a running commentary as she did, and making sure she included several rice and noodle dishes, the options that would fill everyone up for the least amount of money.

"Did you want to try the abalone and fish maw soup, ma'am?" the waitress asked, when Norah finally stopped talking. "Special price today, only $650 per pot, enough for four to six people, very nutritious…"

Norah looked doubtfully at her parents. "Do you want to try it, Mom and Dad?"

She closed the menu in relief when they shook their heads. "Sorry, perhaps another time. That's everything, thank you."

The waitress bowed her head before walking away, her tight ankle-length dress forcing her to take theatrically small steps.

"How's your mom doing, Ben?" Mom said, carefully balancing three peanuts on her chopsticks and dropping them daintily into her bowl.

Ben, who had been spraying sanitizer onto Joey's hands, glanced up at Mom. "Oh, she's well," he said quietly. "Thank you for asking."

This answer seemed too short, so Norah added to it: "We don't live with her anymore, Mom. We moved out of Nai Nai's flat a couple weeks ago."

Dad's eyes widened. "You bought a place? Why didn't you tell us?"

"No, Daddy," Norah laughed, glancing at Ben, who was pretending to be busy with Joey. "We're just renting, still saving up for that down payment. It's twenty percent now, can you believe it? *So* prohibitive."

"We rented at first, too," Mom said, smiling sweetly at Dad before taking a sip of her tea. Their waitress had returned and resumed her position; she promptly topped up her mother's cup. "No problem with that. Whereabouts is the flat?" She directed this question at Ben.

"Not too far from here," he said reluctantly, "about fifteen minutes away by bus."

This seemed absurdly vague. "It's sort of between Tsim Sha Tsui and Hung Hom," Norah continued. "Depends on who you ask, I guess."

"Do you mean Whampoa Gardens?" Dad asked, cocking his head. "That's a nice area." He brightened at the thought of his daughter living in the affluent and sizeable apartment complex by the harbor.

"No, not Whampoa." Norah cleared her throat. "It's not far from there though." This was not entirely true; Whampoa Gardens was at least a twenty-minute walk from their studio. "The landlord is very helpful, though, and the flat is in good condition." *Flat* could mean anything, from a sub-divided unit to a five-bedroom apartment.

Her dad did not look convinced, but thankfully, their order arrived—bamboo baskets with dainty shrimp dumplings and beef balls, golden spring rolls arranged prettily in a tall champagne glass.

Everyone ate quietly for several moments. Just as Norah began to relax, thinking they had weathered the worst of it, she felt her stomach clenching, bile rising in her throat. She took several deep breaths, willing the wave of nausea to pass. She glanced cautiously at her bowl and quickly saw that she would not be able to stomach the remaining half of her dumpling. Was it something she ate that morning? The night before? She hoped she wasn't sick; her parents had made lots of plans for their time in Hong Kong, including visiting Gemma's Gym that afternoon, and she wanted to spend as much time as she could with them. The nausea passed.

Beside her, Ben squeezed her hand. There was concern in his eyes; of course he had noticed that something was off.

"And are you still working at the same studio, then, Ben?" Mom set down her chopsticks and looked expectantly at him.

Ben began coughing violently, his face reddening. The people at the tables around them stared openly at him. He downed his little cup of tea and their waitress refilled it immediately, but it was clear from the steam that this new cup was too hot to drink. Norah held out her own cup of tea in front of Ben's lips and he drained it. Finally, the loud hacking coughs subsided. "Sorry about that," he said to no one in particular, his eyes streaming. "I choked on my spring roll."

"That's alright," Dad said. "It happens to the best of us."

"You were telling us about your work," Mom chimed in helpfully.

"Right," Ben said, swiping at his eyes. "It's been going, uh, pretty well. Summer is usually a busier time for…me, lots of family shoots at parks and things."

Ben was doing great. Under the table, Norah threaded her fingers through his. His hand was clammy and cold.

"Of course, of course," Dad said, nodding sagely. "And is it still the two of you, then, at…what was the name? You told us last time that the studio's a bit of a start-up, didn't you?"

"But growing all the time," Mom added. "Isn't it?"

Their tone was light and friendly, but this was clearly an interrogation. "Mom," Norah began, watching as Ben struggled with the remaining half of his spring roll. It kept slipping from between his chopsticks; his hands were shaking so. "Snapshot…"

"Let *Ben* tell us about his work, dear," Mom interrupted,

putting down her chopsticks. "We're very interested."

Ben didn't quite make eye contact with either of them. For a moment the silence around the table was too much to bear, but just as Norah opened her mouth again, Ben cleared his throat and began speaking. "I-I've also been doing lots of portraits for children who want pictures for their school application portfolios." He finally managed to look up at her parents, but his brow was still furrowed. "I really love working with kids. I have a shoot with a few families this afternoon in Tai Po." He patted his backpack with a strained smile; he looked as though he was baring his teeth at them.

Norah wished her parents would give it a rest. The last thing she needed was to have them berate Ben for losing his job. *What will you do now, Ben? How will you support your family? What are your long-term plans, Ben? You are the head of the household, Ben, and when we let Norah marry you, you made us a promise – do you remember it? Do you remember what you promised us?*

"That's good to hear," Mom said. "Although how a child can be judged on the basis of a portfolio, and whether their photo was any good, is beyond me. The local system is *so* competitive. Oppressive, really." She gazed fondly at Norah. "We didn't want that kind of education for you, dear."

She couldn't tell if she was being oversensitive, but why did all her parents' comments seem so prickly and judgmental today? It wasn't Ben's fault, or Nai Nai's fault, that he hadn't received an international school education like she had.

"Have you guys thought much about where Joey will be going to school?" Dad asked. Norah shifted uneasily in her seat. This was another topic that made her heart race; the last thing she wanted was for Joey to go to some competitive, oppressive school where all that mattered was the students' ranking. Ben agreed. That being said, the way their finances stood, it would be next to impossible for them to send Joey to an international school, or even one of the better local schools.

Norah swallowed. Would Joey be alright in a local school? In recent years many of them had purportedly become less reliant on rote learning, less examination-driven, but in her heart Norah was doubtful that any real change was taking place. What if they turned their precious, naturally inquisitive boy into some exam-taking robot? She envisioned Joey's little spirit being crushed by the heel of some mean class teacher, and shuddered.

Would her tutoring and Ben's budding photography business ever be lucrative enough to afford an international school education for Joey? How many hours would they need to work to make that kind of money? The numbers swam around in her head hopelessly.

To hire a helper would be another several thousand, so that would mean asking Nai Nai to help look after Joey during the day. *Was that an option?* she wondered. Would Joey be safe with her? She felt her heart being pulled in opposite directions—or was it her stomach? The room was beginning to spin, the green jade on the walls swirling around her. She closed her eyes and drank some more tea. She was dimly aware that the teacup was being topped up again.

"Daddy," she said, finally. She tried to keep the little-girl whine out of her voice—she was a married woman, for goodness' sake, married with a *child*—but failed. When Mom and Dad were in Vancouver, she didn't feel this tension so much, this tug-of-war between needing to appear grown-up and independent in her parents' eyes and an almost involuntary return to her childhood ways of pacifying them. But with them here in front of her, their concerned gazes one and the same, she fell back on whining and theatrical sighing. "Joey's only just turned nine months. You're stressing me out, Daddy." Norah reached for Joey's bib and wiped up a bit of drool at the side of his mouth.

Dad held up his hands in surrender, as Norah knew he would. "Sorry, sorry. Let's talk about something else. Want to see some pictures of our yard? The okra's doing pretty well this year."

When the elevator doors opened, revealing Gemma's Gym, Dad sniffed the air appreciatively. "This place smells like candy!"

"Stop it, you're acting like Oatmeal," Mom said, simultaneously rolling her eyes and pecking him on the cheek. Norah hid a grin. It was obvious her parents were still very much in love. *They* certainly never had to live with their in-laws. They had rented at first, just a humble one-bedroom flat in North Point—Norah had seen the faded photographs, the two of them beaming at the camera, their arms around each other—but without a difficult mother-in-law out to destroy their marriage.

Norah planted a kiss on Joey's forehead, trying desperately to clear her mind of thoughts of Nai Nai. She had been reluctant to cancel Joey's lesson, knowing Gemma's policy was to not reschedule unless the child applied for sick leave with a doctor's note, but her parents had jumped at the opportunity to come along and watch. Now she was determined not to let anything ruin this special day out. She hoped they wouldn't ask any more questions about her marriage, or Ben's work situation. She was an adult, wasn't she? They should trust that she could manage her own life.

"Welcome, Joey! Welcome, mummy!" Erin waved enthusiastically from the reception counter, a broad smile on her face. She nodded at Mom and Dad. "Hello, and welcome to Gemma's Gym! I'm Erin!"

"Hi, Erin," Norah said, gesturing at her parents. "This is my mom and dad. They want to observe the lesson from the waiting area today. Is that okay?"

"Of course it is! There is a special area *specifically* designed with grandparents in mind. You are *more* than welcome, Mr. and Mrs...?"

"Kwan," Mom said, clearly impressed by Erin's solicitous welcome. "What a lovely place this is, Erin. I'm so pleased our grandson has his lessons here."

"Oh, *absolutely*! Gemma's is Hong Kong's leading gym for babies and toddlers, and Joey is such a joy to see every week—he's just the sweetest little darling, isn't he?"

With that, Erin led Mom and Dad to the seating area directly in front of the viewing window and fixed them each a cup of instant coffee before returning to the reception counter. "Let me know if I can get you anything else, Mr. and Mrs. Kwan!"

"I'll leave my bags with you, then," Norah said, letting her backpack thud onto the floor beside Dad's chair and taking off her shoes before going inside the gym. There was an enormous air track filling the space today; some of the babies were already crawling towards it and patting at it curiously. Stuart was at the back of the gym, setting up a small obstacle course with foam steps and a low balancing beam. The other moms waved hello.

Norah waved back before gently nuzzling Joey's cheek with her nose. "Time to wake up, sweetheart." Joey's eyelids fluttered open for a moment before closing again. "Hi, baby," she tried again, tickling his chin. Joey let out a little giggle in his sleep before reluctantly opening his eyes. He blinked at her, clearly bewildered. "Oh, sweetheart," Norah said tenderly, kissing him on the nose. "Sorry to wake you. We're here. Ready to have some fun?"

"Morning, little one," Stuart said, appearing beside them. "And good morning to you, too, Norah! It's so lovely to see you both!"

"Say hello, Joey," Norah said, pleased when Joey, despite just waking up from his nap, reached out his chubby arms to Stuart. As Stuart took Joey in his arms, Norah gestured at her parents, who were beaming and waving behind the glass wall. "That's my mom and dad," she said, proudly. She did feel proud of them, and was pleased they were here with her and Joey. They were proper grandparents who hadn't made her parenting journey miserable. Proper grandparents who would never intentionally try and poison their grandson, like Nai Nai had. Norah realized she was scowling and forced herself to smile instead. "They're visiting from Vancouver."

Smiling, Stuart opened the glass door just a crack and waved hello with Joey's arm. "Hello, Grandma! Hello, Grandpa!"

"That teacher should be on TV," Mom gushed after the lesson. "He was *so* good with the children. Handsome, too." She closed the menu. "I think I'm ready to order."

Dad had wanted to go for dimsum, but Mom spotted a hip little all-day breakfast place in one of the side streets by Gemma's Gym and suggested they try that instead. Eggs Etc was both stylish and laidback, with mismatched dining chairs that worked beautifully with the teak wood tables. Norah noted that while the ceramic bowls on the table were all Santorini blue and off-white, they were pleasingly irregular in shape, as though a potter had lovingly crafted them by hand and fired them in a kiln.

"It was a great lesson," Dad agreed. "Was it very expensive, Norah?"

"A bit," Norah said lightly. She knew now that the lessons were indeed too expensive, and that she should have done more research and found a more affordable option. She felt guilty now thinking back to how she had insisted on this, and steamrollered

Ben into giving in. "Joey really enjoys them, though. You're our whole world, aren't you, love?"

Joey was sitting in one of the fancy Tripp Trapp high chairs the cafe provided, and alternating between gnawing on his giraffe teether and squeezing it hard enough to make it squeak. As though he understood, Joey paused mid-gnaw to flash her his signature toothy grin. Norah couldn't get over how blindingly white his teeth were. "Ma," he agreed. "Mama."

"Of *course* he's your whole world," Mom said with feeling. "Investing in your children is the best investment you can make."

Norah nodded as she unscrewed Joey's thermos and scooped out the still-warm sweet-potato mash into one of the restaurant's pretty ceramic bowls. "Absolutely. That's one thing Ben and I agree completely on."

"I'm glad to hear it," Mom said, but her tone was uncertain. "Norah, I'd be lying if I said I didn't still have some reservations about..."

"Mom, please." Norah frowned. She had heard enough about Mom's 'reservations' when she and Ben were dating; surely she didn't need to have them repeated to her now. She finally managed to make eye contact with one of the servers, someone about her age who was dressed completely in black from head toe, from the black bandana around his head to the Doc Martens on his feet. He sauntered over, an iPad in his hand. "I'm starving."

"Eggs benedict, please," Mom said. The server tapped the screen of his iPad before looking up again, a bored expression on his face. "With smoked salmon. I'd love a glass of orange juice as well; thank you."

"And I'll have the French toast with scrambled eggs," Dad continued, "and a black coffee. How about you, Norah?"

Norah was normally a great fan of greasy breakfast food, but this morning even the pictures were making her stomach churn.

She probably needed to see the doctor; it had to be some kind of stomach bug. "Just the poppyseed bagel, please," she finally said, closing the menu. "And could I have a glass of orange juice?"

"Yup," the server said, collecting the menus. Norah noted that he had a tattoo on his wrist, some kind of bird, a raven or a crow.

"Cream cheese for the bagel?"

Norah felt queasy just thinking about cheese. "No thanks."

"Now, Norah," Mom said, after the server had walked off, "I don't have anything against Ben, you know I don't. How can I, you've gone and married him, haven't you? Don't think so badly of your mother! All I was trying to say is that…"

Out of the corner of her eye, Norah saw that Dad had placed an arm on Mom's forearm, as though to say, *Let me take it from here.* "How's Ben's work actually going these days? He didn't seem very forthcoming this morning when he was talking about his work. He said he's doing a lot of shoots, but is he really? I got the feeling that the work may not be very steady."

Norah felt her body temperature rising; she knew her cheeks were burning and she felt exposed and vulnerable. She wished she wasn't so easy to read. She was hoping, desperately hoping, they would avoid this topic. She wondered wildly whether she could pull off an outright lie—*Never better,* then smoothly seguing into a comment about the weather.

"Snapshot's not *that* little, Daddy," she said, trying to make a joke of it, but her words sounded false to her own ears, and it was obvious her parents were not fooled.

"You were the one who told us there's only the two of them," Dad said, gently. "It's a start-up, isn't it? The first couple of years can be rough. Is Ben's income… stable?"

"Pretty stable," Norah said, tucking a lock of hair behind her ear and trying hard to imagine that she was talking to a couple of inquisitive students at Future English, and not her own parents. *I'm here to help! Feel free to ask me anything!*

"Actually," she continued bravely, "Ben recently decided to part ways with Eric. The market's changing, and he's got a solid client base. He's only just gotten started, but things are going great."

She had managed to keep her composure through this little speech, but when she picked up her glass, she was dismayed to find that her hands were shaking. She closed her fingers firmly around the glass and brought it to her lips, downing half of the juice in one gulp. By the time she set it down again on the paper coaster she felt a little calmer.

She turned to Joey, pointedly avoiding making eye contact with her parents. She unstrapped him from the high chair and cuddled him, drawing strength from his warmth. *I will be calm for you, my darling. I will be calm for you.* She was aware that her parents were watching her, their frowns one and the same.

"You never mentioned this to us," Mom finally said, breaking the silence. "When did this happen?"

"Very recently," Norah shrugged, pretending it was nothing, pretending Ben hadn't got laid off, pretending their finances weren't so tight she could barely sleep sometimes, she was so worried. She sometimes wondered whether they might be better off asking Mom and Dad for a loan.

Mom opened her mouth to say something, but Norah beat her to it. "Anyway, it's going really well. He's got lots of clients already, just last week he did, like, what was it, five shoots back-to-back, and he hasn't even done any real marketing yet, it's all been by word-of-mouth. Once his Facebook ads go live, the business is going to be pouring in…'

Norah rambled on like this, exaggerating some of the details—it was three shoots last week, not five—and making up the rest, stopping only when their orders arrived.

Norah immediately slipped half of her bagel into one of the spare Ziplock baggies she always carried with her in case Joey got motion sickness. "I want Ben to try some," she said, by way of explanation. "I'm trying to lose weight."

"Well, it sounds like Ben's doing great," Dad said, without much conviction. "That's good to hear."

Mom didn't say anything.

Chapter 19

Ben arrived home around 5:30, buoyant after a great shoot for a group of kindergarten graduates and their parents at Tai Po Waterfront Park. The children wore purple graduation gowns with matching hats, clutching similarly clad stuffed animals as they beamed at the camera. It was hot, but Norah had packed him a baseball hat and a frozen bottle of water wrapped in a washcloth, so it wasn't bad at all. The parents were very pleased with his service. They paid in cash, and tipped him handsomely for his time. With an extra $2,500 in his wallet and his difficult in-laws safely back in their hotel, he was feeling better than he had in a long while.

When he pushed the front door open, he found Norah curled up on the sofa, her eyes closed. Beside her, Joey was playing in the playpen Norah recently bought second-hand on Carousell. Ben was proud of Norah—she'd gotten good at hunting down bargains on online platforms, and this very lightly used PacknPlay only set them back $400, a real bargain compared to what it would have cost them at BabiesRUs. It was the kind of playpen that could be folded up when not in use, and which could double as a crib in a pinch. Eventually he would need to go back to Ma's to get the real crib, but for now it was nice to have

Joey sleep somewhere other than between them on the sofa bed.

There was an open paperback lying face-down on the floor. In the glow of the floor lamp, their home looked wonderfully warm and cozy, perfect for the three of them.

"Baba!" Joey cried immediately, pulling himself up onto his feet. Ben grinned, holding up one finger to his lips, but Norah opened her eyes right away.

"I wasn't asleep," she said, yawning as she rubbed her eyes. "I don't know why I've been feeling so run down lately. How was the shoot?"

Ben set the bag of groceries down on the counter and went to his wife. She looked so exhausted, his heart hurt. She had messaged him that afternoon, asking if he would please pick something up for dinner—she wasn't feeling well enough to cook.

"Silly," she said, gently batting his hands away when he tried to knead her shoulders, "I'm fine. You're the one who just got home from work." She pecked him on the cheek. "I want to hear all about the shoot. Were the kids cute?"

She was trying so hard to sound cheerful for him, but Ben could see through her, of course. She'd been juggling so much lately, from caring for Joey to finding clients for his fledgling photography business to tutoring students online. On top of all this, of course, were her parents, who were demanding and difficult, even if Norah wouldn't admit it.

"Not as cute as this little guy," Ben said tenderly. Joey squealed as he scooped him out of his crib and held him close. "Missed you! Come keep me company while I get dinner ready, will you?" He turned to Norah. "As for you, Mama, you look like you're coming down with something. Keep resting—I'll wake you when Joey and I've got dinner ready."

Norah shook her head, but when she yawned again, she didn't

resist as Ben spread Joey's comfort blanket over her, Joey at his hip. He kissed her on the forehead. "I love you." She nodded sleepily, her eyes already closed.

Ben strapped Joey into the high chair and placed one of his new high chair toys on the tray. It was a fancy one from Canada, with a suction cup on the bottom and different contraptions for spinning and pulling. Joey studied it carefully, looking exactly the way Norah did when she was poring over a recipe. "Now for a little Baba and Joey time."

Beaming, Joey brought his hands together in a single clap. "Baba," he said, sweetly. "Baba."

"He's doing it! He's really doing it! Honey, come look!"

Tonight Joey had no bowl on his high chair tray. Instead, Norah had arranged placed little lengths of udon and banana for him to try and pick up with his fingers. They were quite small; Norah seemed to have made the task intentionally challenging. But after ten minutes of coaxing and demonstrating, Joey finally seemed to have got the hang of it.

As Ben set down a steaming bowl of udon noodles and dumplings on the table, Joey studied the little strand of udon in his fist, a bemused expression on his face.

"You're really doing it, Joey!" Ben cried, running for his cell phone. He managed to film the moment when Joey brought the noodle to his mouth, and his broad smile as his parents clapped and cheered. He immediately repeated the trick, to more applause.

Ben ladled out some noodles and dumplings for each of them before sitting down beside Norah. The dumplings were nothing special, just frozen pork and napa dumplings from the supermarket, but he had mixed up a nice little dipping sauce with white vinegar, sesame oil, and soy sauce, and Norah, who hadn't had much appetite this week, seemed to be enjoying her meal.

"This is so good, honey." Norah slurped up the broth in her bowl even though they both know it was just chicken essence. She looked at him adoringly. "You should be a chef."

Ben blushed, even though he knew she wasn't being serious. "Are you sure you're feeling better? You were so pale at the restaurant this morning when we were eating with your parents."

"I did feel a bit queasy," Norah admitted. "I hope I'm not coming down with something. Mom and Dad want to go to Cheung Chau tomorrow with me and Joey."

"That's nice." He placed his hand on Norah's forehead. "I don't think you're running a fever." He stroked her cheek tenderly. "You look exhausted, though. Have an early night," he offered, before standing up to gather the bowls and dishes into a little tower to bring to the sink. He gave Joey a little kiss as he detached his tray from the high chair to wash in the sink. "I'll give the little guy his bath after I do the dishes. You don't have any Zoom lessons tonight, right?"

Norah shook her head.

"Then go shower first. I'll just be a few minutes."

As Ben started filling the sink with water, he was aware that Norah was still there behind him. The familiar sounds of Norah unbuckling Joey from the high chair and sitting back down on her squeaky folding chair were the soundtrack of his life. He was about to say, "Go, honey," when she spoke first.

"Ben?"

He switched off the tap and turned around, wiping his hands on his jeans. "Yes?"

Norah had an expression on her face that he couldn't quite read. "Honey, I told Mom and Dad you left Snapshot."

It was an effort to hide his shock. "You did?"

She nodded, clearly miserable. "They kept asking…just like they were doing at dimsum. My parents can be *so* nosy. Growing up, I didn't mind; I liked the feeling that they cared so much despite their work being so busy. They always made time for me, no matter what. It felt…good, I guess, knowing I was the centre of their universe. But now…it's one thing to pry into my life, but to go on and on about your work…"

Ben glanced at her, surprised, as she continued fretfully. She was normally so protective of her parents; she never said anything negative about them, so he didn't dare to either. This was a first.

"I think they're probably just worried about you," he said, sitting down on the other folding chair. He was uncertain whether Norah was truly prepared to discuss the failings of her beloved parents. "They've always been very protective of you, so I guess…'

"Mama," Joey suddenly interrupted, pointing at the Jumperoo.

Pointing was a new milestone Joey had just reached in the last week, and Norah had given in to his requests more than usual to encourage him to do it more. But this time she shook her head. "Sorry, baby. No jumping right after meals, remember?"

Joey jutted out his bottom lip.

"Play for a while in the playpen first," Ben suggested, taking Joey from Norah's arms. He set him down gently in the playpen and stacked a few soft blocks for him to knock over. Joey let out a little squeal as he nudged the tower over with the top of his head.

Norah took in a shuddery breath. "They just wouldn't stop. They have no idea what the job market is like in Hong Kong these days, and how hard you've been working." She glared at the wall, as though her parents were standing there making more mean remarks about him. "*I* think you're doing *so* well, and I'm *so* proud of you, and I have so much *respect* for you, and nothing they say....'

Norah was still talking, and roughly swiping at her eyes with the back of her hands, when he enveloped her in his arms. "Hey," he said softly, burying his face in her hair. These days Norah smelled different; she had just been using Johnson's baby shampoo along with Joey rather than ordering the fancy brand—Giovanni?—from Amazon like she used to. Ben's eyes smarted when he thought of how much Norah had changed because of him and Joey.

Ben wanted to say something eloquent, but he didn't have the words to express just how grateful, how moved, he felt that Norah was siding with him for once, and not with her parents. He had always known that she loved him, but to know that she respected him, too—it meant the world. She was changing, for him. And she respected him, despite everything.

"Thank you," he said, his voice thick with emotion. "I love you so much, you know that?"

Chapter 20

NORAH SWITCHED off her breast pump, thankful that its drone had not woken Ben and Joey, both of whom had fallen asleep hours ago.

Normally sleep came easily to her after making love, but even after a full hour of lying very still beside Ben, she had not been able to drift off. She finally decided to tidy up the apartment a little, before sitting down to try and pump, although her supply had been dwindling more than ever in the past few weeks.

Norah now held the Medela bottle up to eye level and frowned at what she saw: 60ml of breast milk, barely a third of the little bottle. She focused on thinking warm maternal thoughts about Joey as she tried to express a little more by hand. Despite her efforts, her breasts only managed a few weak sprays each, bringing the total to a measly 70ml. She would try again in the morning.

She screwed the yellow cap onto the bottle and put it in the fridge beside the butter. Back in the early days, when she was doing well, she sometimes had three or four bottles of breast milk lined up in the fridge, waiting to be reheated and served to Joey. Nai Nai sometimes pretended she couldn't see them and turned to the can of formula instead.

To Norah's surprise, this memory did not upset her as sharply as it used to. When she thought of Nai Nai in her silly Barney suit, sitting regally on her armchair like some matriarch from one of her period soaps, Norah felt an unexpected wave of emotion wash over her.

Were in-law relationships always like this? Did they always cause this much heartache? If Norah was honest with herself, she knew that the bitterness and dislike went both ways—Nai Nai was often unnecessarily mean and critical of her, but Norah harbored a lot of dislike and distrust towards her mother-in-law, too.

Until Norah arrived on the scene, Nai Nai had never needed to listen to anybody. She had singlehandedly raised her son, who heeded her every command and agreed with all of her opinions without question. Norah smiled wanly, thinking of how much heartache she must have caused her mother-in-law.

Thinking back, Norah could recall a few instances of kindness. When Norah came home from the hospital after giving birth, she found that Nai Nai had attached little stockings filled with dried ginger peel to every tap in the apartment. "For this month, Norah should only use warm ginger water to wash her hands and to bathe," Nai Nai ordered. "This is the easiest way. You will suffer joint pain and headaches all your life if you wash with plain cold water. That's what happened to me."

Traumatized and delirious from her very long and drawn-out labor, Norah laughed at the ludicrousness of the little bags of ginger, but Nai Nai was unfazed. "This is *my* flat. No one is allowed to remove my ginger bags until Joey is one month old. Is that clear, Norah?" Then, under her breath, she had muttered, "So ungrateful. Nobody did this for me when Ben was born."

Back then Norah's mind had been consumed with her newborn, but now she recalled how Nai Nai had changed the ginger peels for her every day to ensure maximum potency. The apartment had smelled of sweet vinegar; Nai Nai had prepared an enormous ceramic pot of vinegared eggs and pig trotters, traditional food for the new mother during the first month. "Eat," Nai Nai had insisted, pushing the steaming bowl of black vinegar towards Norah, even as Norah was longing for instant noodles and potato chips. "You need to build up your strength."

Her emotions felt all out of whack today, and thinking of Nai Nai was making her tear up. She would have to remind Ben to go back and visit sometime with Joey, maybe buy her some fruit. Visits would be fine, surely; she wouldn't try to feed Joey anything if Ben were there, would she?

Her phone buzzed. When she picked it up she saw it was not a message but a notification from her Flo app prompting her to log her period. During the day she usually ignored all the notifications from her apps; it was busy enough trying to keep up with messages from actual people like Ben and her parents, and her growing list of Zoom clients. Just as she was about to swipe up and clear her screen, a speech bubble popped up: *Your period is late (5 days). Would you like to find out why?*

Yawning, she tapped on the little x in the corner; she had read that article before. It was a long list of possible causes, from *stress* to *dietary changes, pregnancy* at the bottom as the last possibility. She had been so stressed lately; it wasn't unusual at all for her periods to be a little irregular, was it? Her skin had been breaking out, but that could be because of the stress, or perhaps because since moving out she hadn't had any of Nai Nai's nutritious broths. Five days was not so many days, was it? Then she thought of the way her stomach had been acting up in the last few days, the nausea she'd been feeling all week, and a chill crept down her spine.

Her watch read 1:23a.m. For a moment she was immobilized

with indecision, but then her fear got the better of her and the next thing she knew she was kneeling beside Ben and shaking his arm.

"Ben," she whispered. "Ben, wake up!"

Ben's eyes flew open and he sat up, rubbing his eyes. "What's going on? Is it Joey?" Even in his groggy state, he instinctively knew to whisper back.

"Joey's fine."

He patted the floor for his glasses. "Are you feeling dizzy again?" He peered at her face, his expression so tender and concerned Norah's heart ached with love for him. "I'll make you something to drink. There's a lemon in the fridge, I think, and I can put in some—"

Norah threw her arms around him with such force that he lost his balance and collapsed onto his pillow. "Whoa, babe." They let out matching nervous giggles. "Whoa."

She rested her head on his chest, listening to his heartbeat. "Honey…I think I'm pregnant."

For a moment, no one spoke or moved. Ben's heart rate seemed to be speeding up, but perhaps she was imagining things. When he stroked her hair, she could feel his hand trembling. "H-have you done a test?"

Norah shook her head. "Not yet, but my period's late." She hesitated. "Five days. And I've been nauseous all week, and…"

Ben pressed his lips to her forehead, stopping her. "I'll go down and buy a test from 7-11."

Norah glanced at her phone again. It was 2:03 but she was so abuzz with nervous energy that she didn't feel tired at all. All she could think about was how much she needed to pee, but Ben would be back in a minute with the pregnancy test, so she resolutely avoided looking at the bathroom door.

She tiptoed over to the playpen to check on Joey, who was sound asleep, his legs extended in a ninja kick position. She dearly wanted to kiss him, but the playpen was too low to the ground and she couldn't reach him without scooping him up and waking him. Instead, she planted a kiss on one of his pudgy little feet through the mesh side instead. As expected, Joey ignored this completely; he was such a good sleeper when he wasn't itchy, and lately he'd been doing great.

"Are you really in there?" Norah whispered, placing her hands on her tummy, the thumbs and index fingers meeting to form a heart. She took ten deep breaths, then another ten, before allowing herself to imagine the possibility of another life growing in her.

"In case you are," she said, "hello."

The truth was that she desperately hoped the baby wasn't there at all, but she was afraid of making her little guest feel unwelcome. She read somewhere that babies could sense their mothers' thoughts very early on. "I'm happy you're here," she added hastily, for good measure.

Opening her eyes again, she was faced with the reality of their little studio, clean but cramped. How would they possibly fit one more child in here?

Chapter 21

The moment Ben walked in the door, Norah grabbed the box from his hand and rushed into the bathroom.

When she re-emerged, her cheeks were flushed. "I did it," she said breathlessly, the test wrapped in a bit of toilet paper. She set it on the dining table before sitting down on one of the folding chairs. "Five minutes to wait."

Ben hid his fear by standing behind his wife and rubbing her shoulders.

Norah placed her hands over his. "Are you scared?"

He wanted to say no, of course not, but he was terrified. "A bit," he finally admitted. He let out a little laugh to try and ease the tension. "A little bit, same as you."

If only they weren't so strapped for cash. When he was at the 7-11 downstairs, he saw an ad for part-time cashiers; $48 an hour, $55 for the graveyard shift. He filled out one of the green application forms and was assured that the manager would call him back the next day. If he worked the graveyard shift a few times a week that would mean an extra five or six thousand dollars a month. With the drastically reduced *gayong* he was giving Ma these days, that might be enough for them to get by while he continued to build his client base.

Ben was calculating these numbers in his head, his hands kneading Norah's shoulders, when she suddenly gasped. "Ben," she said, her voice catching. "Oh God, Ben."

He sat down beside her, and the two of them bent over the pregnancy test together, the tops of their heads touching.

Ben felt a sharp jolt of electricity as he saw that second pink line, faint but unmistakable. Norah stared at the twin lines in the little testing window for what seemed like minutes, her expression inscrutable. When she blinked, a single tear rolled down her cheek. In the harsh glow of the lamp, she looked vulnerable and haggard.

"I'm sorry," he said, hanging his head, and he was, for everything, but especially for not wearing a condom that one time, although he couldn't remember exactly when this baby was conceived. It must have been shortly after Norah got the playpen; they hadn't been able to make love before then, not when Joey was sleeping between them. He and Norah had never been very intentional about either using protection or tracking their love-making; Joey had been a surprise, too. Ben felt a lump forming in his throat. "I'm so sorry, Norah."

But Norah didn't hear his apology because she spoke at the same time: "I'm scared," she said, covering her face with her hands. "I…I'm h-happy, of course, it's j-just…'

Ben wrapped his arms around her. He was sorry as well as scared, but he found comfort even as he was extending it. He stroked her back until her breathing steadied.

"Joey's going to be a big brother," she finally said, freeing herself from his grasp. "You're lucky, little one," she said, trying to smile at her belly, but the expression on her face was more a grimace than anything else. "You have a great big brother. I mean, he's still a baby, but…but…" She let out a heart-wrenching sob. "Oh, Ben, how are we ever going to manage? We don't have enough money for another baby, do we? I know you've got clients, lots of clients, but…but…I'll need to go back to work, won't I, and…"

"We'll be okay," he interrupted, sounding more confident than he felt. "We're going to be okay."

Norah looked at him doubtfully, but Ben could tell that, all at once, she was too tired to protest.

"Come," he said, holding out a hand to her. "Let's go to bed. This baby won't be here for another nine months. We still have time."

"Say hi first." Norah grabbed his hand and rested it on her belly. "Say hi," she insisted.

"Hello, baby," he said awkwardly. "It's me, Baba." He paused, imagining another little person growing inside his wife, a tiny baby who would grow to have her mother's eyes and sweet dimpled smile. *This one's a girl*, he thought, with odd certainty. "I love you already, little one."

"I love you back, Baba," Norah whispered fiercely.

Chapter 22

The little girl on Ben's laptop screen was missing one top and one bottom tooth, but she smiled confidently at the camera, at an angle, as Ben instructed her during the shoot. It was a great picture, one that really showcased her confident personality; any principal perusing her kindergarten application would be pleased to accept her. He adjusted the lighting slightly, cropped the photograph so six pictures would fit on a single 4R frame. He added a narrow white margin, then sent four copies by Bluetooth to his Canon Selphy printer. The Canon was a necessary investment since he no longer had access to Snapshot's industrial-grade photo printers. Eric had either sold them or set them up in his apartment. Ben didn't know; they hadn't been in touch. He suspected Eric felt guilty about the way things ended up.

Even as he worked, as he sliced the photograph into six equal passport-sized pictures, his emotions swung wildly from excitement about the new baby to pure panic, the kind of panic that made his fingers slippery and his breathing shallow. Maybe he should go for a run a bit later; that would calm his nerves.

Norah and Joey were on a day trip to Cheung Chau with her parents today. He had very much wanted to stop them from leaving the house that morning, because it was a terrible idea, really; he could only imagine how nauseous Norah must be feeling on the ferry. But he also knew how unwilling Norah was to disappoint her parents, and he hadn't wanted to add to her stress. In the end he had packed her a thermos of ginger tea and some mints; it was all he could do for her.

Now he kept glancing at his phone, ready to send her reassuring messages and kissy face emojis, but so far she'd been silent—perhaps too dizzy to look at her phone. Ben hadn't been invited to join them, even though he didn't have any photo shoots lined up for today. It was for the best, of course—he never knew what to say to Norah's parents without sounding either defensive or self-deprecating, so a day trip would have been difficult—but still, he wished he could have gone along to take care of Norah and Joey.

His phone suddenly buzzed in his pocket. He grinned in anticipation, certain it would be a selfie of Norah and Joey, but it wasn't. It was Ma. He studied his screen for several long moments to make sure it was actually her number, that he wasn't imagining it. Ma hadn't picked up his calls or answered his texts in three weeks.

"Ma?"

He could hear her breathing.

"Ma, how've you been? I'm sorry we left in such a hurry, I..." his voice trailed off. "I'm sorry."

She cleared her throat. "I've cooked Joey some soup. It's just plain chicken broth, nothing else," she added hastily.

"That's so nice, Ma, thank you. Are you home? I'll come pick it up."

"I want to come over and see the baby." She didn't say, *And I want to see whether you've really been able to manage on your own,* but Ben could hear it between the lines. "Where are you exactly?"

Ben shifted nervously in the folding chair. When it squeaked, he stood up and paced around the small living area. "It's so hot out today, Ma, how about I just come by? I miss the apartment. We could have lunch together at the Golden Phoenix, what do you think? I feel like a barbecue bun."

"I said I want to come see the baby."

"Right, of course," Ben said, glancing anxiously around the studio. It was not a mess, exactly, but it would need to be tidied up. The plates and mugs from breakfast were still in the sink and Joey's toys were strewn about on the linoleum floor. These were minor details; what worried him was their studio's proximity to Universal Funeral Parlour. Ma was going to be furious when she found out their location.

"Send me the address then," she said impatiently. "You're not going to stop your own mother from coming to your home, are you?"

"Joey's not here," he tried again. "He's gone out with Norah." He didn't mention Joey's Gong Gong and Paw Paw, didn't want to add more problems to the churning pot. It was hard to say whose parents disliked their child's spouse more, but just as Ma couldn't stand Norah, his in-laws disliked him. The only time they had all been together was at the wedding two years ago, and it had been an awkward affair indeed. "Ma, of course you're welcome, it's just that..."

She hung up.

When he tried to call her back, it went straight to her voicemail, meaning that she had rejected his call. He tried and tried, and gave up after the fifth attempt.

In despair, he sent her their address.

Chapter 23

The ferry chugged languidly towards Cheung Chau Island. The sky was more hazy grey than picture-perfect blue, but Norah was content. So far, the seas had been calm and the rain had held off. She was a little dizzy, but not too bad.

Norah shared a bag of pork jerky with Mom, the sticky kind that made them lick their fingers after each slice. Every now and then Mom reached across the aisle to feed Dad a piece. Joey was asleep on his chest, one of his arms wrapped around Dad's neck. It had been bittersweet to see her baby bonding with her parents; they only had a few days left. If only they didn't live so far away. She resisted the urge to rub her tummy. Would they be able to bond with this baby from such a distance? They had with Joey, but still, she wasn't sure.

This thought brought with it a pang of guilt. Was she doing the right thing in wrenching Joey from Nai Nai? In the heat of the moment, Norah had been certain she was right, but now she was not so sure. Ben really should take Joey to visit his Maa Maa soon. She would remind him tonight.

"How've things been between you and Ben lately?" Mom asked casually. Across the aisle, Dad glanced at them, then looked away again, feigning disinterest. He began patting Joey's back intently. Her parents were terrible actors.

"Good." Norah was careful to keep her tone light and avoid sounding defensive. "Things are great." She squeezed Dad's arm. "I know you're listening, Dad. We're doing great."

"If you say so," Mom said, but she sounded doubtful. "We were surprised to hear you'd moved out of your in-law's place so suddenly. You never mentioned that you were planning to. I'd always thought if you ever decided to move out it would be to move in with us!"

"You also didn't tell us you quit your job," Dad added. "Or that Ben lost his."

Norah crossed her arms against her chest. "Hey," she said, jutting out her bottom lip. "You guys are ganging up on me."

"We love you, is all," her mother said. "It's hard for us to not know what's going on in your life. We want to know if things are... not working out. We want to be able to help." Across the aisle, Dad was nodding in earnest.

"I know you care about me," Norah paused, wondering if she should go on. "But sometimes it seems like you still don't believe Ben and I are going to make it." She sighed. "We love each other, Mom. We've been married for two years. We're happy together. Don't you want me to be happy?"

Dad sighed. "Of course we do. We just want to make sure he's providing for you and Joey, that you're living... comfortably. You know we had reservations when we found out you were going to be living with your mother-in-law. And now, with both of you out of work, some of those old concerns are coming back. We keep telling you, we've got plenty of space in Vancouver, and..."

"I know." Norah tried not to sound as impatient as she felt. "I know, Dad. But Ben isn't out of work, and anyway, this is my home now. Here, in Hong Kong." When Dad looked away, hurt, she added, "I miss you and Mom all the time and wish more than anything that you could move back here," as an olive branch, but he sighed some more and didn't say anything.

Norah glanced out the window, wondering what she could say to salvage their trip, now that she had upset her parents so. In dismay, she saw that while they were talking, the sky had grown dark.

"It's raining," Mom said, sadly. "I was really looking forward to playing with Joey on the beach."

Norah was about to respond when their ferry bounced violently, as though an invisible hand had picked it up, then dropped it back on the waves. The hand proceeded to rock their ferry roughly, to and fro, and Norah's stomach lurched in protest. She felt sweat beads blooming rapidly on her forehead; some of them gathered to form rivulets that ran down the side of her face. She struggled to swallow the sour, bitter taste of bile in her mouth, but her efforts were futile. It was only by a stroke of luck that she was able to grab the sick bag from the seat pocket in front of her in time.

Her parents immediately began fretting over her as though she were a young child, fanning her with the ferry's safety card, buying her M&M's, wiping the sweat from her brow. She threw up again, violently, into the sick bag.

Norah was embarrassed by the sound and stench of herself vomiting, but she was too dizzy to stand up and head for the washroom. At first she tried to ignore the stares of the people sitting around them, fearing their judgment, then decided she was too ill to care.

"I think we should get you home," Dad said, finally, after several moments. He took the soiled sick bag from Norah's hand and handed her a fresh one. Someone handed them a vial of White Flower Oil, that pungent cure-all, and Mom dabbed it anxiously at Norah's temples, the insides of her wrists.

"Of course we should, but how is she going to manage another hour on a ferry? She's so pale, dear. I'm scared she's going to faint."

Norah tried to smile at them, to reassure them, but found she couldn't quite manage it. She glanced briefly at Joey, saw he was still asleep, and closed her eyes. She hated the smell of White Flower Oil, had always associated it with illness and the very old, but was surprised to find the strong scent of menthol a welcome distraction from her nausea. She breathed in, counting to five, imagining her womb filling up with warmth and space for her baby, before exhaling. She liked the image. She did it again and again, until she was asleep.

Ben stood outside the entrance of their building, his phone in hand, waiting for Ma. He kept checking for new messages but there'd been nothing since the 'OK' she sent upon receiving their address. She was likely already disapproving of their proximity to the funeral parlour, but that could not be helped.

He studied the hubbub across the street uneasily. Like his mother, he was afraid of death. He remembered attending only one funeral, his grandmother's. The sight of her body in the coffin had given him nightmares for weeks.

Growing up, his greatest fear was that Ma would die, and he would be left alone in the world. Despite how cranky and moody she could be, he wanted her to live forever. He had Norah now, and Joey, and Baby Two, but the thought of losing Ma was no less frightening.

He felt unsettled by the sight of the many floral wreaths being delivered into the funeral parlour but couldn't seem to look away. There were different styles: most were circular, but some look like paw prints, and there were two hearts, and one cross made entirely of lilies. All of the wreaths had a pair of thin black banners hanging from them, with messages carefully written in white paint.

You are always in our hearts, Beloved Grandma. Your Second Grandson Siu-Keung, Second Granddaughter-in-law Ka-Ying, and Great-Granddaughters Tsz-Yan and Tsz-Lam.

Most Respected Father, I will always miss you. Your daughter, Theresa.

Yui-Ling, journey safely. Your golden sisters, Hiu-Fong, Yuk-Wah, and Bo-Zhu.

The wreaths had a strange hold on him and he read one final message after another. He wondered dully what messages would be on Ma's funeral wreaths when the time came. His eyes welled up, and for a moment he feared he might start crying right there on the sidewalk.

His phone buzzed in his hand; it was a notification for a text message from his father-in-law. He frowned, anxious. His in-laws never messaged him, they didn't have that sort of relationship, so something was almost certainly wrong. He took a deep breath, bracing himself for the news, but just as he was about to unlock his phone and read the text, a taxi pulled to a stop in front of him. It was Ma.

He tried to open the taxi door for her but it was locked. When she stepped onto the sidewalk, Ben saw that she was wearing her special purple outfit, complete with the purple sequined loafers. She had a large thermos in one hand, a cloth bag of groceries in the other.

Ben reached for her things, and was relieved when Ma allowed him to take them. She smiled sadly at the sight of him. "You've lost weight," she said, finally. "Hasn't Norah been cooking for you?"

He hadn't noticed any changes in his weight; they didn't

have a bathroom scale at the studio. Anyway, he had been the one doing most of the cooking lately. Their kitchenette was too small to cook anything too elaborate, so mostly they'd been on a noodle rotation: vermicelli, rice noodles, *hor fun*, udon. But the few times she had cooked it had been fun. Last week she made some kimbap rolls using a box of rice she bought at the take-out store downstairs.

"Sure she has," he said, a little too earnestly. "All kinds of nutritious things. Joey can eat pork now, Ma, did I tell you? And tomatoes, and broccoli, too. He loves broccoli. Isn't that strange for a baby? Norah calls them baby trees." He was talking too much and too fast, but Ma wasn't saying anything and he felt the need to fill the space between them as they took the elevator up to the studio.

He fumbled with his keys and dropped them when he tried to unlock their door. As he picked them up, he noticed for the first time how dusty their doorway was. He jammed the key into the lock for the second time and gently pushed the door open.

"It's not as nice as home, of course..."

She elbowed past him and studied the space without speaking. "But where do you sleep?" she said, finally. "Where's your bed?"

He laughed nervously. "That's a sofa bed. Our landlord bought it just before we moved in. It's pretty comfortable."

Ben led Ma to the little dining table, fixed her a cup of tea. They only had peppermint tea bags, the cheap Tesco ones Norah bought. They both sat down, the folding chairs squeaking loudly beneath them.

"How've you been, Ma?"

She didn't say anything, just fiddled with the string of her teabag. They never used tea bags at home; it was always looseleaf Chinese tea, always pu-erh, in the chipped blue and white teapot. Finally, she looked at him. "The first few nights I kept waiting up for you, kept thinking you would come back."

"Ma, I'm sorry." Why hadn't he gone back to see her? He had been meaning to. Why hadn't he?

She took out the fruit from the grocery bag—bananas and six enormous Korean pears—and added them silently to the dish on the dining table. "How's Joey?"

"He's fine. He's cruising really well now. We think he might start walking pretty soon."

Ma nodded. "You started walking at ten months. I wouldn't be surprised if Joey started walking around the same time." There was another long pause. "Also, I got your *gayong*."

"Oh, good," Ben said, flustered. "That's good the transfer went through."

She sipped her tea.

Ben watched her, anxiety building in his chest. Was she going to comment on how little money he'd given her this month? He reached for a washcloth and started wiping the table.

He didn't like the way she kept looking out the window. The studio itself was small but quite cozy, really: their mandarin oranges were arranged in a little pyramid on a plate, Joey's best finger-paintings were blue-tacked neatly to the wall above the sofa bed, the linoleum floor had been freshly mopped. But she kept staring out the window at the third floor of the funeral parlour.

He went to draw the curtains. "There's no sea view," he tried to joke. "But, well..."

"Why are you home?" she interrupted. "It's a weekday. It's noon. Why aren't you at work?"

Ben opened his mouth, then closed it again.

"Did you lose your job?"

His phone buzzed in his pocket again, more insistently this time, and he suddenly remembered that his father-in-law was trying to reach him. He realized that there was nowhere to take a call in private.

"Sorry, Ma, be right back," he muttered. He rushed into the washroom.

He pulled his phone out and tapped frantically on the green circle. "Dad?" he said, breathless. "Is everything okay?"

"We're downstairs," he said, his tone curt. Ben could hear Joey wailing in the background.

"Is Joey..."

"You didn't get my messages? Norah's been throwing up all morning. Joey's pretty upset. Come down and give us a hand, please."

Chapter 24

THE TAXI smelled of cheap air freshener and the driver's sour body odor. Norah clutched the sick bag Mom swiped from the ferry in her fist.

Dad had Joey in the carrier, but Joey had been struggling to climb out of it ever since he woke up from his nap, when the four of them got in the taxi outside the ferry pier in Central. He was now crying inconsolably.

"There, there, sweetheart," Norah murmured weakly, reaching out a shaking hand to stroke his hair. She knew he wanted her to hold him, but she was nauseous, mere moments from vomiting again, and her limbs felt weak and jelly-like, like tentacles.

Mom and Dad insisted on taking the return ferry from Cheung Chau and bringing her and Joey home. Norah tried to convince them that she and Joey could go home on their own; she hadn't wanted them to see their flat or their neighborhood, but they wouldn't take no for an answer. Norah finally agreed, knowing she wasn't strong enough to take Joey home on her own.

When she told the taxi driver, "Universal Funeral Parlour, Hung Hom", her parents had raised their eyebrows, but Norah quickly closed her eyes and pretended to be asleep.

The driver finally swerved onto Cheong Hang Road and pulled to a jerky stop in front of the funeral parlour. "Do you need a receipt?" he asked, turning to them. He was missing most of his front teeth, and the remaining few were stained brown. She climbed unsteadily out of the taxi as Mom handed the driver a $100 bill.

She leaned against the peeling wall of the funeral parlour, knowing she would not be noticed among the many deliveries, but the pungent scent of the funeral lilies was unbearable. With trembling fingers she uncrumpled the sick bag and vomited violently into it.

When she looked up again, she saw Mom pacing up and down the sidewalk, bouncing Joey in her arms. He had finally quieted down, his wails reduced to whimpers. Poor baby.

Norah swiped at her streaming eyes with the back of her hand. "Let's go up," she said, walking towards them, but her legs felt wobbly beneath her.

"Ben's coming down," Dad said, frowning. "I was hoping he'd be here to meet us."

It wasn't like Ben to not be attentive to her and Joey. "Maybe he was in the washroom, Daddy," she said. "Look, there he is now."

Ben rushed across the narrow street to them. "Hi Mom, Hi Dad. Sorry to keep you waiting," he said, clearly anxious. He repeated this apology until Mom and Dad nodded coolly at him. He finally turned to her. "Are you okay? Is it…is it…"

She slipped her arm in his, allowing him to take some of her weight, and rested her head on his shoulder.

Joey stretched his arms towards his daddy. "Baba," he cried, his tears starting up afresh. "Baba!"

Ben reached for Joey, but Mom wrapped her arms protectively around him and kept bouncing him up and down. "Oh, don't worry about Joey," she said. "You help Norah." Ben's arms fell back to his sides.

"Let's go up, then," Ben said, his voice hesitant. It often was around her parents. "We're just on the third floor."

Norah had never noticed any particular smell in their elevator before, but today it smelled of sweat and garbage. The ancient elevator struggled audibly under the weight of so many people. Norah closed her eyes and tried to think tranquil thoughts. Perhaps her parents would only stay for a short while. Perhaps they would not say anything. She desperately needed to lie down, and she wouldn't be able to if everyone was sitting on the sofa.

When they reached their front door, Ben slipped the key into the lock, but didn't turn it. He looked at Norah, a guilty expression in his eyes. "Ma's here," he said quietly. "She wanted to see the flat."

Chapter 25

BEN GINGERLY pushed the door open. Ma was sitting on the sofa, her eyes on her cell phone. "I'm back, Ma," he said, gently, but he knew she would be startled no matter what.

When she looked up, her eyes grew wide. There was a moment of strange quiet as everyone took in everyone else.

"Nai Nai, I'm so glad you came to see us," Norah finally said. Ben felt a great surge of love for her. "This is my mom and dad, they're visiting from Vancouver this week. You met them at the wedding," she gestured weakly at her parents, then disappeared into the washroom.

Ben could hear her switching on the shower faucet, and the sound of her vomiting was muffled by the running water, but there it was all the same. Poor Norah.

"Maa Maa," Joey suddenly cried, seeing Ma. He flailed in Norah's Mom's arms like a fish out of water. When she finally released her hold on him, he crawled towards Ma with an urgency that made Ben want to cry. Despite everything, there was this bond between Ma and his son. When Joey reached the sofa, he pulled himself up and cruised the remaining meter into Ma's outstretched arms.

"Joey," she said, tenderly. She held him close. "My Joey."

"Mom, Dad," he said. "Please, have a seat." They did, but warily, as though afraid the plastic chairs were too flimsy to hold up their weight.

The parents exchanged a few awkward hellos from across the narrow room. It felt very crowded.

Ben wanted to make his in-laws some tea, but they would have to share a mug; they only had two, and Ma was drinking from his. He quickly filled the electric kettle and flipped the switch. Norah would need some ginger tea for her nausea, but she wouldn't mind drinking from a rice bowl. He quickly peeled and sliced a small knob of ginger to make a simple ginger tea for her. At first he reached for the honey, then opted for a small spoon of sugar instead; he couldn't remember if it was safe for her to eat honey in the first trimester. He would have to check.

It was very quiet; the conversation behind him had quickly fizzled up. He set the mug of peppermint tea in front of his in-laws. "Please have some tea," he murmured, his head bowed. They ignored him, of course; they were very busy studying the studio, alarm in their eyes.

Norah finally emerged from the washroom. There was nowhere left to sit except beside Ma on the sofa, so Norah sat cross-legged on the floor at her parents' feet. Joey immediately climbed out of Ma's lap and crawled back to his mother. Ben placed the bowl of ginger tea in Norah's hands.

"Thank you, honey," she whispered. The sound of her voice seemed very loud in the silence.

"You're still so pale, dear," Norah's mom said.

"What's wrong?" Ma asked. "Are you sick?"

Norah tried to smile, to laugh. "I'm fine, I..."

But Ma was not finished. She gazed steadily at Norah, as though she could see through her. "You're...you're not expecting, are you?"

Norah turned crimson. "It's possible, I suppose, Nai Nai, but…"

Dad stared at Norah in disbelief, then whipped his head around to glare at Ben. "She's pregnant?"

"How long have you known, darling?" Norah's mom's face turned ashen. "Joey's still so little, not even one yet."

This last remark felt like an accusation, and Ben knew some kind of explanation was in order, but he didn't have any.

"We just tested this morning," Norah finally said. "We only just found out."

Norah's mom chewed on her bottom lip. "Well, congratulations, we're very happy for you, but…"

"How will you fit another baby in here?" Dad interrupted, his voice rising. He directed this question at Ben. "It's a tight squeeze isn't it, even for the three of you? How will you fit one more?"

"Honestly, the location doesn't seem terribly well-suited for raising children," Mom added. "I mean, we're not superstitious people, but, well…"

The grey linoleum beneath Ben's feet seemed to be shifting and sliding, like he was on a boat. He took a few deep breaths to try and steady himself; he felt like he was about to faint. Just then, Norah's hand slipped into his, an anchor.

"We'll definitely need to find a bigger space," he began, clearing his throat. "I'll start looking today." He glanced at Ma, who had been so quiet. She was looking out the window; she must have parted the curtains. Another funeral was in session at the parlour. Ben noted that the funeral was a closed-casket ceremony.

"Daddy, I know you're worried," Norah said earnestly. "We're going to be okay. I can go back to work at Future English anytime. You remember Ivan, he's always telling me how much the students..."

"And what about Joey? What about when the baby comes? I have half a mind to bring you and Joey back with us to Vancouver," Dad interrupted. He was not quite yelling, but close to it. "Our daughter, living in a dump like this, another baby on the way..." His voice broke then, and he buried his face in his hands. Mom squeezed his shoulder, but he didn't look up.

Norah withdrew her hand from Ben's grasp. "Daddy," she said, her bottom lip trembling.

"I'll find another place," Ben said, desperately, to Dad, to Norah, to everyone. "A better place, I promise." But even as he said this the dwindling numbers in his bank account flashed before his eyes. He would have to take a loan somewhere. There were places that required nothing more than your phone number and a photocopy of your ID card, he'd seen the ads. And he was waiting to hear back from the 7-11 manager. He could do more than a few graveyard shifts a week; he could work every night. He could...

"Ben, I know you're trying your best, but we can see you're struggling." Mom's voice was kind. "Norah told us she's quit her job to care for Joey. And you're freelancing now, isn't that right? How exciting." By this point it was evident that she was not being kind, but condescending. "The income isn't terribly stable though, I suppose. It can be hard at first, can't it?"

"He's got quite a few clients now, though, Mom," Norah piped up. "He's taking pictures for Gemma's Gym next week, aren't you, honey? Staff photos for over thirty people. And..."

Ma cleared her throat, cutting Norah off. "The only sensible solution is for them to move back in with me. I can care for Joey. I have done, since he was born. See how attached he is to me? We've just got the two rooms, but for now..."

"Please don't take offense, Mrs. Tam," Norah's dad said. "But

I imagine they must not have been very happy staying with you, or why would they move here?" And then, almost to himself, "Who would want to move here?"

Ma's cheeks reddened, but her gaze remained steady. "Surely, Norah, for the sake of your family..."

Norah was already shaking her head, but Ma continued. "You must think of what's best for Joey, not just yourself..."

"Mrs. Tam," Dad interrupted, loudly, "surely you can see that moving back into your flat isn't at all a long-term solution. Your home, as you said, only has two bedrooms. They will soon be a family of four."

"It seems to me that the issue does not lie with Norah," Mom said, pursing her lips. "Call me old-fashioned if you must, but I've always believed that the husband should bear the brunt of the responsibility for providing for the family. When we agreed to the marriage," she paused, sighing heavily, "we did worry that this would be a concern. If not at the time, then eventually. Now here we are."

This *was* an accusation, and Ben was filled with shame. He had always known that he didn't deserve Norah, couldn't afford Norah. He had done his best, but it hadn't been enough.

"Don't blame my son," Ma growled.

"I mean no harm," Mom said lightly. "You'll have to forgive me for being concerned for the well-being of my daughter and the grandchildren. Now, Norah," she said, as though Norah was a very young child, "would you like to come back to Vancouver with me and Daddy?" Out of the corner of his eye, Ben saw Dad nodding.

"No. That's not..."

"Not forever, of course, I would never suggest that. Just until Ben works things out, gets a proper home set up for you and the children. He can move back in with Mrs. Tam here, can't he? Save on rent? We want to take care of you during your pregnancy, is all. And Joey, love," she said, her smile saccharine, "don't you want to meet Oatmeal? He's *so* much fun. We could get a bouncy castle for the yard, a swing set, whatever you like. Wouldn't that be fun, Joey?"

At the sound of his name, Joey clapped, but he quickly stopped, as if he could sense that it was not an occasion for celebration. "Mama?" he asked, tentatively. He tilted his head so he could see Norah's face. He grabbed onto her shoulders and pulled himself up so he was standing on her thighs, then wrapped his little arms around her neck.

"Mom," Norah tried again, "I know you love me. I know you're worried. But I can't just leave Ben in Hong Kong. Being apart isn't an option for us."

"And do you think this…" here Mom paused, waving an arm around the studio, at Ben, "is an option for us? Just leaving you to… to *fester* in this place? Who knows what could happen?"

"It wouldn't be responsible of us to just leave you like this," Dad added, standing up. "Right then. I'll book a seat for you on the same flight as ours. Joey will need a bassinet…"

"Dad, wait," Ben protested. How had things developed so quickly? They wanted to take Norah, and Joey, too.

"A bassinet, but that can be easily arranged," Dad continued, ignoring Ben. "It's settled then. Excellent. Pack your things, Norah, but there's nothing you can't buy over there, of course. Shall we go, Edith?" He put on his shoes and turned the doorknob. "Bye-bye for now, Joey!"

"Dad, wait," Ben said, loudly, at the same as Norah cried, "Daddy, stop!"

"Now, Ben," Mom turned to him, smiling. "You are welcome to visit us anytime you like. You're *always* welcome." In that moment, Ben realized he hated her. They both knew that he would not be able to afford such visits. "Thank you for the tea," she continued. "Get some rest, Norah. I'll message you the flight details once they're confirmed." She waved regally at Ma. "Goodbye then, Mrs. Tam. A pleasure to see you again." She closed the door behind her before Ma had a chance to respond.

"I'll go talk to them," Norah cried. She set Joey in Ma's lap and rushed out the door after her parents.

Chapter 26

"I'll just change Joey's diaper," Ben said quietly. Ma nodded, mute. He scooped up the baby from her lap. "They'll listen to Norah, surely."

Ben laid Joey on the changing mat, his hand cupping his little head so it wouldn't bump against the floor. Joey stretched out his pointer finger and touched Ben's nose, giggling as he did. Normally Ben would giggle back, but today it was all he could do not to cry.

"This tea is no good," Ma said, abruptly breaking the silence. "It's sour."

"It's just mint tea, Ma," he said, although just then it was hard to see why the quality of their tea mattered. "Norah seems to like these teabags, but I prefer pu-erh, too."

"I keep swallowing, trying to make that vinegar taste of rotten soup go away, but it's stuck in my throat." Her fingers touch her neck, indicating where she means. She shook her head, distraught. "Maybe it isn't the tea. That sour taste…it's coming from my heart."

"Ma," he said, his voice catching. "All this… none of this…" Ben tried to take a deep breath but it turned into ragged gulps. He felt like he was drowning. In desperation, he held Joey to his chest. He kept hoping that any minute now, Norah would open the front door and announce that her parents were joking and none of this was real. He never cried in front of Ma, ever; he could not remember the last time. But now the tears were flowing and he was powerless to stop them. He could see his anguish reflected in his mother's eyes.

"Son, seeing you like this… it's like my heart is being sliced open with a cleaver." She placed her hand against her heart, as though she was in physical pain. "How dare they speak to my son like that! How dare they!"

Ben wanted to comfort her, but all he could think of just then was Norah and Joey. "Norah won't really go with them, will she, Ma? They can't make her, can they?" Ben tried to control the growing edge in his voice, but he felt as powerless as a child. "Ma, what am I going to do?"

Ma's expression hardened. "Better to advise a man to beat his child than to teach him to part with his wife—that's traditional Chinese wisdom. You don't go and break up your child's marriage, no matter how hard things are." She sniffed. "*I've* never told you to leave Norah, have I? Not once, not even when she was driving me crazy, which was all the time."

Despite everything, Ben felt a wry smile playing at his lips. Ma and Norah sure drove each other crazy, that was for sure.

"Norah is… not submissive or soft-spoken, the way I hoped my daughter-in-law would be. She doesn't listen to me or trust my advice on anything. Because of her, you have made some decisions that I… do not agree with. But I also know you are happy because of her." Ma gazed at him steadily. "I am not blind, Ben."

She had never said anything like this to him before. All he had ever sensed from Ma with regards to Norah was disapproval. "Ma…"

But she interrupted him. "Go pour out the chicken broth for Joey. I want to take the thermos home and… make some more for next time." Neither of them acknowledged that there might not be a next time. She reached out her hand to stroke Joey's hair. "It really is nothing but chicken, a whole fresh chicken from the market."

Ben knew this was as close as she would come to an apology for what happened with the fish congee, and he accepted it as such. "Sure, Ma. I'll go do it now."

When Ben set Joey in Ma's lap, Joey leaned on her chest and yawned. Ma wrapped her arms around Joey and began humming a lullaby that Ben hadn't heard since he was a child.

Ben poured the golden broth into one of Joey's bottles, careful not to waste a single drop. The fragrance filled their small space and as Ben turned around, he saw Joey sit up again, licking his lips like a puppy. He noticed the way Ma was tenderly stroking Joey's head, her eyes studying his scalp with an expression that he couldn't quite read. Was she thinking of the day she shaved Joey's head? That afternoon seemed like a lifetime ago.

Just then, the door swung open. "They won't listen, honey," Norah was saying fretfully. She yanked the scrunchie from her hair and ran both hands through her hair; this gave her a wild, frenzied look. She seemed to not have noticed that Ma was still here. "I've never seen them like this before… they just kept talking over me like they couldn't hear me. I kept trying to say…"

"I'll be going now," Ma interrupted quietly. After a moment's hesitation, she gestured at the hill of pears on the table. "I bought the pears for you, Norah."

Norah stopped talking, clearly surprised. Ben could see that Norah was both taken aback and touched. It was like Ma was a different person. Ben could not think of a single time when Ma had gone out of her way to be kind to Norah. "Oh, Nai Nai, that's so sweet of you. Thank you so much…"

But Ma didn't say anything else as she passed Joey to Norah. She picked up her leather handbag and thermos, then left the studio without another word.

Chapter 27

Norah stared at the door. "Your Maa Maa bought me some pears," she said to Joey. "What do you think of that?"

Joey just grinned back at her. "Maa Maa," he agreed good-naturedly. Norah was proud of how differently Joey said 'Mama' and 'Maa Maa' now. There was no confusion at all. "Maa Maa!"

Norah pecked him on the nose before setting him down in the Jumperoo. The familiar music filled the studio as Joey began bobbing gently from foot to foot.

"Come sit down," Ben said quietly. He chose the largest of the six pears and took it to the sink to wash. "I'll cut one for you."

When Ben sat down across from her, Norah noted his red-rimmed eyes and nose. *Silly*, she wanted to say. *I'm not going anywhere.* But she did not want to interrupt him as he made the first cut into the golden-brown skin of the pear, and a thin, winding strip emerged from his hands. As the fruit's snowy flesh was revealed, she watched in quiet reverence. He must have done this for her a thousand times.

"Dad kept acting like he couldn't hear me… he called their travel agent right in front of me and booked our tickets." She thought of how crazed Dad had looked as he spoke to his agent, his cheeks flushed. Mom had stood beside him, quietly approving.

"They kept ignoring me right until the end, when they waved goodbye from the taxi window like nothing had happened. It was crazy. They really think we're going with them."

With sudden force, Ben sliced the pear in half, the knife striking the plate below with a startling crack. "Sorry." He set down the knife, his face flushed. "Are you?"

"Of course not. I've thought this through—we just won't show up at the airport. I'm married, with a child. Two children, actually," she said, rubbing her flat tummy. "They can't make this decision for us."

She made this sound like the most natural thing in the world, like she wasn't terrified of a severed relationship with her parents. She was certain that by insisting on staying here with Ben, everything between her and Mom and Dad would change, for good. There would be no going back to being Mom and Dad's little girl. Would they cut things off with Joey, too?

With sudden clarity, she recognized that although she had never admitted it, not even to herself, she had always seen going back to Vancouver as a back door, an emergency exit. She felt her cheeks warm as she remembered all the times she'd threatened Ben with this; it happened every time they argued. *Oh, Ben. I'm so sorry.* She reached for Ben's hand and squeezed it so tightly he winced. "Sorry," she said, blinking back tears. "You're stuck with us, mister."

He kneeled in front of her, taking her hands in his. "I was afraid that if I tried to stop you from going with them, I'd be holding you back. It wouldn't be fair for you, or Joey. But..." His face contorted, and Norah saw how hard he was trying to hold back his tears.

"I couldn't bear to lose you. I don't know how I could go on without you." He hesitated. "Norah, I've been thinking...maybe I can ask Ma for a loan. Maybe she would say yes. I'll pay her back once the photography business is doing better. Maybe your parents wouldn't be so worried if we had, you know, a bigger space...'

She stared at him. In all the years that she had known him, he had never once mentioned borrowing money from Nai Nai as a possibility. The topic was strictly off-limits. Money went one way only—from Ben to Nai Nai, in the form of *gayong*.

As though he could read her thoughts, Ben continued: "I—I never wanted to, before. I was too afraid of her reaction if I tried to suggest that we move out. With her money." He smiled sadly. "I've been such a coward, Norah, I'm so sorry. Anyway... she might still say no. And if she does... we'll think of something else. I'll find more work. I'll do anything. I'm going to take care of you, Norah, I..."

Ben's phones buzzed loudly against the table, cutting him off. "It's Ma," he said, frowning at the screen. "She's saying...' But he stopped talking as he read the message, his brow furrowed. "N-Norah, come look."

Ben had never invited her to read Nai Nai's messages to him before, so she felt like she was trespassing as she read over his shoulder. It was a long message, in Chinese; Norah struggled through it, character by character:

> *Ben, my son:*
> *When your father left us 27 years ago, I promised myself I would not despair. I would not let you come to any harm.*
>
> *When you were young, Ma was often strict with you. In hindsight, I know that I was too hard on you. Forgive me, son. All these years, I wanted to keep you close to me, free from danger and unhappiness.*
>
> *Your* gayong *over the years has made me feel loved and secure. After all, Chinese wisdom teaches that having money within reach is of more worth than your own flesh and blood.*

But I know now Chinese wisdom doesn't get everything right. I don't always get everything right.

You are my heart and my liver, my reason for living. All I have ever wanted is for you to be happy. To have better luck with love than I did. To have a place of your own to call home.

Love always,

Ma

P.S. Look in Joey's pocket.

"Go," he heard Norah saying gently. "Go get Joey."

Ben was unsteady on his feet as he stood up. Norah, too, felt a fluttery feeling in her stomach—but the sensation seemed distinctly unrelated to the morning sickness from earlier on. When Ben switched off the Jumperoo, and the studio was suddenly silent, Norah sensed that this next moment would change their lives, and they would remember it for always.

Despite Joey's protests, Ben scooped him out of the Jumperoo and brought him over to the table. When Ben reached into the little striped pocket of Joey's blue onesie, his hand trembling, Joey giggled, thinking his Baba was tickling him, playing with him. Ben tugged out a pale yellow square. Even before it was completely unfolded, Norah recognized it for what it was: a cheque.

"Oh my God," Ben muttered, staring at the cheque in disbelief. He held it out to Norah, his hand shaking so badly Norah had to grab it from his hands to get a proper look at it.

It was a check for $500,000.

Norah screamed. Joey spun around, taking one questioning look at his mother before joining right in. Ben watched, his laughter mingled with tears, as they screamed and they screamed, delirious with joy and relief and gratitude.

Epilogue

"Don't come in yet," Norah cries. Ben catches a glimpse of her running back into their bedroom just as he is pushing the front door open. Joey is nowhere in sight. Ben closes the door again in a hurry. He can hear Norah yelling from within: "I mean, happy birthday, honey! I love you! But wait outside, please!"

Ben grins and tries to feel excited rather than nervous. He runs one hand over the custom engraving on their front door as he waits. It was his idea, his design, but Norah was the one who finally found a carpenter willing to engrave the intricate image he had in mind on their door. It is the stylized picture of two gingko trees, one big and one little, leaning against each other, and if you look closely enough, their surname, *Tam,* is hidden among the fan-shaped leaves and branches.

The flat itself is bright and airy, the walls cream-colored and the curtains a cheerful creamy yellow that makes Ben think of the mango puddings Ma likes so much. A rainbow of handprints and footprints form a frame around a large collage of pictures of their family and all those who love them. The prints are mostly Joey's, but some of them are Ben and Norah's; she wouldn't take no for answer, and had stroked the loaded paintbrush against his bare foot until he was giggling helplessly.

All of the air-conditioners are silent, top-of-the-line appliances, gifts from Norah's mom and dad. Their reaction to Norah's refusal to go with them had been surprising. At first, they acted like they were angry at Norah for staying with Ben, but in the end their relief that Ben and Norah now had the means to move into their own flat had eclipsed everything.

Mom and Dad had also gifted them with all the lighting. The day before Mom and Dad were to fly home, they all went to a three-story lighting specialty shop in Mong Kok, and insisted that they choose whatever they wanted. Ben had followed along, but was happy to let Norah take the lead: she gleefully picked a Tiffany-style lamp for the dining area ('So we can pretend we are eating out every night!") and an energy-efficient ceiling fan and light combo for their living room. For their bedroom, Norah chose a pair of hanging rattan lanterns that reminded Ben of the light fixtures in their villa in Sanya. She spent the longest time choosing a light for the children's room, and in the end, she settled on an ensemble of backlit clouds that would be installed on a wall rather than the ceiling. As the cashier rang up the bill (Ben had gulped, seeing how much it all cost), she had thrown her arms around both her parents, everything forgiven. "You must visit us all the time," she had cried. They had agreed, tearfully, to be back in time for the birth.

In another three months, Joey will be sharing his room with his baby sister. Norah wants to name her Kit. Ben agreed immediately; he likes the meaning—baby rabbit—and likes how easy it is to say. There is a trundle bed in the children's room, in case Ma ever wants to spend the night. But although she visits regularly, always with a steaming thermos of soup and a cloth bag of fruit, she always leaves right after dinner. Their apartment is in Sham Shui Po, only a fifteen-minute minibus ride from Ma's apartment, so he tries not to worry too much about her. He always walks her to the bus stop, and at the last moment, just before she climbs onto the minibus, he always presses her *gayong*—just a token amount, five hundred dollars—into her palm. She always waves goodbye from the open window, the wind in her hair.

Work has been going well, too: he has such a steady stream of happy clients who immediately recommend him to their friends that he is booked solid for the next six months. When Eric contacted him, asking—pleading, really—if he wanted to work together again, Ben had marvelled that he had the option of turning him down. And turn Eric down he did, because he needs his schedule to remain flexible and on his own terms so that Norah can return to Future English two afternoons a week while he is home with Joey. It is only a few hours a week, but that time Norah spends with her students at the centre has brought back a great deal of her former vitality and confidence.

"Okay, you can come in!" Norah cries.

As Ben is opening the door for the second time, he hears Joey crying, "Baba!" right on cue, as though he and Norah have rehearsed this moment. Her tummy bulging, Norah pushes a sleek three-wheeled stroller with rugged-looking oversized tires out into the living room to meet him. Joey is strapped inside, his Fedora hat on his head. Joey flashes Ben his signature grin. These days, with four teeth, it is the toothiest, goofiest grin in the world. He waves as he cries, "Baba, HI!"

"Happy Birthday, honey!" Norah cries, kissing him on the lips. "Surprise!"

"Wow," Ben says, slightly taken aback. Such a fancy piece of baby gear must have cost a lot of money, but he keeps smiling, unwilling to spoil the moment. "Thanks, guys. Wow. It's a nice stroller."

"Not just any stroller! This is a *running* stroller," she explains, clearly very pleased with herself, "so we can go training with you for the Standard Chartered." She attempts to demonstrate, pushing the stroller forward while jogging a few steps. It was bigger and brighter here in their new flat, but still not big enough for Norah to do more than a few performative pushes. "Do you think your running club will mind?"

Ben laughs in spite of himself. The two of them could be in a stroller commercial, they really could. "Of course not. I'll tell them we can join them next week. This is perfect, Norah. I love it."

"It's only second-hand," she says, shyly. Ben pretends not to be to relieved, but this is the best thing she could have said. "I've been looking on Carousell for this model for ages, Runners' World says it's the best, and I finally found a seller last week. A new one would have cost an absolute fortune, but I got this one for less than a thousand dollars! The seller was in a terrible rush to get rid of it because they're moving to the UK, like, next week." Norah's cheeks are flushed with pleasure as this spills out. "What do you think?"

Ben wraps his arms around her. "I think it's perfect."

He means the stroller, of course, but also more, so much more.

About The Author

Jane Lo is a Chinese-Canadian writer and English teacher. Shortly after Lo was born in Hong Kong, her family moved to Vancouver. In university she studied Biblical Hebrew and English Literature and loved both: she pursued further studies in one (Hebrew) and a career teaching the other (English). Over the years she has worked and studied in both cities, but she is now happily settled in Hong Kong, and lives with her husband, their two sweet but boisterous children, and their extremely shy leopard gecko, Snowy. Reading and writing are her passions. *ALL I EVER WANTED* is her first novel.